GOING GREEN

A NOVEL

FOR SOME IT HAS NOTHING TO DO WITH THE ENVIRONMENT

GOING GREEN

A NOVEL

FOR SOME IT HAS NOTHING TO DO WITH THE ENVIRONMENT

CHRIS SKATES

BRIDGE LOGOS FOUNDATION

Alachua, Florida 32615

Bridge-Logos
Alachua FL 32615 USA

Going Green
For Some It Has Nothing to Do with the Environment
By Chris Skates

Edited by Hollee J. Chadwick

Printed in the United States of America.

Library of Congress Catalog Card Number Pending
International Standard Book Number 978-1-61036-094-4

ACKNOWLEDGMENTS

Write what you know—that's the most common advice given to aspiring writers. My previous works were historical fiction, so, in writing **Going Green**, I was actually doing that—writing what I know. I enjoyed the experience immensely.

I am thankful to all the hard working and dedicated personalities that I've worked with, and continue to work with, in the industrial realm. I drew on traits of many of you that were admirable and, in some cases, humorous. I would like to thank Glenn Clayton, Mark Guard, Joseph Mion, Keitha Dobbs, Annette Tanner, Connie Sommer, Bethany White, LeGail Tudor, and Ashley Lievers—industry professionals all—for reviewing my manuscript or sharing their research with me.

Also for my friends, Dan and Judy Tankersley, Jack and Patsy Marshall, Alice Story, and Tonya Shea who were willing to read revision number three: Thank you.

My wife Tracy, a recovering English teacher, is always my first (and almost always right, no matter how much I want to differ) editor.

I am grateful to the Bridge-Logos team: Thank you for seeing in this novel what I saw. It is cliché but, "thanks for believing in me." Hollee J. Chadwick has been a wonderful editor to work with, and for all you aspiring writers out there, Kathleen Campbell is the best publicist in the business.

ACKNOWLEDGEMENTS

PROLOGUE

A male and female madtom catfish swam lazily along the bank of a Midwestern river. The male was the one surviving member of the female's most recent clutch of eggs. Contrary to their normal habits, the little male had remained alongside his mother throughout his life.

He was feeling good today, adventurous, and he darted with lightning speed from the line his mother was swimming in the safety of the weeds to deeper water and back. His mother didn't deter him. It was not in her neurological program to protect an adult offspring. She merely continued to swim her line parallel to shore in search of the aquatic insects she needed for food. She observed dispassionately as the smaller, younger male darted in and out of her field of vision.

Suddenly a dark shape blocked the sun's rays from above the water line. An extremely effective predator, the largemouth bass, had followed the male madtom from the deeper water. Instantly, instinctually, the mother madtom dove toward the base of the weeds. She lay deadly still, hugging the muddy bottom. Her offspring soon joined her but something was wrong. He was swimming along on his side, awkwardly, crookedly. The bass could not follow here for the water was too shallow. Only now, the bass was not the biggest worry.

The young male was wounded and thrashed awkwardly. He was now more like a sail than a knife through the water. A cross current was pulling him. The mother effortlessly corrected for it with her dorsal fins and was able to remain in place. The wounded male however, could not right himself. He could not fight the cross current that they had both swam through hundreds of times before.

He flailed pitifully, then grew weary and began succumbing to the current. For some reason the female followed. She watched her offspring. Mortally wounded, he would die within a few hours in any case. Normally with this type of wound, it would only be a question of time before he was consumed by some predator. Today, that unavoidable end would be delayed. The female watched the madtom flutter futilely one last time. He was then sucked into a massive steel tunnel. The water near the female was filled with the roars and whirrs of machinery. Then suddenly, the little male was gone. His carcass would never be seen in this part of the river again.

1

Ashley Miller turned down the radio and cocked an ear as she speed shifted into fourth gear. She had just accelerated out of a sharp turn and now had the Mustang on her favorite straightaway. She was taking the opportunity to "blow out the carbon" as her Dad was fond of saying. As she made the shift from third and the engine RPM's rose, she'd detected a slight ticking sound from the engines lifters.

"Hmm, better adjust those valves this weekend."

It was nothing serious. In fact, most mechanics would have advised her to leave the valves alone as long as the ticking was so subtle. But Ashley wasn't most mechanics. She was a perfectionist, and her '66 white Mustang with the powder blue trim was her passion. It looked perfect and she kept it running perfectly. Now the 289 V8 engine showed its stuff as Ashley barreled down the straightaway, the speedometer needle passing the 95 mph mark and headed for 100. She was as comfortable driving at these speeds, as most people would have been puttering along at 50. Up ahead she saw a farmer drive a tractor pulling a hay wagon onto the highway. He didn't look in her direction.

Probably used to this road being empty at this time of the morning, Ashley thought. With that, she expertly slid the toe of her right shoe over, applied the brakes lightly, downshifted into third and accelerated around the farmer like a white blur, sliding the shift lever smoothly back to fourth gear as she returned to her lane.

"There go your darned lifters again." Ashley spoke directly to the Mustang now. She would definitely make that a priority on Saturday. But for now, any tweaking of the engine would have to wait. She glanced down at her watch. It was 6:30 in the morning—time to head for home. She would need time to swap to her little Chevy Pickup and head to work for her usual 7 a.m. start. She certainly wasn't going to subject the Mustang to the parking lot at the coal-fired power plant where she worked.

Ashley braked hard and made an abrupt left onto highway 45, which would take her back towards home. The back end of the car broke loose a little and Ashley couldn't help but smile as she lifted her foot from the accelerator to bring the car back under control. Fifteen minutes later, she was the picture of a safe driver as she tooled along casually in her pickup on the way to the plant.

2

Muhammad Raschi, *aka* Ian Flannery, tied the belt on his thick terry cloth robe, picked up his cup and saucer, and stepped out onto the patio to enjoy his tea in the cool morning mist. He seated himself by the little table in the corner, smoothing the silk fabric of his lounge pants across his knee. He rested the fine china saucer on the table and slowly sipped from the cup. The hot tea felt good on the back of his throat, still scratchy from the desert sands. Ian hated the desert.

From his vantage point in the corner, Ian could watch the activity along the boulevard below as the Capitol began to come to life. At the same time, he could keep an eye on his sliding glass door as he awaited his guest. The morning was foggy but at least today the temperature had warmed somewhat. It had been a record-breaking cold Fall already in Washington, D.C., even though it was only the tenth day of November. Most people down at the street level had traded the heavy coats they wore only the day before for light jackets. Many looked up expectantly as rays from the morning sun peeked through the low clouds here and there. *Perhaps today we will see the sun,* Ian thought.

Ian was enjoying his time in Washington, almost as much as he had enjoyed New York. Atlanta had been pleasant as well. The southern women were the most beautiful by far. But Atlanta had lacked the excitement, the "hustle and bustle" of the other two. In New York, the activity was centered more on the nightlife. Here in D.C., the people projected an image of importance. Not self-importance or arrogance, but actual importance. It was apparent that most of them felt they were working in a field that was worthwhile. In their own way, the people now beginning to fill the sidewalks and board the trains were serving their country. Ian admired them for it despite the fact that he hated the country they served.

His thoughts were suddenly interrupted by the sound of the opening front door of the suite. Ian smiled broadly, his perfect white teeth momentarily dazzling his guest. Though Earl Worthen had seen pictures of Ian Flannery, he'd never had the pleasure of meeting him in person.

"Mr. Flannery," the jaunty Brit spoke with enthusiasm as he stepped through the already opened glass door. "I've so been looking forward to our meeting." Worthen had been a citizen of the United States for nearly a decade. He had found engineering work here after graduating from the Royal College of Engineers and he was quite good at it.

Unfortunately, Mr. Worthen had also developed a passion for gambling. He was so far in debt that he was on the verge of losing everything. That was what Ian liked about him most. That made Earl Worthen useful.

"I have looked forward to it as well," Ian replied joyfully, standing to shake the professor's hand. His English was perfect; two years studying at Oxford had helped with that. He made a mental note to tone down the charm a bit. Worthen was already enthusiastic enough. No need to overdo it.

"Shall we sit and visit out here on the patio?" Worthen asked.

"Oh no, it's still much too damp and cool out here. I've arranged for tea and biscuits inside," Ian replied waving an arm toward the tea service arranged on the table in front of the sofa. The two men took seats on either end of the sofa.

Worthen eyed the tea service for a moment, and then said, "Lovely of you to have selected my favorite tea, Mr. Flannery."

"It was my pleasure to have my staff acquire it," Ian replied, knowing full well that the tea had been provided by room service and that it was a complete coincidence that they had sent up Worthen's favorite.

As Ian poured tea in a cup, Worthen, quickly entered the electronic combination, and popped his briefcase open.

"I don't mean to be rude, but shall we conduct our business first? I'll enjoy tea with you afterwards but then I really mustn't tarry. I have a flight at noon for the Caribbean, you know." Worthen was clearly delighted at that prospect.

"Well, if the documents you brought meet my expectations then I would say you have earned a nice holiday," Ian said as he spread strawberry jam across one of the thin shortbread biscuits.

"Oh, I think you'll be most pleased." With that, Worthen took out a folder, placed the case on the floor, and unfolded a large blueprint and spread it across his lap. "You may need to slide over here to see the level of detail present, but this technical drawing is an excellent example of others that I have with me."

Ian scooted closer, sliding his right arm across the back of the couch and behind Worthen so that the two almost looked like a couple.

"You can see these drawings of the infrastructure are extremely detailed. There is a separate drawing for each subsection broken down by state," Worthen continued.

He turned towards Ian to gauge his reaction. He was certain that the rich Arab would feel that he was getting considerably more than he had hoped for. He had no idea why Flannery wanted these drawings but he was sure that he did not have the best of intentions. However, Earl Worthen was not in a position to question anyone's motives just now. He was desperate. He was not going to tell his wife that they were going to lose the house. He had been through too much to get to where he was. All he needed to know was that Ian Flannery seemed a gentleman and that he paid well. He paid very well.

Ian looked up and smiled proudly so that for a brief moment the two men's faces were in uncomfortably close proximity—but only for a moment. With a lightning quick upward thrust of the hand Ian had across the back of the couch, he drove a stiletto into the soft tissue just at the base of Worthen's skull. As the blade entered the man's brain, Ian applied a leftward twisting motion to the blade's handle. With no noise and little fuss, Worthen slumped over, his body resting against the arm of the couch.

Ian clutched the cuff of his own sleeve tightly in the hand that had held the knife and wrapped his arm tightly around Worthen's neck. He allowed the warm blood to soak into the absorbent sleeve of the terry cloth. Then, rising slowly, he carefully pulled himself out of the robe and wrapped it around Worthen's head, neck and shoulders. Standing bare-chested before the coffee table, he reached over and picked up a small silver bell in one hand and his jam covered biscuit in the other. He rang the bell lightly as he stepped toward the desk phone, taking a bite from the biscuit as he moved.

In seconds, two larger Arab men entered the room with a neatly folded body bag. Ian, acting as though the two men and Worthen's body were invisible, dialed room service.

"Yes, can you have someone bring another robe to my room? I plan to take two of them home with me when I check out. Yes, of course, place it on my bill."

3

Ashley hurried out to her truck. She had cut it a little too close and now she was going to be late for work. She stopped in her cabin just long enough to change from her fireproof racing shoes to her steel-toed work boots. As she found the key to the truck and was about to put it in the ignition she heard a tap at the window.

Oh no, she thought. She knew who it was without looking up. It would be her neighbor Ray Harrison. "Not now," she mumbled to herself. Still she rolled down the window and smiled at Ray.

"Hey, Ashley," Ray said sheepishly. "Listen, I'm really embarrassed to ask you this. But my scooter won't start again. Tammy needs the car today 'cause the baby has a wellness visit with the pediatrician..."

"Get in, Ray," she said, rolling her eyes much more than she intended to.

Ray didn't hesitate. He ran around the front of the truck, hopped in the passenger seat, and buckled himself in. The two headed down the highway in silence. The auto shop where Ray worked was well out of Ashley's way. She would definitely be late now. Ray knew this. Ashley knew Ray knew this and she knew it embarrassed him. After about five miles, Ray finally spoke.

"Ashley, we are gonna get another car. We're gettin' some bills paid off and then we can save..."

"You don't have to explain yourself to me, Ray. It's really not a big deal."

The two rode silently for a few moments more until Ray finally said under his breath, "It's a big deal to me."

She knew Ray would resent it, but she actually did feel sorry for him. Many evenings she saw the single headlight of Ray's scooter pulling into the driveway of their small house next door. She usually saw the same headlight heading out in the morning when she was just getting out of bed. She sometimes did the math and realized that Ray was putting in thirteen and fourteen hours per day in the unheated, non-air conditioned auto shop. Tammy took the baby with her four days a week to sit in a playpen while she cleaned houses for the people who lived on what was known as "silk stocking lane."

Ashley sometimes thought of the old country song that talked about "trying" when she observed this couple. These two smart, resourceful, and hard-working people just kept on trying.

She wheeled the truck onto the gravel parking lot of the shop and stopped next to a '92 Blazer with the hood up. Ray didn't get out right away. Instead, he sat there staring straight ahead.

"That the one you were talking about with the throttle body injection problem?" Ashley asked.

"Yeah," Ray answered.

"You know those spiders on those old injectors were notorious for not holding fuel pressure," she said.

"Yeah, I checked that. That ain't the problem on this one," Ray changed the subject. "Guess I'll catch hell from the guys for not havin' my own ride," Ray said, staring at the dashboard. "I'll have my own shop someday, Ashley, and when I do, I'll pay you back. I promise."

Before she could say anything in protest, Ray abruptly grabbed the door handle and was gone. Ashley stared after him a moment, then said, "Blessed are the meek."

4

Ashley swung her pick-up into the first parking spot she came to. She was already five minutes late and didn't want to make a further spectacle of herself by driving around looking for a closer spot. She walked hurriedly toward the security gate of the 50-year-old coal-fired plant. Even though she had been with Sinclair Power Generation, or SPG, as it was better known, for five years now, she still couldn't believe she was here. It seemed like only yesterday she was in college carrying a sign that protested the same type of plant in which she now worked. She'd been determined that she'd be a part of closing all the old plants down for what they did to the environment. That lasted right up until her first job interview during the last semester of her senior year.

SPG had been one of the companies that attended a job fair looking for Environmental Engineering and Biology majors. No one else that day had been terribly interested in talking to her, so she swallowed her pride for the interview and became downright enthusiastic when she was offered a job. For a month or so, she was still skeptical. She'd accepted the job assuming it would be a temporary stepping-stone. Five years later, she was still here with no intention of leaving.

Ashley pulled open the glass door on the security shack.

"Hey, we start work around here at 7 a.m. You might make a note or something," said Mike, the security guard.

"Very funny," she replied as she placed the frozen lasagna entrée she'd brought for lunch onto the conveyor belt so that it could be x-rayed. "What're you doing here anyway? You mean they actually let you off midnight shift?"

"Twice a year if I'm good," Mike replied as he stared into the monitor. "No bombs in the tomato sauce again today. Good. A few more months of this kind of behavior and maybe I can talk them into taking you off the 'suspicious employees' list."

Ashley walked through the explosives detector and waited for the green light at the top. Stepping through, she grabbed her lasagna off the conveyor. "Why can't all the dayshift guys be as funny as you," she said, smiling sarcastically.

"Send 'em by. I'll try to work with 'em," Mike shouted after her as she walked out of security and into the plant.

It was looking good. She was pretty sure she was actually going to make it to her desk without anyone noticing her tardiness.

"Hey, Ashley!" someone shouted from the area near the intake.

Ashley stopped and turned in that direction. There she saw Dan Dortery, the president of SPG.

"Great!" she said under her breath as she walked toward her boss's boss who was now curling his index finger at her, signaling her to come toward him. She felt a knot begin to form in her stomach. As she approached, she wondered what exactly the penalty was for tardiness and why the one day she was late, the highest-ranking management employee in the entire company had to be standing right there. Dan normally resided in the corporate offices in St. Louis. Today, as luck would have it, he had apparently decided to visit here.

"We may have a problem," Dan said. "Walk with me."

As the pair headed for the river, it began to dawn on her that Dan had not beckoned her across the front of the plant site to talk about her being late. They were going to look at something of more significance.

They approached the river and Dan swept a hand in the direction of the discharge canal. "One of the operators reported rainbow sheen."

She saw it right away. The discharge canal sent river water that had made one trip through the plant for cooling purposes back to the river. On rare occasions, despite diligent efforts to the contrary, some oil would be spilled near a floor drain that connected to this canal. Ashley suspected that's what had happened this time.

"Well, they did a nice job with the booms," she sighed with relief. "I'll look closer and make sure it stays contained. Then we can get a crew down here with the skimmer to start the clean up."

Ashley made it sound easy. It wasn't. Responding to an oil spill was a dirty, difficult, and stressful job. It was times like these she felt she really earned her pay.

Dan asked the obvious question. "Do you think any has made it to the river?"

"Don't know. I'll have the lab start pulling samples all along the riverbank. We should have some results in a couple hours."

She knew the state and federal regulations stated they were only required to report a spill if a visible sheen was present in the "waters of the state," which was not the case. She also knew that SPG's self-imposed limits were even tighter than that. If the lab results showed any trace of the oil in the canal, the procedure would require her to report it, which would be a paperwork nightmare.

"Well," Dan said, slapping her on the shoulder. "Looks like your morning won't be boring."

They walked back toward the offices so Ashley could get the process started. As they had leaned on the bright yellow handrail that overlooked the canal, neither noticed the bespectacled man hiding beneath the bridge underneath them. He'd heard most, but not all, of their conversation. He couldn't afford to be caught. He was trespassing and was already on probation. He'd known better than to remain here past daybreak. Rethinking the potential consequences, the man decided to leave for now. He stepped carefully and quietly in his thigh-high rubber waders and was soon lost from sight in the bulrushes.

5

Muddy waders lay crumpled on the tiny deck of the Airstream camper where Shelton Leonard lived. Inside, the sound of snoring could be heard. The dinette table could barely be seen, it was so covered with glass jars filled with formaldehyde. A detailed topographical map of the area was spread across the tops of the jars. Dirty bowls, encrusted with the remnants of dried cereal or ravioli, filled every remaining space on the table.

A folding card table adorned the center of the small living area. An HP color printer sat on one corner of the table, printouts of digital photos in the printer tray. A few more were strewn on the dingy carpet beside the table. Each showed a different angle of the plant where Ashley worked. Beside the printer was a half-empty pint of Johnny Walker Black. Alongside it was a slice of half-eaten pizza, the leftovers from the previous night's meal.

Finally, on top of the pictures and beside the pizza, lay the reason that Shelton had set his alarm for 4 a.m. He would spend the early morning hours along the bank of the river downstream of SPG. Once there, shivering in the cold, he would stare into the water, wearing a small headlamp, hoping to attract a fish. He would wait not for just any fish, but a very special fish. He had risked everything, sacrificed everything for this fish. He lived in a camper and ate cold, stale pizza so that he could invest all the money from his parent company in his website and on the law firm he kept on retainer. He had to find this little fish—a fish just might change his whole life.

6

The oil spill had been contained and the skimmer was in place. Ashley glanced at her watch and was pleasantly surprised that she would make it to the lunchroom on time to eat with the others.

She keyed her radio, "Hey, Leroy Allen?" She waited ten seconds…nothing. She tried again, "Hey, Leroy Allen?"

"Gorehead," Leroy's voice boomed through the radio's speaker. Proper plant etiquette was to answer a radio call with something like, "Go ahead for Leroy." But there was no personality in that, and Leroy definitely was not lacking in personality. She smiled every time he answered with his version of "go ahead" even though she had heard it a thousand times.

"Leroy, have you got any results for me on those river water samples?"

"Enjoy your dinner," he replied. "You ain't got nothin' to worry about. The first two showed less than ten PPB. I can run the others after dinner. But there wasn't no oil made it to that river, I can already tell you that now."

She blew her bangs out of her eyes in a sigh of relief. "10-4, Leroy, that sounds good. Thanks for the info. I'll come by and sign the analysis reports after lunch." She released the key on her microphone and clipped it back to the row of buttons on the front of her shirt. Leroy's voice came back through the speaker once more.

"I'll be right here if nothin' bends or breaks, I suppose."

She smiled again and rolled her eyes. "You guys did a great job," she said to the crew of laborers who had been working diligently throughout the cold, damp morning. "Go ahead and take your lunch break. We can finish up here afterwards." The guy standing nearest to her, a new employee who was close to Ashley's age, looked up.

"Sure thing, miss," he said. "You've been really nice to work with." Immediately a look of regret came across his face. He had overreached and he realized it. Ashley saw the other workers covering their mouths with gloved hands, trying to hide their laughter. The younger man's face flushed a deep shade of red. Ashley decided to help him save face.

"Well, thank you. You guys have been great, too. I'll see you in a half hour or so."

With that, she turned and headed up the bank. Once she was well out of earshot one of the workers clapped the youngest man sharply on the back.

"Whoo hoo! This boy just lights up like a Christmas tree every time that little redhead gets within a hundred yards of him."

"Oh shut up, Stank. You'd do the same thing if you weren't so scared to death of that wife a yours."

"Hup, hup," one of the workers said. "He's got ya there, Stank." He looked back again to watch Ashley walk up the hill. "I can't say as I blame either one of ya though. She sure is a pretty little thang."

Without any agenda on her part, Ashley had spent her entire life shattering stereotypes. When people met her for the first time, they assumed that she might be a model. They certainly never imagined her as a tomboy whose primary hobby was rebuilding cars with her Dad and competing in road races and car shows. She'd been the only girl in the entire engineering department at her University. In that environment, as well as during her first weeks at SPG, the assumption was that she was not up-to-snuff technically, and that she used her looks to get what she wanted. That line of thinking didn't last long once Ashley began to rise to the top of the class rankings. At SPG, it only took the other engineers a month or so to realize that this young lady was very serious about her work, and very capable of pulling her weight.

By the time she entered the lunchroom, most of the other engineers had heated their food or opened their lunch boxes and were already half-finished eating.

They all looked up at her. Ashley had worked here long enough to know what they were thinking. She would have been thinking the same thing about them if the roles were reversed. "Man, am I glad I'm not you today," was foremost in their minds. Ashley knew, as did the others, that on some other day it would be their turn. They would be the ones at some point with a problem in their systems that made them the center of everyone's attention, but not today. Tony Sanchez, the engineering department head spoke first.

"How's it lookin'?" he asked, looking up over his glasses as he tried to read the fat grams off the back of a bottle of salad dressing. He then referred to his food log to determine how much he could have on his salad.

"We're gonna be okay," Ashley answered. "It doesn't look like anything made it to the river. Looks like B shift did a great job of catching it in time."

"That's good news on two fronts. It's good for compliance but also good because now you'll have time to attend a special meeting called in your honor," Tony said.

Ashley froze in her tracks, one hand still on the handle of the refrigerator door. The others in the room, including Tony, smiled at her posture.

"Not to worry," Tony went on. "Just go and see Dan when you're done."

Once her food was heated and Ashley had taken her usual spot at one of the corner tables, she looked at the faces around the room. The conversation had turned from the environmental near miss to a debate over the best way to rid one's yard of those pesky moles. Ashley began to eat and looked from one face to the other. This was a good group of guys. Sure, they were engineers, and several of them could be a little dry at times, maybe a little too technical, but they were conscientious and hard working. In fact, they and the other employees at the plant had completely changed the perspective that Ashley had once had of the people who worked in industry.

Only five years prior, Ashley had been determined to save the world from evil, greedy, industrial giants. She wanted to thwart those whose manufacturing plants belched black toxic smoke into the atmosphere and drained poisonous fluids into the rivers. With that mindset, she had focused her engineering degree in the specialty of Environmental Engineering. Her professors were full of anecdotes of devastation wrought by people running everything from nuclear power plants to tire factories who cavalierly sacrificed entire communities without so much as a second thought. But when Ashley needed a job after graduation, SPG had stepped up to the plate first.

The interviewer had taken her aback. She'd been professional, courteous, and expressed a real commitment on the part of SPG to being a good steward of the environment. In the following days, after what seemed a whirlwind of interviews, Ashley had found herself a somewhat reluctant employee of the very type of company she had railed against at rallies in college. The first time she drove up to the plant, Ashley felt as if she were stepping over to the dark side.

There was smoke coming from the stacks all right, but it was white. The waste products that during Dickens' day turned the smoke black were constantly being removed. Ashley would soon learn that multi-million dollar equipment was in place to monitor constantly all plant emissions and alert operators of anything that approached the arena of harm to the environment.

All in all her real life experience was completely different from her preconceived notions. She scanned the room and saw people who genuinely wanted a clean, safe environment as much as she ever had. But she also saw a group of realists, a group that recognized the fact that with six billion people on the planet there was a dire need for reliable and affordable energy. These days she was actually quite proud to be a member of a team that wanted to accomplish both.

7

Ian, *aka* Muhammad Raschi, rolled the British racing green Jaguar slowly and smoothly up to the curb. He always drove slightly slower than the posted speed limit. Despite the car's capabilities, Ian was much more interested in what driving it said about him than he was about performance.

He stepped out into the damp, cold afternoon air, and handed his keys to the valet. The sun was starting to burn off the morning fog but the day was still gray and dreary. By the time he handed his keys to the valet and walked up the granite steps of The Pine, Ian was already starting to catch a chill.

"Mr. Flannery," the *maître d'* snapped to attention as Ian walked in. "So wonderful to have you back with us. Your table is ready."

To have a table at The Pine restaurant in Washington was to be a true power player. Only the most influential lobbyists and politicians could elicit such a privilege. In almost any other city in America, a restaurant like The Pine would also have catered to the famous and the very rich. But this was D.C. This was the exclusive hangout of the powerful and those most likely to gain influence with them. Even junior senators and congressman were very rarely invited to enjoy a meal with their more senior fellows.

Ian had only been seated a moment when Senator Aaron Hatcher walked in. Senator Hatcher had been in Congress for most of his adult life and had been in Washington for his entire life. His late father had been in the Senate up until his death in 1979 when his son narrowly won the seat in the mid-term election that followed. He'd represented the State of Maryland ever since. That is, until the November elections the previous year. In a shocking defeat, he had been beaten by a young upstart conservative who ran as an independent. The loss had been an embarrassment to Hatcher's family. Hatcher still hadn't gotten over it and he wasn't nearly ready to go back to Maryland.

Ian stood to greet him.

"Ian Flannery, so nice to see you again," Hatcher said. Hatcher had no clue about Flannery's true identity—Muhammed Raschi.

"It has been too long, Senator." said Ian.

"Yes," Hatcher said. "Yes, it has."

The senator's blue eyes were gleaming and his smile was at maximum wattage. He had long been considered the "heartthrob" of Washington. In his first two terms, he'd been a favorite of Hollywood actresses and had been in the press more often regarding his celebrity girlfriends than any legislation with which he was involved. That had changed when he finally married his college sweetheart and decided to get serious about politics.

To an unknowing observer these two men would have looked like two male models meeting over some upcoming photo shoot. They were two completely contrasting types; Flannery the dark, handsome man of Arab descent and Hatcher the blue-eyed blonde-haired, Ken doll of the Washington scene.

"How are your parents?" Hatcher inquired. "Are they well?"

"No," Ian replied. "I am sorry to report that I have lost them both since we last met."

"I'm terribly sorry. Of course I hadn't heard or I wouldn't have brought it up."

"Oh, it is quite all right; you had no way of knowing," said Ian. *Too late,* Ian thought sarcastically, *he has already moved on.* As he looked into the senator's eyes, he could tell that he'd already sped past regret or empathy for Ian. The senator was obviously thinking of his next remark—he certainly wasn't listening to Ian's explanation. Of course, Ian didn't care either. He'd never known his parents.

The "parents" the former senator was referring to were an elderly English couple who had been paid handsomely to adopt Ian when he was twelve years old. By then, he'd already had four years of intense training in Iraq. Nine years later, on the day he'd completed his studies at Oxford, Ian left their house without so much as a goodbye. He never saw them again. However, their English name and the photograph of them he kept handy in his wallet had been most helpful in adding credence to his alter ego. As long as Americans perceived him as a boy raised English by his loving, adoptive parents, they were ready and willing to give him the benefit of the doubt.

"I appreciate you inquiring about my family, Senator, but I am actually much more interested in how you are doing. How is a man with your competitive fire handling this unfortunate turn of events?" Ian had succeeded in moving the conversation to an area that the Senator was much more interested in—himself.

Hatcher got testy. "How would you imagine I am handling it, Flannery?" He shot back. He took a moment to gather himself. "Obviously, I'm unhappy. And I have every intention of holding public office again very soon. But I have no interest in being out of circulation for the next three years until it's time to campaign. I'm looking into a number of arenas in which I might serve until then."

Ian thought for a moment about other overpaid positions where former senators like Hatcher often found themselves "serving." Lobbyist, consultant, and corporate board member came to mind. That wasn't in Senator Hatcher's future, however. Ian knew full well what Hatcher was about to disclose. It was the only reason Flannery was here.

"That's why I wanted us to meet for lunch," Hatcher went on. "And by the way, I appreciate you inviting me here. I always loved The Pine and haven't been here since election night."

"The pleasure is all mine, Senator. I..."

Hatcher interrupted, "Flannery, I've got a vision that I want to share with you. It's my hope that it will become your vision, too."

I am certain that you do, Flannery thought, *a vision of you sitting in the Oval Office.*

Hatcher continued, "I want to give you an opportunity. I know we don't know one another well, but your reputation precedes you."

Flannery laughed—a relaxed and charming laugh. "And what reputation would that be, Senator?"

"You've a reputation of being one of the most successful lobbyists in Washington for causes that you believe in. Your efforts to support environmental activism and particularly climate change legislation through your foundation have not gone unnoticed. Many people don't realize how passionate *I* am about environmental stewardship. And I believe that's an area where we could join forces."

"I have seen you often lately on some of the talk shows and in public appearances with like-minded celebrities," Flannery said. "It has been a very impressive thing to watch—your success in raising awareness about climate change. I must confess I was beginning to grow weary of the uphill battle we have been waging. Recently, however, you have provided inspiration even for one who has been in the game as long as I, Senator."

Hatcher smiled broadly and sat back in his chair. "You've no idea how much that means to me," Hatcher said and he pressed a knuckle to his lips. Then suddenly, realizing he was over-acting, he took his hand away and began again.

"Your lobbying efforts have been particularly effective in the area of environmental protection. That's why I want you to join me as a driving force—behind the scenes. I'll be the public face, of course."

"Oh, of course," Ian said, matter-of-factly. "But Senator, I could never..."

As he spoke, Ian held up his hand in a mock gesture of protest, though he had no intention of protesting. This would allow Hatcher to feel that he had used his superior powers of negotiation to sway Ian to his way of thinking.

"Now hear me out first, Ian. I know there are plenty of groups and organizations vying for your time, but none with the particular focus I'm talking about. I'm going to give you the opportunity to effect positive change in this country in an area that you care very dearly about."

Hatcher leaned closer and placed a hand on Ian's forearm, gripping tightly, the way he had been taught by his politician father when he needed to communicate "real" passion about a topic.

"Ian, I want you to help me change the world."

8

Ashley fidgeted nervously in her chair. She was sitting in what was known as the small conference room just outside of the office Dan used whenever he came down from corporate. This was not to be confused with the large conference room where all the most important meetings took place. Watercooler legend had it that the small conference room was more intended for group interviews of job applicants, committee meetings, inquisitions, and lynchings—things of that sort. It seemed like days ago, instead of four years, that Ashley sat in this same seat waiting to start her first post-college job interview. She'd been nervous then, too. But that was a very different kind of nervous.

Even though she thought she was ready to get this over with, when Dan walked into the room she found herself wishing for five more minutes of delay. Then again, she knew when that five minutes ran out she would only wish for five minutes more. To make matters worse, Tony stepped into the room only a minute or two later. The two of these managers meeting with her at the same time was most definitely not a good sign.

"Okay, first things first. What is our obligation this morning? What do we need to report?" Tony asked.

Dan sat down in the chair across the table from her. He took out a pair of half-lens reading glasses from a metal tube that was always in his shirt pocket and began glancing over the contents of a file. Ashley rose slightly in her chair but couldn't see what the file contained. She'd always perceived Dan as something of a corporate statesman. His knowledge of even minute details of the plant and how things worked was impressive to say the least. He was demanding of his employees but always fair. He was one of those managers who fooled you—just when you were beginning to think he didn't even remember who you were, he would ask a question about an ill relative or something that you had mentioned in passing several weeks before.

"Ashley, what do we need to report?" Tony repeated.

Ashley snapped to attention. Now her antenna was up. *Why were a department head and the corporate president meeting with her about this small spill?* The dormant environmental activist within Ashley shook itself awake.

"What do you want me to report?" Ashley wished she could take back the question almost as soon as she spoke it. Tony's eyes told her that its tone had in fact irritated him.

"What kind of question is that? What have I always told you to do in these situations? I want you to report *every single thing* that we are legally and ethically required to report...but no more. And I hired *you* to know the regs and to advise SPG on your determinations. So I say again, what do we need to report to them?"

"Them" was a term painted with a relatively broad brush that everyone in the room knew meant state EPA, USEPA, county officials, the Coast Guard, concerned citizen groups, and anybody else that might be owed an explanation.

"Sorry, I jumped to a conclusion. I suppose being in the conference room has that affect on me." Ashley laughed awkwardly at her own joke but no one else in the room even smiled. Instead, both men stared at her, clearly waiting on their answer.

"We don't have to report anything to anybody," Ashley continued. "I have viable data that indicate that not one drop of the oil made it to the waters of the state. Our permit is clear. As long as the oil was contained in our canal and cleaned up there, then we've fulfilled our responsibilities. The guys are going to continue to collect samples of both the canal and the river through tomorrow. But I see no sheen on either surface and I don't expect to detect any oil in the samples. We got it all, gentlemen."

Ashley waited for a response. When she got none she said, "We done good here, guys," using a little plant slang for affect.

Both men sat and stared at her for what seemed like a long time before saying "good" almost simultaneously.

"I finished reading your proposal on that instrumentation purchase. Nice write-up," Tony said. Ashley was beginning to get the sense that Tony was stalling, protecting her, maybe.

She had to think a minute about which project Tony was talking about. She certainly hadn't expected to come here and talk about one of her projects. Could this be all they had summoned her for? If so, this was her lucky day. But it didn't make sense. The project wasn't that important.

"So you want to spend eighty-thousand dollars of my money to monitor ash pond chemistry and send the data via radio signal back to the plant where it will be relayed to our computer network and even to your Blackberry?" Dan asked, without looking up from his reading.

She gathered her thoughts a moment. "Yes, well...uh, it would allow me to receive alarms 24/7 and I...uh...well, I could contact the plant about potential countermeasures so that we could minimize the risks of a violation..."

Dan interrupted her. "I like it. You make an excellent case in your write-up and you'll get the money." Dan looked over his glasses, making eye contact with Ashley for the first time during the meeting. "Tony and I have a big problem we hope you can help us with. So let's move on to the business that we're really in this room to discuss."

Ashley felt her stomach do a little flop. She was starting to regret having lasagna at lunch.

Dan went on, "Could you share with us exactly who Riverguardian is and tell us a little about your affiliation with them?"

As Dan spoke, he closed the file and laid it on the table. For the first time Ashley was able to read the label on the tab. She felt the hair on the back of her neck stand up. It was her personnel file.

"I'm sorry, I don't know of any group called Riverguardian and I certainly don't have any affiliation with them."

Tony spoke up now. "Ashley, it appears they're an environmental activist group."

"Yes, and from the letter I received from them in St. Louis the other day, they seem determined to either meet with us here or else they'll go to the media and make a case that we're environmentally irresponsible," Dan said. "The reason we're asking about it is the letter names you as a source of their information. Says here you told them we were impinging thousands of fish on our river intake screens and that we weren't responsive to spills." Dan slid a copy of the letter across the table toward Ashley.

"Dan, Tony, I haven't given any information to any environmental group of any kind since the day I was hired. And I certainly wouldn't tell them that our environmental record was shoddy. That'd be a negative reflection on me," Ashley insisted.

Tony spoke while staring down at his hands folded on the table. "According to the letter you've been trying to get us to change since you've been here and we won't listen."

"Put yourself in my position for a moment. Here I have a relatively new employee. You just reached your five-year anniversary date a month ago. And to me you seem like a model employee. Then suddenly I get this letter from what certainly appears to be a semi-hostile activist group in which my model employee is mentioned by name multiple times. Then something occurs to me. I remember a conversation we all had last summer at the company picnic. You were keeping us all entertained with some pretty funny stories about your college days and the time you nearly got arrested as an environmental protester."

Ashley groaned inwardly. No wonder Dan wanted to meet with her. She hadn't thought of how this must look from his perspective.

"Dan, I was telling that story to illustrate how naïve I was. I ..."

"Ashley, I am just going to come out and ask you. Are you feeding some kind of information to these people?"

Ashley reacted with a little more emotion and volume than she intended, "No! My gosh no, Dan. I would never do something like that. I love it at SPG."

"I believe you. At least I really want to believe you. But you can see why I asked the question."

"Yes sir, I can. But you can rest assured that I don't know anything about these people or this group."

"Well, they're demanding that we meet with them and I'm inclined to agree to it if for no other reason than to draw them out of the shadows. Let's see who's behind this propaganda. You'll need to plan on sitting in on this one, that's for certain. But be careful what you say. Let me do most of the talking. If I want you to speak on a topic, I'll prompt you. Personally, I've never had dealings with a group like this, but I've made some phone calls and our attorneys want to have a couple of people there as well. I'm setting the meeting up for this Thursday. These folks could very well be a little hostile towards us, even though they probably know nothing about our company or our employees' dedication to the environment. They *don't* know us, do they, Ashley?"

"Dan, I'm not sure what or who they know," Ashley answered. Her confidence was gradually coming back to her. "But I do know that other than a name they got from some company directory, they sure as heck don't know me."

9

Ian slid the Jag's shift lever into first and eased out the clutch, merging smoothly into traffic. It wasn't until he checked the oncoming traffic in the rearview mirror that he caught a glimpse of his reflection and realized he was smiling. The lunch meeting had gone better than expected. Not only did he not have to convince Aaron Hatcher to include him, Hatcher was so anxious that Ian had barely needed to speak. The honorable former senator had responded perfectly to all the months of preparation. He'd practically run the meeting for him and was now committed to everything in the plan. The masterstroke was that Hatcher actually believed all of this was his idea.

Ian was more than pleased. Today had been the culmination of years of preparation and things had gone so perfectly, had so exceeded all expectations, that he felt most deserving of congratulations. After having spoken with his superiors by satellite phone, he'd been given blessings from Allah. Now, his work temporarily completed, Ian would treat himself.

To some of his fellow believers, Ian's upcoming activities might seem terribly hypocritical but Ian felt that he could be allowed leeway in this one indulgence. After all, he was in Allah's complete service. And Allah was surely pleased with him today. He didn't wait until he arrived at his destination to begin his search. He was watching the sidewalks closely as he drove past Pentagon Place. The sprawling mall was full of bored housewives at this time of day. Alongside them were recent college graduates and new hires of the powerful from offices all around the city. Many of them came here on their lunch break to purchase five-dollar cups of coffee or a salad more fattening than a fast-food burger. He shook his head in contempt at the thought.

He felt his car cooling slightly as he entered the mall parking deck. He'd make a round through the garage to see if there were any worth following. He'd succeeded like this before on more than a few occasions. Women were drawn to his dark good looks and his perfect British accent—lots of women. Ian never ceased to be amazed at how ridiculously trusting some were after only knowing him a few minutes. After they were in his secondary apartment and were getting dressed, some stupidly began to assume they'd established a connection with him. They, in turn, began to ask questions, too many questions. A day or two later they would end up as stories on the six o'clock news—"missing but presumed dead."

Rounding the corner, Ian saw just what he was looking for—tight white jeans and high heels, leaning over to place something in the trunk of a Lexus.

Gorgeous, Ian thought. His heart had already begun to race as he slowed slightly. Then, as he made his first pass by the car, he saw the woman's small child still strapped in its stroller, which was parked between the Lexus and the car in the next slot. He accelerated rapidly, irritated at the intrusion into his newly formed fantasy. He didn't have the time or the motivation for this today. He was more interested in a sure thing.

Aggressively, he pulled the Jag out onto Fern Street. The tires chirped slightly as he shifted from first to second, dashing ahead of an oncoming panel van, the logo of an overnight delivery company emblazoned on its side. He glanced at his Rolex and quickly calculated that he could be in the red light district of D.C. in about 25 minutes.

10

Ashley puffed out her cheeks as she reviewed the letter that had been delivered to Dan by courier that morning. It was the fourth time she had read it and she was still numb. The letterhead read Riverguardian. All she'd been able to find on Google in the two days since the oil spill and subsequent meeting with Dan and Tony was a very slick-looking web page. Riverguardian was indeed an environmental activist group that was primarily interested in the protection of fish and marine life, but beyond that she'd found nothing. Ashley had no idea how they'd gotten her name.

In preparation for the meeting, Dan had given her a copy of the letter that had been sent to him. In it, the group demanded a meeting with plant management regarding SPG's "abuse of state wildlife." The letter had mentioned Ashley repeatedly by name as being frustrated in her role as the company's Environmental Specialist. Even though Ashley had little experience in legal matters, the tone of this letter screamed high-priced law firm. Although she had no indication that there were any ill effects being realized by fish in the river near the plant, she was scared. She was intimidated by everything from the letterhead, to the website, to the use of her name so prominently in the letter. The meeting with Riverguardian was scheduled for the following week and she was already nauseous with worry. What would they want? And just what was it Dan expected her to say?

"What are you reading—a ransom note?"

Ashley jumped at the unexpected voice. She'd been lost in thought and totally focused on the letter in her hand. She looked up to see her best friend at SPG, Connie Winters, standing in the door of her cubicle. She must have looked confused because Connie felt the need to elaborate.

"Whatever you're reading, you look like you just saw a ghost."

"I'm afraid I have. The ghost of what was a promising career as an Environmental Engineer. By the way, you look great as usual and you need to understand that I resent you for it."

Connie had been with SPG for -4 years and she looked at least 10 years younger than her age of forty-six. Her role as plant librarian allowed her to dress significantly more chic than Ashley was willing to, considering her work environment. Today she wore a brown suede jacket, brown boots, a crisp white blouse, and jeans.

When Ashley first started working at the plant site, she and Connie had almost immediately clicked. For now, Connie did what she always did when complimented. She diffused it and turned the attention away from herself.

"Don't be silly, you look cute, too, in your little top. I did notice it this morning. It's new. You've been shopping. Very nice."

Ashley replied, clearly not buying Connie's praise, "Yeah, I have a new top on that coordinates wonderfully with my coal-stained jeans and my steel-toed boots. I am sure the phone will ring any minute and I'll be asked to do the cover of *Vogue*."

"I think we were about to talk about the letter," Connie said, changing the subject.

"Ah yes, the letter. Well, I guess I probably shouldn't even talk about it, so consider yourself sworn to secrecy."

Connie held up two fingers. "Scout's honor."

"This is from an environmental activist group and...oh, here."

Ashley abruptly handed the letter to her. Connie finished reading and said, "Yikes, sounds like they are pretty intense. Are we killing lots of fish or something?"

"No!" Ashley was a little surprised at the question. "I mean, we occasionally pull in some small baitfish on the screens but they're usually already dying from something else. Some of the baitfish species die by the thousands naturally when the seasons change. When they become stunned by cooler water, they get caught in our intake screens. But any healthy fish is used to swimming against strong currents. They live in a river, for Pete's sake. Other than that, I don't know what they're referring to. Forget the fish; what scares me is how often they mention me by name. More than that, I have to give some of their members a plant tour next week. What if I say the wrong thing or something? I mean, I don't even know what they're about. I wish I could find out a little more about them before meeting with them but there really wasn't much on the web."

"You know who I bet could find more for us?" Connie asked. Ashley smiled slightly at Connie's use of the word "us." It made her feel good to know Connie was already standing alongside her in this.

"You're going to say Annette, aren't you?" Ashley groaned. "Connie, I don't want to ask her. She hates me."

"You're blowing it way out of proportion," Connie cautioned. "She doesn't hate you. She just has her own way of expressing herself. And she is the closest thing I've ever known to a real live computer hacker. If anybody we know can find out something about these folks, she can."

The two stared at each other for a moment. Ashley's expression reflected that she detested Connie's idea and had every intention of remaining seated right where she was. Connie, eyebrows slightly raised, countered with a look that communicated just how obvious it was that she was right and that she was determined they should proceed to Annette's office immediately.

After a few more seconds, and without another word being spoken, the pair rose from their seats and began walking down the aisle between the rows of engineer's cubicles. Ashley led the way, arms crossed to show her mild protest. Both were subconsciously aware that a couple of the engineers had rolled their office chairs to the edge of their cubicles so they could watch the two of them, but they had long since grown accustomed to it and ignored the gawkers.

Annette Boone was SPG's computer programmer. She could write code for computer programs that would perform functions as varied as turning a steam valve or balancing an accounting ledger. Her office literally bristled with computers and computer accessories. A couple of framed snapshots of her and her husband on vacation fought for shelf space with circuit boards and disc drives. When the ladies first walked in they thought Annette was out of the office. They soon realized that she was hidden behind the three large flat-screen monitors on her desk. With one hand, she was typing away on a laptop on a side table. With the other, she was manipulating a mouse for one of the other computers and clicking rapidly. Suddenly aware of the ladies' presence, she stopped typing and looked at them from between the monitors.

"Oh goodie," she said. "Malibu Barbie and racer gal Barbie in my office at the same time."

Ashley shot a look at Connie.

"Ashley," Connie said. "Do you ever get the impression that Annette doesn't like you?"

Ashley ignored the question and got right to the business at hand. "Annette, I could really use your help."

Annette wanted to be annoyed but the sound of desperation in "racer gal Barbie's" voice was too intriguing for that. Ashley continued. She told Annette about the upcoming meeting and told her what little she had been able to find on the internet so far.

"So, do you think you might be able to find out a little more about them?"

"No," Annette replied and returned to her programming.

Ashley and Connie looked at one another, perplexed as Annette returned to clicking and typing. Finally, looking up, Annette spoke again.

"I don't *think* I *might* be able to *possibly* find out a *little* more about them. I *know* I can find out a *lot* more about them, but then that would require a little more than just typing their name into Google, which is all most of you engineers know how to do." She stopped typing again and looked up, expecting one of them to challenge her. Instead, Ashley just looked relieved and for the first time Annette began to feel a little sorry for her.

"If you could get me some information before I go into a meeting with them it would be a huge help."

Annette hesitated a moment, then smiled and said, "Sure. Come by before you leave for the day. I'm sure by then I'll have some stuff printed out for you. It's work related so I won't wait till I get home to look into it."

Both women thanked her and were about to turn and leave when they noticed Deidra Saunders, Dan Dortery's secretary and right arm, standing in the door.

"Ashley, Dan and Tony want you to come back to the conference room right away."

"Why?" Ashley asked. "Is something wrong?"

"You could say that," Deidra replied. "Three representatives of the group Riverguardian just drove up to the gate."

11

Ian's skin was turning red and beginning to chafe. The scalding water of his third shower was beginning to be too much for him. He slapped angrily at the gold-plated handle of the faucet, shutting the water off. He snatched open the curtain and yanked a thick towel from the rack. Instead of drying normally, he scrubbed at his skin with the towel as though it were yet another step in the necessary sterilization process. He felt he could still smell the woman on his skin. The thought of it made him shudder with disdain. It was always like this. It would take him two days at least to stop feeling contaminated.

Momentarily, as he buried his face in the towel, he had a mental image of this one. Her curly, bleached hair framed a pretty face. Her body, obviously surgically enhanced, had been nothing short of spectacular. Briefly, Ian allowed the mental image to please him as the woman had for a time. Then he abruptly shook his head.

"American infidel whore," Ian said under his breath.

They were all whores. Every woman he met in this immoral land was the same. They were just like the English girls he'd lain with back at Oxford. He felt no sympathy or compassion for them. He felt he was just contributing further to the cause of Allah by making sure there would be one less infidel to destroy later. He also felt Allah would give him credit for all the potential offspring that would never be born. It was sort of like killing a female spider or rat or some other vermin. Eliminate her and you eliminate all her future generations. No, there was no compassion. There was only revulsion mixed with relief.

He stepped out of the shower and hot tub and walked to the double vanity. His lip curled in disgust at the sight of the twisted pile of dirty clothes he'd been wearing. Though they had been covered by disposable Tyvex coveralls, he still intended to throw them away. He always went the extra mile and took maximum precautions. One could never be too... the sight of blood on the cuff of one trouser leg stopped him cold. He looked across the floor and saw another streak of blood there. How could he have been so careless? The coveralls had always protected him in the past but the cuff must have slipped out beneath the elastic band at the bottom of the pant leg. If there was blood streaked on the bathroom tile. then where else could it be?

He ran naked toward the front door where he'd kicked off his shoes. These were not the shoes he'd worn when he killed the girl—those were incinerated in the bundle along with her body. These were his "escape" shoes. He always kept a new pair in his trunk for such occasions. When Ian saw the heel of the left shoe, his heart rate began to slow. There was no blood there. Perhaps he hadn't left a trail until after he had removed his shoes. He began to retrace his steps from there to the bathroom. There, a spot right there on the rug. Nothing along the hall, none behind the couch...no... no, there was some. Ian's breath became ragged as he went into the kitchen to look under the sink. He would have to clean it, that's all. He would stay up all night if he had to. Then he would need to retrace his steps back toward his car.

Ian cursed himself for being so careless. If the people he worked with ever learned that he'd risked this operation because of his own weakness, his fate would be much worse than death. If he caused the police to begin any type of investigation, they would make sure that his death would take days.

12

Shelton Leonard pulled his shirttail out for the third time as he stepped out of his Honda Prius. Then he tucked it back in again. On the one hand, he wanted to be perceived as a professional, on the other, he wanted to appear aloof and unconcerned. He waited for two of his fellow officers in Riverguardian to get out of the car. As he waited, he thought that despite the fact that he'd never held a job in any corporate cubicle prison or a foreboding factory, he was every bit as capable of conducting himself in a professional setting as any of the dolts they were about to meet with. By the same token, Shelton refused to succumb to their corporate, buttoned-down mentality. He refused to allow them to judge him by their warped, closed-minded standards.

"The clothes make the man, my rear end," Shelton thought.

"Summer. Stacey. You guys ready for this?" Shelton asked.

"Oh yeah!" the pair answered, oddly in unison.

Shelton didn't intend to tell anyone at SPG this, but he, Summer, Stacey, and two others comprised the activist group known as Riverguardian in its entirety. Expensive parchment letterhead, raised letters on their business cards, and a very slick website provided the impression of a much larger organization. That was precisely what he wanted. In any case, they had all they needed. They may have lacked research staff, any semblance of a real base of operations, or even viable data to support the accusations they routinely hurled at industry, but the very expensive lawyers they kept on retainer more than made up for those shortcomings. They received adequate funding from their parent organization to make sure of that.

They walked slowly across the parking lot. They approached the SPG facility like soldiers walking into battle, constantly scanning the area. Although they were outside the fence of the plant proper, the sights and sounds of a twelve-hundred megawatt facility were intimidating. The SPG generating station was capable of producing enough electricity to power an entire city the size of St. Louis. Even as they walked, massive amounts of energy were leaving the plant—energy that would keep lights on in dozens of schools, heat on in hundreds of homes, and heart/lung machines running in scores of hospital rooms.

Energy production of this magnitude required massive and clangorous pieces of equipment—turbines whirred, massive fans hummed noisily as they maintained the proper airflow in three hundred foot-tall boilers, and steam hissed through giant valves. To the Riverguardian team, the entire scene was surreal and downright creepy. This was the closest any of them had ever been to a hulking industrial plant. They didn't like what they were seeing one bit.

13

Ashley sat at the long table in the large conference room with her legal pad in front of her, still slightly out of breath from the jog across the plant site from Annette's office. To say this was a hastily called meeting would be putting it mildly. Dan had wanted to turn Riverguardian away at the gate and not permit them entry since they showed up with no appointment. This was clearly a power play on the part of these people. Much discussion had ensued between Dan, Tony, human resources, and the PR spokesman, Robert Jenkins. The consensus was that it would be a PR mess to turn them back. Better to let them in and talk with them. At least that way they could figure out who they really were.

Ashley could actually hear the clock ticking on the wall. Tony sat toying with his Blackberry. Dan had his palms together in front of his face with his fingers spread, his index fingers poking at his chin. June, the front receptionist and the first face visitors to SPG would see, had hurriedly prepared the side table for the hastily ordered lunch of sandwiches and chips. SPG would make every attempt to show hospitality and hear Riverguardian out. Despite this effort, it was clear to Ashley that no one, least of all her, wanted to be there. Each individual in the room had about a dozen other high priority jobs they needed to be working on. They were, after all, trying to run a 350-employee power plant.

Clyde Jenkins came whisking into the room, his ever-present day planner under one arm, his fountain pen in the other. Under duress, Clyde had begun to use cutting edge electronics like laptops and cell phones. It was even rumored that he had successfully sent a fax recently. Clyde made no bones about it, though—he was a pen-and-paper kind of guy. No Blackberries for him.

He'll probably be scheduling his own funeral in that darned planner thirty years from now, Ashley thought.

Ashley had just decided to break the tension with a little quip but as she leaned forward to whisper her attempt at humor to the two men, June walked in followed quickly by the two women representing Riverguardian—Summer and Stacey.

Just as I suspected, never saw them before in my life, Ashley thought.

Ashley's jaw dropped. The only man she'd ever dated—the man that she had once mustered the courage to say, "I love you" to—walked into the room. She'd not seen him in five years, since the beginning of her senior year at U of I, but he'd changed very little. Shelton looked around the conference room and then his eyes settled on Ashley. It was obvious, at least to Ashley, that he had some kind of reaction at seeing her. But what?

Though he'd fully expected Ashley to be in the meeting room, seeing her look at him had an effect that he wasn't anticipating. With all of the times he'd sat parked along her road and watched her drive by, with all the times he'd followed her as she drove into town, even after he'd watched her work near the river two days prior, he still wasn't ready for this.

Dan rose from his chair and extended his hand. "Is this everyone?" He seemed to have been expecting a larger group.

Shelton had apparently come to the meeting in an already hostile mood. "We're the management team of our organization. We didn't feel we needed to bring the entire staff along for a simple meeting."

Dan attempted to diffuse the immediate tension, "I'm sure that's true. I'm happy to meet you all. I'm Dan Dortery."

Shelton looked at Dan, then at his hand still extended in the offered handshake, then back at Dan again before reluctantly giving in to the greeting.

Ashley and Tony stood and exchanged cool handshakes all around. Ashley could feel a huge knot forming in her stomach. The other day she'd assured Tony and Dan that she didn't know anything about this group. She'd never even considered the fact that Shelton might be involved with this. She was certainly not surprised that Shelton had maintained his interest in the environmental movement that he'd been so passionate about. She'd even heard once that he was working for the EPA. But when she saw her name in the letter, she never considered this possibility. She found herself hoping that upon seeing her, Shelton would reconsider telling everyone the embarrassing truth about their relationship.

Shaking Shelton's hand, Ashley kept her grip very loose and started to pull away rapidly but Shelton gripped her hand tightly. Their eyes met for what seemed to be a very long and very noticeable moment. Finally, when he was ready, Shelton released her hand and took a seat.

Power play, Ashley thought, becoming angry. *Typical Shelton maneuver.*

She could still feel her heart beating in her throat and she was aware she was starting to perspire, but it most definitely wasn't due to any remaining feelings for Shelton. His handshake had instantly taken her back to the way she'd felt in the final dying weeks of their relationship. She'd thought she loved Shelton even when she left him, but she'd been unable to tolerate being with him anymore. Shelton never stopped competing and never stopped complaining. That, as much as anything, had ended their relationship. He always looked for an advantage. He never stopped trying to gain the upper hand, whether choosing a restaurant for dinner, preparing for exams, or as now, meeting in a boardroom. And no matter how much things went his way, Shelton always seemed to manage to emerge from the process feeling slighted.

Ashley shook herself out of her reverie. Dan was speaking, "Well, Mr. Leonard, Riverguardian insisted on this meeting, so why don't you tell us what your beef is with my company?"

The gloves are already off, Ashley thought.

Dan had noticed Shelton's body language toward Ashley and he didn't like it. Whenever Dan felt that SPG or its employees were being unfairly treated or when he felt someone was trying to take advantage, his speech became possessive. And he didn't generally use words like "beef" unless he was perturbed.

"Our 'beef,'" Shelton curved his fingers in air quotes, "as you call it is with the cavalier way in which this company treats the rivers of the state. State EPA mandates..."

"We know precisely what state EPA mandates," Dan interrupted. "We are not interested in having you lecture us on that topic. I have Mr. Sanchez and Ms. Miller here to make those determinations in full cooperation with our regulating agencies. What I *would* be interested in hearing is which of those obligations we're not meeting in your opinion. I would request that you be specific."

By Ashley's assessment, Shelton was clearly taken aback. Dan wasn't done. "Let's get something straight, Mr. Leonard. In your letter, you made some very strong accusations against this company and the people that work for me. They're accusations that I don't believe are based in fact. You cite Ms. Miller here as a primary source of your information and she's never spoken to any of you in her life. She'd never even heard of any of you until a few minutes ago."

Shelton spoke. "Ashley, is that what you told your bosses?"

Everyone in the room looked at Ashley. She didn't want to look back at Dan or Tony. She saw the self-satisfied smirk on Summer's face. The realization hit her: *I'm being set up!* She knew smug when she saw it. Her instincts told her that Summer and Shelton were dating. Summer had expected this awkward moment. Shelton had talked to her about it in advance. But why?

She didn't know how to respond. What could she say that would minimize the damage?

I'm about five minutes away from losing my job.

Finally, Tony spoke up.

"Ashley, you *don't* know these people, right?" he asked. "I mean, that is what you told us."

14

She had to say something. She decided the truth was her only option.

"I know Shelton. I *didn't* know he was affiliated with this group. I haven't spoken with him in several years and didn't even know he was in this area," she said quietly.

"Oh come now, Ashley," Shelton said sarcastically. "If you want to count multiple phone calls and two meetings in the last year as 'not speaking' then I guess you can play that game."

"That's a bald-faced lie!" Ashley shot back. She realized how unprofessional she'd just sounded, and how defensive.

Shelton realized that all he had to accomplish was to put the possibility in Dan and Tony's minds that inside info may have been leaked to him. If that were the case, then they couldn't be sure just what it was that Shelton might know. That being the case, they would be much more pliable, much more determined to keep him away from the press.

For a brief moment, watching Ashley as her face grew paler, he felt sorry for her—but then he steeled himself. *The ends justify the means.*

"Everyone stop right there," Dan stepped in. He looked quickly from Ashley and then back to Shelton a few times as though he were watching tennis. "I'm not sure what's going on here but I don't care for your tactics, Mr. Leonard." He looked at Ashley intensely for a moment, silently letting her know that he and she would be having a discussion later. Dan went on, "Unless you want this meeting to end immediately, I think you'd better tell me exactly what you really came here for."

"We have evidence—documented evidence—that your facility is having an extraordinarily adverse effect on the fish population in the river. Your intake pulls in hundreds, perhaps thousands, of fish every day. There they are impinged on your intake screens where they become trapped and die." Shelton paused for affect.

Summer picked it up from there, "That is what we know. In addition to that, Ashley seems to think that many of your employees have warned your management team about this and you've refused to spend any money to alleviate this slaughter. So my question for you is, does SPG care about being a good environmental steward, as your brochures and radio ads purport, or is that just more corporate propaganda? Because if it is, then we think our lawyers would be interested in hearing about that. They might want to file a formal complaint with the EPA about that."

The Riverguardian team didn't realize it but the entire tone of the discussion had instantly changed with the invocation of the "L" word—lawyers. Dan and Tony now looked at one another, both pretty certain that they had a good idea of what this was about.

"First of all," Dan started to reply. "Ms...I'm sorry I didn't get your last name."

"Summer. Just Summer. That's my legal name."

"All right, Summer, first of all, if you want to call your lawyers then please go ahead and do that now. As you're doing that, I'll be calling mine. They would be very interested in hearing the slanderous accusations you just made. There's a whole big office chock full of 'em that will be down here to talk to you and your lawyers faster than you can spell fish. Now, on the other hand, if you would like to test your accusations against reality, then that might be something that we could work toward together."

Dan let that sink in for several seconds. He only gave a sideways glance to Tony, who was looking at him as if he'd lost all his marbles. Tony slid a note over to Dan. He'd written it in bold caps: NEED TO TALK TO ASHLEY OUTSIDE THIS MEETING. AM CERTAIN WE ARE NOT SEEING ANYTHING LIKE THESE NUMBERS OF FISH ON OUR SCREENS!

Dan leaned in close to Tony. "I'm sure you are right. That's why I want to play it this way," he whispered.

Shelton was unsettled. He hadn't expected such a suggestion. What he'd hoped for was a confrontation that he could use with the media and in the lawsuit he wanted to file against the EPA. From his perspective, a study would only delay what he wanted to do. But now, what he was being offered was full access to the intake. He could use that.

"What are you proposing when you say, 'work together,'" Shelton asked.

"I'm telling you that SPG would be willing to fund a study. We could hire an independent marine biologist to oversee the study. We can try to find out just how much effect we're having on the fish population. We'd be willing to share information with your group. If we find that we're having as significant an effect as you propose, then we'll come up with a plan to mitigate that effect. On the other hand, if we can demonstrate that we're not having a significant impact, then you drop all these lawsuit and media threats."

Ashley was becoming incensed. "Dan, you don't have to cave to them! I assure you I've never spoken to any of them, they don't have anything..."

Shelton interrupted. "I didn't want to invade anyone's privacy but I have some printouts here of emails from Ashley to me." He began to rummage around in his briefcase.

Tony held up his hand. "Ashley, I think it would be best right now if you left the meeting and headed back to your desk. The three of us will meet separately later."

"Tony, I..."

"Ashley, please."

She rolled her chair back hard against the wall, glared at Shelton, and walked out, slamming the boardroom door against the stop as she opened it. She wanted to be angry. She wanted to lash out. But that was not what she really felt. Instead, she felt the worst hurt she could ever remember.

No one spoke for a time. Shelton hadn't foreseen this offer. Now the wheels were really turning. *Mr. Tough Guy Dan doesn't realize that he is offering up his beloved SPG to me on a platter,* Shelton thought.

Dan leaned closer and looked Shelton intensely in the eye. "You accuse us of not caring for the environment. I'm giving you an opportunity here. You can be a part of research that might provide huge benefits to the river you claim to care about."

"How long would the study be? What would be the protocol?" Shelton was stalling. He didn't know whether to take Dan's offer or to continue to pursue his original strategy. He wasn't sure which would provide him the greatest advantage.

Tony was catching up to what Dan's intentions were. "We can provide details for you in a separate meeting, after we've selected a consulting biologist."

"The clock is ticking, Mr. Leonard. SPG is extending a hand of friendship here despite the way you approached us. Why don't we shake on this and then have some lunch?" Again, Dan extended his hand.

Shelton looked from Summer to Stacey, both of whom only shrugged. The decision was his to make.

Shelton stood, turned his smile up to maximum wattage, and extended his hand.

15

Ashley paced back and forth behind the locked door of the ladies restroom. If someone had to go they would just have to walk across the building because she was about to lose it and she didn't want anyone around to see it happen. She was genuinely unsure of what was happening to her. She wanted to scream, cry, pitch a fit—something! This was not like her. She was always cool under fire. She'd been in race cars traveling at 120 miles an hour that suddenly went into an uncontrolled spin in a curve and never felt this sense of panic.

It wasn't just that Shelton, for reasons she couldn't comprehend, had blindsided her. It was also that Dan and Tony had believed him over her. Had she established no credibility in her five years of loyal service here? And what was Shelton's problem? Why try to destroy her career? She thought back to when she broke up with him. She'd given him the classic, "it's not you it's me" speech, and he'd taken it almost in stride. If anything, she'd been a little miffed that he hadn't taken it harder. Had he been harboring bitterness ever since?

And what about SPG and the river and the fish? Shelton had been a marine biology major. He did love the water and marine life, and when they were dating he was much more political than she had been. But she never saw him as being particularly anti-industry. Ashley couldn't make sense of any of this on her own. As she thought more and more about what had just transpired, she became less hurt and more angry. She may have been dismissed from the room in shame, but Shelton could be sure that they'd be having another private conversation before he left this plant site.

"How long is it going to take them to eat a stupid sandwich?" Ashley wondered aloud. From her bathroom stronghold, she could hear the boardroom door open. She had to come up with a plan. She couldn't just march up to Shelton in the hall in front of Dan and Tony and have a screaming match. Thinking of Dan and Tony made her realize anew that she may very well be unemployed at this very moment and not realize it.

"He is not going to cost me my job," she said to her reflection in the mirror.

At that, she set her jaw, splashed water on her face to freshen up and reached for her truck keys. She stepped out into the hall and without a word to anyone, she walked to her truck, started it up, and wheeled it around to park behind the Prius, blocking it against the curb.

"You're not leaving until you talk to me, you lousy..." she said, pounding the steering wheel with her hand. She stopped just short of really doing some damage, to the wheel or her hand.

Mike in Security took all this in through the monitors in the Security shack. He didn't know what was going on but he decided he'd better be prepared. He reached for his hard hat and slid his billy club into the loop on his belt.

By the time Shelton shook Dan's hand at the front door of the office building one final time, Ashley had composed herself for the coming confrontation. The last thing she wanted was to come across as hysterical, but she knew she could reach that point easily right now.

It wasn't until Shelton was fiddling with his door key that he looked up and realized an old pickup had him blocked in. Frowning, he started to look towards security when he heard the door of the truck open. Ashley didn't bother closing it but walked to within an inch of Shelton's nose.

"What is your problem?" Ashley startled herself for a moment. She realized her voice sounded like someone else.

Shelton smiled smugly and took a step around Ashley. Ashley sidestepped to block him again. She wanted to hit him. She wanted to knee him where it would really stop him but she didn't dare—that would guarantee her firing. Unexpectedly she got a mental picture of her father and wished he were here.

Realizing he was not going to be allowed to leave without talking to her, Shelton spoke. "I've been wanting to ask you the same question, Ashley," Shelton spat. "What is *your* problem? Why have you become everything we fought against? Why do you enrich yourself at the expense of the nature that you once claimed to love so much? I always thought you were smart but I guess you're as stupid as those people are." Shelton jerked his head back toward the office building.

Ashley was taken aback and felt tears welling up. "Where's all this hostility coming from? We ended on friendly terms. Why are you trying to get me fired?" she asked.

"Oh please, don't flatter yourself. Do you actually think I have been sitting around pining for you all this time? My team identified this as a problem plant long ago. It was strictly coincidence that I later found out you worked here," Shelton said with deep disdain in his voice.

"What's this all this about emails and phone calls?" she asked. "You know full well we haven't spoken since before you graduated."

"You'll have a lot harder time proving that we haven't talked than I will have proving that we have, Mustang64andahalf." Shelton shot back.

This stopped Ashley cold. Shelton had her Hotmail address. How on earth had he gotten that? Suddenly Ashley became aware that Summer and Stacey were standing right behind her. The scene was starting to look like a group of playground bullies picking on the new kid. For a second Ashley felt the knot of nerves starting to form in her stomach once again. Then she glanced a little further beyond Shelton and the others.

A few feet away she noticed Mike, two other security guards, as well as Leroy and a gathering of mechanics holding very large wrenches, some still chewing bites of sandwich from their lunchboxes.

"These folks giving you trouble, Ashley?" Mike asked.

Ashley couldn't help but smile a little, especially when she saw a hint of fear in Shelton's eyes as he eyed the group of men. With the way her morning had gone up until now, it was nice to know some people still had her back. She was very tempted to scream "help" just so she could watch Shelton get pulverized.

Instead, she answered, "No, Mike, I think they were just leaving."

16

The strategy session was about to begin. Muhammad looked around the back room of the Chicago mosque. Here, in this setting, he could breathe a sigh of relief and leave his alter ego of Ian Flannery at the door. Here he could speak his native language, which he had practiced every day since leaving Arabia. He felt a chill as he remembered the cool dampness of the basement of his adoptive parent's home in Coventry. He would hide there as a boy to read from the sacred book and to recite in Arabic. In their presence, he was a good Anglican. It was all part of who he had to become, of what he had to be, in order to please Allah.

The strike team assembled and Muhammad looked from one face to the next. Abraz, Nadeem, Dahi, and Adeem, dedicated servants of Allah, one and all. He could trust these men. Muhammad unrolled the cylindrical structural drawing that Earl Worthen of the Royal Engineers had lost his life to deliver to him.

"I've marked the exact location for the charges. There will be six of them. Each one placed counter from one another, here and here." Muhammad said. "It will be critical that the charges be accurately mounted. You will only have three inches leeway in either direction. If you are off in your placement by any more than that, the structure will remain standing."

"What if that should happen?" Dahi asked.

"It must not happen." Muhammad's anger flared as he punched the table hard enough to make the large drawing bounce.

Each of the men recoiled. Muhammad, inwardly embarrassed at his show of emotion, continued. "It must not happen. But if it does, Nadeem and Abraz will go in again. The rest of us will form a perimeter and fight off security with small arms and grenades. But a failure of that type may jeopardize everything I...we have fought for. Even that much of a loss of the element of surprise could give them time to take countermeasures. We cannot allow that."

Muhammad didn't notice it but Adeem had been glaring at him from the time he hit the table. Adeem, only twenty-three years old, had reacted much more than the others to Muhammad's flash of anger. He stared at the man, twenty-four years his senior now, and remembered the terrible day that they'd first met.

He'd been playing outside the sheep's fold with his little sister and brother as the sight of a dust cloud in the distance caught their eye. Trucks were approaching. Adeem's attention was drawn to Muhammad, standing behind the machine gun of an antiquated World War II British half-track. Adeem's father came running in from the fields, his shepherd's staff waving in one hand. He was calling out to them but with the high winds that day Adeem could not make out what he was saying. It was only clear that his father looked afraid. It was the first time Adeem had seen fear in his father's eyes.

Before he could close the distance between him and the children, Muhammad felled him with a short burst from the machine gun, then another short burst stilled him as he clawed at the parched soil.

Adeem barely had time for the horror to soak in before his mother ran from the house. The fear that gripped him made Adeem's feet feel glued to the ground but he willed himself to run. He called out to his brother and sister to hide as he ran to place himself between his mother and the men, who were now jumping from the vehicles wielding AK-47's or pistols.

Muhammad had been ruthless. He had jogged right past Adeem and easily caught up to his three-year-old sister. He grasped the little girl roughly and clamped her under a powerful arm. Muscles bulged beneath a tan army-issue t-shirt as he held the little girl so tightly she could barely breathe, much less cry. At the same time, one of the other men had Adeem's six-year-old brother. Adeem was proud of the way the younger boy fought. But then the man threw him down hard on the ground and then jerked him up by his collar. He punched the small boy in the solar plexus, paralyzing his diaphragm and rendering him unable to move.

Adeem gritted his teeth and took a step toward Muhammad, his fists balled up tightly. Before he could do anything to help his siblings, however, his mother's scream wheeled him back around. Two of Muhammad's men had fallen upon her. Blood splattered as one of the men busted her lips with the butt of his rifle. The others were tearing her clothes until Muhammad caught up to them. He drew a pistol with his free hand and shot the man closest to him. Everyone stopped and looked at him, even Adeem.

"You will follow the orders you were given," he called out. "I will not have my men conducting themselves beyond my orders. Now bring the woman over here. You take this child and bind her. Over there, take her over there with the brother." Muhammad didn't care about protecting the woman. It was only that he had intended to take her for himself. Now the others had soiled her with their touch and she was no good to him.

Adeem ran towards Muhammad as he spoke this. From his belt, he drew a small straight knife. His father had told him only last month that he was now old enough to have one. He held the knife up as he ran and he felt a growl of rage rise in his throat. Suddenly as he drew near Muhammad, the man turned and met him with a kick that sent him flying in one direction and the knife in another. Muhammad stepped with cat-like quickness toward the boy and before Adeem could gather himself, he was jerked off the ground. Muhammad punched him so hard on the side of the head that Adeem thought he would black out.

"This one will serve Allah well," Muhammad laughed admiringly. "He has the heart of a lion. We will have to aim him toward the right enemy. That process starts now."

With that, he threw Adeem down to the ground again and drew a second pistol from his belt, this one a revolver. He opened the cylinder and fed in one .38 caliber slug. He snapped the cylinder closed and cocked the revolver.

"Seize them," he called out. As he did so, the men that had tied his sibling's hands behind them drew large curved swords and placed them at the children's necks.

Adeem couldn't seem to think clearly. His mind was reeling from the way that his life had been destroyed in only a few moments' time and from the blow he had taken. He saw his baby sister squirming against the knife as a trickle of blood ran down her throat.

"Sari, do not move or you will be cut. Just be still and I will come to help you," he called out. His own voice sounded strange to him. It was as if he was shouting from inside a well. He heard his mother trying to comfort her children. He was aware that she was having trouble speaking through broken teeth.

"I give you one chance to make the correct choice, boy." Muhammad stepped over in three large strides and lifted Adeem easily from the ground by his hair.

"You will take this pistol, it contains one cartridge, and you will prove your loyalty to Allah. You will kill your mother with it or you will be responsible for watching your brother and sister die."

Adeem couldn't comprehend what he was hearing. He couldn't process it. At first, he heard his mother scream. But as she looked back and forth from Adeem to her younger children, she forced herself to be calm.

"Adeem, do what you must do," she said. "Save the children. I have lived. Give them a chance to live. Do as they say, Adeem. You have no choice."

It was all too much. Adeem just stared at the pistol as if he didn't know what it was. The pain in his scalp was numbed by the shock of what was occurring in the yard where only moments before he had laughed and played with his siblings.

"You have ten seconds before they all three die. Do you think we will hesitate? Did we hesitate to kill your father? Ten...nine....eight . . ."

"Adeem, take the gun," his mother screamed.

"No, Mama!" It was the first time he had heard his brother's voice since the men had arrived.

"Seven...six . . ."

Adeem reached out for the pistol but Muhammad jerked it back.

"Don't get any ideas boy. There is only one bullet. If you point this at one of my men, you will all die. And it will be a slow death." With that warning, Muhammad handed the gun to Adeem.

"It's okay, son. I love you. I want you to do it," his mother said. "You are not taking my life; you are saving Sari and Jaktar."

Adeem could not see. Tears burned his eyes. He couldn't feel anything. His limbs were numb.

"Five...four...three..."

Adeem raised the gun but he couldn't pull the trigger. The gun felt so heavy. It waved around wildly as he tried to make himself squeeze the trigger.

"Two..."

Adeem heard his baby sister cry out. He steeled himself, and then heard his own scream rise in his chest. Suddenly the gun went off and his mother's body went limp. Adeem kept screaming. He couldn't stop.

He felt himself snatched up by the collar and was aware that he and his brother were being carried to the half-track. Just before he was tossed into the sweltering enclosure of the half-track, Muhammad grasped his face roughly and forced him to look toward his sister.

He watched in horror as the man with the sword slit her tiny throat.

"You shouldn't be so easily swayed, boy," Muhammad said with contempt as he clamped Adeem's hands to a bulkhead in the half-track. As the tailgate was closed, Adeem took a mental picture of his family, lying in pools of blood on the desert sand.

He never forgot that picture. He didn't forget during the years of intense training in Al-Qaida training camps. He never forgot during the hours of intensive study and brainwashing under radical Imams.

He saw the image clearly now as he had heard the same anger in Muhammad's voice. Adeem wondered where all that anger, bitterness, and hatred had originated. It didn't matter really. All that mattered to Adeem, all that he lived for, was the day when he could kill Muhammad Rashi. When this mission was completed, that day would be at hand.

17

Ashley downshifted to third and accelerated past a red Toyota as she headed for the long straightaway on Highway 45. She shifted smoothly back to fourth and felt the therapeutic push in the small of her back as she floored the accelerator. Her eyes scanned the horizon for deer approaching the road, as this area enjoyed a large population of whitetails. She glanced at the gauges as the next curve approached rapidly—120 mph—way too fast an approach. She slid her heel over to the brake, keeping her toe on the accelerator. She peeled the speed rapidly down to 70, downshifted to third, and then used her toe to accelerate through the sweeping turn. Heel and toe braking, just the way her father taught her—it would add a good 10 mph to a driver's exit velocity through a curve.

She heard the tires squeal and had to fight a little to keep the Mustang's back end from swinging around on her. She was at the absolute limit of what the car was capable of and she knew it. Ashley always drove fast when she was really angry. She also drove fast when she was really happy, sad, or just bored. But this was different. Ashley was taking out her frustrations today. She wished that the gearshift was Shelton's neck. She could have easily strangled him about now.

Her speed was back up over a hundred as she approached the area in front of her house. She intended to drive right on past, but slowed considerably on the outside chance that one of Ray's kids was playing near the road. Instead of seeing a child, she saw Connie Winters leaning against her Harley in the driveway in front of Ashley's house.

"Well surprise, surprise," Ashley said aloud. Actually, there was nothing surprising about it. She had known Connie would show up sometime today. Ashley had sent out a terse text after she left the parking lot, telling Tony she was taking a half day of vacation. Then she'd peeled out of the parking lot in the old pickup without further explanation. Over the course of the rest of the day, she'd alternately cried, shouted, and thrown things.

Now she didn't alter her normal parking pattern in order to accommodate the big Harley. As usual, she pulled past the driveway, backed the Mustang in, and drove over onto the grass so that she could get around Connie and back into the garage. Connie had become her best friend, but right now, she didn't feel like talking, not even to her. Secretly, she hoped her abrupt demeanor would send that message. As the garage door closed, Ashley drug her bomber jacket out of the front seat and shrugged into it as she headed for her house. Connie wasn't deterred in the least.

"Did I ever tell you that I think it's cool the way your little back window and trunk thingie come together?"

"It's called a fastback, not a trunk thingie. Connie, I gotta be honest with you—I really don't feel like talking right now."

Connie was following her step for step just behind her right shoulder. Her motorcycle boots clumped onto the wooden front porch and her leather chaps made swishing sounds as she walked.

"Oh, you don't feel like talking. As if it's fair for me to be frozen out of the juiciest tidbit to come out of SPG in years. Why don't you think about somebody besides yourself for a change?"

Ashley refused to let Connie see the faint smile forming at the corners of her mouth. She was going to be really hacked off if Connie made her laugh. To prevent that, she shoved her hands deeply in her jacket pockets, spun around, and plopped down heavily in the porch swing.

"You mean Gary finally said it was okay for you to drive his Harley?"

"He said it with his eyes," Connie answered as she looked affectionately back at the Sportster. "That's the great thing about 21 years of marriage. We don't need to talk in order to communicate. I could even read his thoughts while he was engrossed in watching the Salukis. By the way, I need to leave soon. Gotta get this thing back before the game ends," she nodded towards the bike.

"You know that environmental group I never heard of before?"

"Yeah."

"Turns out my ex-boyfriend is the president of it."

"And he's the one that showed up at the plant today?"

"Yes."

"And you hadn't spoken with him, didn't know he was coming?" Connie asked.

"Nope. Not a clue. I haven't heard one word from him since we broke up five years ago. He blindsided me, Connie. He set me up so that he could embarrass me in that meeting. I might really get fired over this." Ashley began to cry. Then she got angry with herself for letting it get to her and pounded a fist on her thigh.

Connie softened her tone. "Well, first of all I am pretty sure from what I was able to overhear that you will NOT be getting fired." She noticed Ashley's inquisitive look and then said, "Hey, a gal can't help the conversations that she happens to hear through her air vent."

"Really hard to avoid overhearing when you stand on that chair, huh?" Ashley laughed despite herself and dabbed at her eyes with her finger.

"I know you're angry right now but you've always told me you were over this guy long ago," Connie said.

"I don't have to still love the guy to be hurt when he throws me to the wolves the way he did today. Why would he do that?"

"Only one reason can suffice. He's a jerk. What did you say his name was?"

"Shelton."

"Sounds preppie. Or maybe it reminds me more of a dog. Here Sheltie, come here, boy." Connie quipped.

"Oh, he was definitely preppie, especially when we met. His parents were both lawyers and then in college he got really into Ecology and the environmental movement. I didn't have a problem with it. In fact, I kind of liked it. But he grew more and more intense about it. It got real political for him."

"Is that why you broke up?"

"No, not so much. I think I just got tired of his arrogance. It was clear that things would always be his way and that I counted significantly less than he did. Once that became clear, I got out."

Connie and Ashley talked for over an hour but they couldn't come up with a good answer to Ashley's "why" question. As darkness began to fall, Connie turned down a lift home in the Mustang and headed out on the Sportster. Ashley made Connie promise to text her when she got safely home.

What had been a crisp but pleasant afternoon was rapidly turning frigid and Ashley thought for a moment about what a cold ride her friend would have on her way home. Then she went to her bedroom, traded her driving shoes for her sheepskin-lined bedroom shoes and put on a pot of coffee. She went with a breakfast blend but chose the decaf because she didn't want to lie awake tonight. She needed to fix a bite to eat, but was too tired to cook. "Maybe I'll eat cereal tonight," she sighed.

A few minutes later, she was lying on her couch, munching on biscotti and thumbing through a sports magazine. She stopped on a headline entitled, "How Global Warming Will Affect Baseball."

"Oh, brother," Ashley rolled her eyes and let her head drop back onto the sofa cushion. "Why don't we just write an article on how global warming will affect hangnails while we're at it," she said sarcastically. She began to read the article. "Global warming is no longer a theory; it is a fact of life," the article began.

"Yeah, you're right. It isn't a theory. It hasn't risen to that level yet. It is a hypothesis, nothing more," Ashley said, growing frustrated. Before she could read the next line, she thought she heard a knock at the door. Ashley cocked an ear, not sure of what she had heard. *Knock, knock, knock*...there was the noise again. It sounded more like a tap than a knock. Ashley blew her bangs out of her eyes and murmured under hear breath as she set down her coffee mug, put her slippers back on, and shuffled to the door.

"Can't a person just have a few minutes of quiet around here without somebody...?"

She didn't complete the sentence but instead flung the door open unceremoniously. At first, she didn't see anyone there. Then she looked down. There, standing approximately two feet-nothing, was her neighbor, Emma, staring up at her with those incredible brown eyes. She held a white kitten under one arm. The kitten raised its head briefly to look at Ashley but then let itself go limp again with its front paws dangling. The kitten didn't seem to be under stress but instead seemed willing to accept whatever Emma wanted to do. Emma was the youngest child of her neighbors Ray and Marsha. She was an adorable child whose head was covered with natural blonde curls.

"Hi, Emma!" Ashley said. "Boy, your kitty sure does seem relaxed."

"Yeah, he always goes with me. He ate too much ice cream. I tol him not to eat all that bowl but he didn't wanna save any for later."

Ashley couldn't help but smile at that one. "So you've been feeding the kitty ice cream?"

"Yeah, his name's Mr. Tinkles. My Daddy named him that for some reason. He had ice cream at my party." At that, Emma looked up and smiled her adorable little smile, her tiny white teeth in a perfect row.

"Oh, that's right. Today was your third birthday, wasn't it?"

"Yeah. I mean, yes, ma'am. I was just wondering if you would like to come over to my party."

Ashley poked out her bottom lip slightly. She wanted to make Emma happy but she really didn't feel like attending a party full of three-year-olds.

"Emma, that's so sweet of you to ask," Ashley said. "But I've had a really long day and I don't much feel like partying tonight."

Emma looked up at her, clearly disappointed. She reached up and brushed her curly bangs out of her eyes. She wasn't quite ready to give up that easily. "If you came, I thought you would like to play a game with me. My mommy got party games from da store and we couldn't have my friends over this year 'cause it costs too much money for a big party and my brothers don't wanna play the games after Mommy made 'em play already. My Daddy is cooking on the grill and you could eat with us."

Ashley started to protest again, but Emma was beginning to get a pleading tone to her voice. Ashley looked down, still hesitating, until Emma sealed the deal with a smile that could melt an iceberg. Even the kitten got in on the act with the sweetest little meow Ashley had ever heard.

"Okay, kiddo," Ashley finally answered. "Come on in while I put on some shoes and a jacket and we can walk over together, but the kitten stays on the porch."

Emma positively beamed.

18

Shelton leaned forward on the musty couch in his trailer and poured two fingers of Buffalo Creek Bourbon. He then picked up the warm Coke can he'd been using for a mixer, shook it, and threw the empty can in the general direction of an overflowing trash bin with a clang. Across his lap, covering the table and scattered on the floor were photographs. There were 8x10's, snapshots, and pictures on printer paper. They were all of Ashley.

Shelton slurped the bourbon and let it warm the back of his throat. He had passed through the stage of a young Southern gentleman sipping whiskey about two hours prior. Now he was just a sad drunk.

"You're so stinking beautiful," he said to one of the photos, this one of Ashley smiling beside him as they attended a dinner for the Sierra Club. She'd been happy with him that day. "You're so beautiful. Why did you have to give up on me? Why did you have to abandon what we were trying to accomplish?"

Shelton threw the photo and watched it sail like a badly folded paper airplane toward the corner of the tiny cluttered living room.

"She never got it," he said as he drank another swallow. "She never saw the big picture. She doesn't see it now. She's part of *them.*" He was talking to himself now but he had said the same things to Summer a couple of hours ago. Finally, she'd tired of hearing about Shelton's old girlfriend and stormed out; slamming the trailer door so hard that it ricocheted off the doorjamb and remained partially open. Cool damp air flooded the small living area but Shelton could barely feel it.

"She's one of them," he said. "She is *they.*" Shelton laughed at his joke but it was a halfhearted laugh.

He picked up another photo, this one an 8 x 10 of the two of them. She'd gotten him to wear a tux for this one. It was some stupid dance and banquet for an engineering association she'd been a member of. Shelton recalled how miserable he'd been that night. What could be more boring than a room full of engineers?

"A little army of potential industrialists just waiting for their opportunity to screw up the earth," Shelton said aloud. "Just waiting to line their pockets." Shelton's vision was beginning to blur, so he held the photo up closer to his face and zeroed in on Ashley's brilliant green eyes.

"You were going to be different," he said. "You were supposed to become a part of the solution with me." Tears began to well up in his eyes. "And now you're one of them," he said. "So now you can suffer with the rest of them."

Shelton had plans—big plans. He was going to fight for what he believed in and become a star. The problem was Shelton didn't know what he believed in. He envisioned himself as some type of crusader. He considered the meeting with SPG and his traitor ex-girlfriend to be yet another battle in that crusade.

Despite this self-important image, deep inside Shelton was tormented. He didn't fight *for* a cause because the cause was too subjective. So he consumed himself with fighting against almost everything. He was against capitalism, against development anywhere for any reason, against exhaust from cars, toilet paper, hunting, horseback riding in national forests, controlled burning to enhance quail habitat, and logging.

Shelton never said so aloud but more than anything else, he was against people's right to breed like maggots. What constituted an adequately clean environment on a planet that contained six billion people? Shelton was tormented because he knew that even if he was successful against SPG, it would be like scooping a small cup of water out of an ocean of polluting, writhing, putrid humanity.

Shelton didn't believe in God but sometimes he fantasized about being God for a day. He thought often about how much better a place the earth would be with at least half the people gone. He would start with the people like the ones at SPG. "If only their mother's had aborted them, think how much better off Mother Earth would be," Shelton said to Ashley's photo. "Don't worry, baby, I would spare you. I would spare you and make you completely enamored with me. I'd make sure you never left me again."

Shelton shivered at the words coming out of his own mouth. Sometimes he wished he didn't drink. When he drank, it was more difficult to keep his crusader mask on and Shelton was forced to see his real face. He'd seen within himself too many times. That's what tormented him the most. Something had happened to Shelton at some point, perhaps during college but he really didn't know when.

Something had hardened within him and he had become deeply resentful and bitter. He wasn't sure exactly what it was that he was so resentful about, but he knew it was there. It had become a part of him. Perhaps it had become him. In any case, it was at moments like this that Shelton had to face what it would be like if he were God. Deep down, Shelton knew what he was capable of and the thought of it terrified him.

19

Aaron Hatcher sat in his blue leather office chair wearing tennis shorts and a white polo. He was an excellent tennis player who'd made it to the semifinals of the NCAA tournament when he'd been a student at the university. The chair in which he sat had been a gift from his father. It was finished in hand-tooled leather in the university colors. The official seal of his home state was prominently displayed on the backrest. Hatcher had been answering some emails and was now logging off so that he could arrive at the club in time for his 10 a.m. match.

As he swiveled his chair around to stand up, a framed 8 x 10 photo caught his eye. Though it had been there on the shelf of his home office for years, it had been a long time since he'd really looked at it. In the photo, his dad stood behind the very chair in which Hatcher now sat. His father's hands were on Aaron's shoulders as he sat proudly in the chair that had just been presented to him. Both men were beaming. It had been one of the few days in his life where both he and his father were truly happy to be in one another's presence. Just two days prior, Aaron had given his acceptance speech as a brand new United States senator. He'd achieved his father's expectations for him to enter national politics. And the timing couldn't have been better. Hatcher had won the seat vacated upon his father's retirement.

Aaron smiled at the memory. But just as quickly, as he began to enjoy that recollection, thoughts returned to him of how bitterly disappointed his father was when he lost the seat after only two terms. He'd lost to an up-and-coming conservative Republican. At the time, there hadn't been a Republican U.S. senator from Aaron's home state in over a century. The loss had been a disgrace for the Democratic Party and more painfully, it had been a disgrace for the Hatcher family.

The old man had made sure that Aaron was aware of his disappointment. He'd reminded him of it each and every day. Over the years, he'd grown accustomed to power. He'd served eight terms in the U.S. Senate and had no experience in handling defeat. He was a tough and sometimes ruthless old man who intended to motivate his son to fight viciously to win his rightful seat back in the next election. Unfortunately, he didn't live to see that wish become a reality. He died only ten months after Aaron lost the election. Aaron knew in his heart that his failure had killed his dad. He hadn't even sought re-election.

"Just you wait, Dad," Hatcher said to the photo as he stood and grabbed his racket off the divan. "Soon I'll be more respected and revered than you ever dreamed of being."

20

Ashley hoisted herself up on the picnic table. It was entirely too cold outside for grilling but she had played one too many games of pin the tail on Barney and was ready for some quiet.

"Burgers are almost ready," Ray said cheerfully. He was huddled over one of those cheap hibachi grills that usually rusted out after a season or two. The burgers were taking forever as it was tough to get enough heat out of the cheap charcoal on such a chilly night.

"Ashley, it was really nice of you to come over," Ray went on. "Emma thinks the world of you. I think she looks at you as more of a big sister than as a grown up. No offense, of course."

"None taken," Ashley held up a hand. "And I'll accept that as a complement, by the way. It was no trouble at all to come over. To tell you the truth I was in a pretty cruddy mood before I came over and all the laughing I did with Emma and the boys really cheered me up."

"Yeah, funny thing," Ray said. "The boys didn't want to play any of those little party games and then, all of a sudden when you show up, they're fighting over who goes first."

Ashley blushed slightly and merely smiled back before looking down at the ground.

"So what put you in a bad mood before? Something happen at work?" Ray asked.

"Yeah, it was kind of a tough day. You might say we had a rough meeting and I was the main subject of it."

"That doesn't sound like much fun. So how are things at the plant?" Ray asked. "How's the electricity business?"

"Believe it or not, it's not that great. I always thought that when I got a job in a power plant that I sort of had it made, you know, job for life and all that?"

"Yeah, that's kind of what I always thought," Ray replied.

"Well, it could be that way but I'm afraid it's not going to be."

"Why not?" Ray asked.

"Too many people out there don't like us. Or maybe that's not a fair way to put it. Too many people out there think we're bad for the environment. I think lots of folks would like to shut us down."

"Are you bad for the environment?"

"I don't think so. I mean, as you know, that's the area I work in. So I see all the money that's spent by my company to protect the environment. Sure, there are some emissions from a coal-fired plant, but we have multimillion-dollar equipment to minimize all that. You know, at some point I have to wonder if we're not getting to a point of diminishing returns with our environmental regs. Do I want a clean environment for my children? Sure I do. But I also know that people have to live on this planet. And if we make a decision to pull the plug, so to speak, on hundreds of coal-fired plants, then hard working people like you are going to start paying a heck of a lot more for energy."

Ray, who was finally starting to take the burgers off the grill, looked up. "Tell me about it. Why do you think we aren't having a real party for Emma? Just in the last couple of years, my electric bill has gone from ninety dollars a month for this little house to nearly two hundred. My natural gas bill for my furnace has done the same thing. I'm a mechanic; Tammy's a teacher's aide. That's a couple hundred a month coming out of some pretty small salaries. We don't have that to spare. We literally did not have the money this month for Emma to have a few friends over."

"Yes, that's exactly what I'm talking about. Much of those increased costs are coming as a result of environmental regulation. Let me give you one example of what I'm talking about when I say diminishing returns. When it comes to the environment, we answer first and foremost to the state EPA. Well, some study, which has been questioned by many, showed that there was mercury getting into the fish, like in tuna. The study proposed that the mercury was coming from coal-fired power plant emissions into the air and then settling in the water. So the state decided to regulate mercury. That meant that we had to find a technology to take the mercury out of our stack gas. Another way of saying that would be to say 'out of our smoke.'"

"Okay, I'm with you," Ray said. "You sound like you're about to start preaching, but I'm with you anyway."

"Sorry, I get a little passionate about some of this stuff" Ashley said. "So the best way that could be found to remove the mercury was to inject this specialized activated carbon.

"So how much mercury are we talking about here?" Ray asked.

"Ray, we burn thousands of tons of coal each year and with all that coal burned, we only emit ninety pounds of mercury. Now mercury is a heavy substance so I could easily put 100 pounds of mercury in that water bucket you have over there."

"You guys have to do all that to protect us from ninety pounds of mercury?"

"You haven't heard anything yet. It takes a great deal of equipment to inject all this carbon. We had to build silos and pipelines and install blowers and control devices. The whole set-up cost over five million dollars. Then we have to buy the carbon. The carbon for one year will cost us ten million more dollars."

"Man!" Ray said. "No wonder my power bills are so high."

"I'm still not done," Ashley continued. "After we put in the equipment and bought the carbon to inject, then we also had to build a landfill. You see, when we burn coal we get two by-products. Bottom ash is one. That's the stuff you see the highway department spread on the roads when it is icy. It doesn't have much value. But the other by-product is fly ash. Fly ash can be recycled and used in drywall and concrete. We used to sell our fly ash to those types of plants."

"You mean like recycling?"

"Yeah, exactly like recycling. But we can't recycle anymore. The carbon that we now have to inject spoils the ash. In other words, it messes it up so that it's no good for concrete or other products. So we had to spend millions more to build a landfill. Now instead of recycling the ash, we're going to pile it up in a great big pile. We have a permit from EPA to pile the ash 100 feet high. That'll take about ten years. After that..."

"After that you shut down?" Ray said.

"Yes, or we hope some new technology comes about."

"Gee whiz," Ray said. "Our government at work, huh?"

Ashley snorted derisively. By now Ashley had absent-mindedly walked over and started helping Ray place buns face down on the little hibachi as he tried to balance the platter of smoking burgers.

"You know what the worst part is?" she asked.

"There's a worst part?" Ray said.

"While people like us are paying a hefty price for all this regulation, the Chinese and the folks in India barely do anything to limit pollution in their power plants."

"So while our economy tanks, theirs thrives and booms," Ray said sarcastically.

"Something like that," said Ashley.

Once everyone was inside, the kids took over the conversation and cheered Ashley up once again. After a couple more rounds of games, Ashley caught herself yawning and decided to head home. Ray and Tammy showed her out.

"Ashley, it was so nice of you to come over," Tammy said.

"It was really nice of you to invite me. It made my day."

Both Tammy and Ray looked genuinely pleased. "I'm glad," Tammy said. "It was the least we could do what with all the rides you've given to Ray lately. Listen, Ashley, I didn't want to say anything in front of the children but you have a right to know as our neighbor."

"Tammy, don't say anything about this." Ray said. "It's probably not gonna happen."

"Now Ray, we talked about this before Ashley got here and you agreed. Ashley, we're probably gonna have to sell the house. We won't be your neighbors much longer."

Tammy got choked up and Ray's eyes glistened.

"She's overreacting, Ashley," Ray said. "I'm not going to let that happen. We dreamed about a little house like this for so long."

"Guys, I am so sorry to hear that. I hope it works out. Is there anything I can do?" Ashley asked.

"Oh no," Tammy said, she was clearly trying to put on a brave front. "You do enough things for us already."

"Like coming to our girl's birthday," Ray quipped.

After another awkward moment of heartfelt but inadequate sympathy, Ashley headed across the dark yard toward her house. Her mind was flooded with thoughts. She thought of how it would be to have ownership of an eleven hundred-square-foot frame house be your dream, and then to have even that taken away. She thought of how blessed she had been so far in her life: an idyllic childhood, great parents, an opportunity to go to a top flight engineering school and a good paying job. Then she thought about what she'd face as she went in tomorrow. And she wondered if she'd soon be planting a for sale sign in her own yard.

21

Lillian Hatcher, wife of former Senator Aaron Hatcher, could not believe her eyes. Everywhere she looked, there was another celebrity. What was a country girl from Possum Trot, Kentucky, doing at a party with Hollywood's elite? Lillian couldn't believe it but she had to admit she was loving the attention.

She looked across the room and saw Aaron. He was staring at her, and when their eyes met he gave her a wink. He was talking to one of the most downloaded internet pinup girls of all time and her producer/director boyfriend, but he was staring at her. That realization made her breath more deeply and her pulse quicken. After twenty years, she was still very much in love. Because of that, she was even more gratified than he was to see him finally getting the acknowledgement he deserved.

A few short years ago, this same group of people was regularly making fun of Aaron. Everyone from the cable talk show host currently standing by the smoked salmon, to the upstart comedy writer sitting on the couch beside the costar of her sitcom, had taken their shots. They'd had great fun talking about how stiff Aaron was and how much of a stereotypical Southern white male he was. When rumors were spreading that he was having an affair with a famous supermodel—Lillian had never for a minute doubted that they were indeed rumors—Aaron had become every comedian's favorite target. The media onslaught had lasted for weeks and had been a miserable time for Lillian and the children.

Lillian ran a finger along the rim of her champagne glass and turned slowly to look around the room. She'd long since gotten used to her handsome husband getting all the attention at the hundreds of political fundraisers and charity events the pair had attended. She didn't normally mind her solitude in the midst of a crowd. Tonight, however, was quite different. Tonight there were a few people she wanted to talk to. Her current dilemma was that she couldn't decide where to start. At that moment, the nightly anchor for GIN news made her decision for her.

The anchor, dressed in a three thousand dollar designer cocktail dress, sat on the opposite end of the couch from Tawny Ray, the comedy writer. These two had been among the harshest critics of Aaron when he was in office, one through satire, the other through what Lillian interpreted as smarmy comments whenever the anchor reported on him. The opening on the couch between the two was too inviting to pass up.

Both Tawny and the anchor, Seneca Fox, looked shocked when Lillian wedged in between them. Lillian realized that prior to that moment, they hadn't even noticed she was at the party.

"Good evening, ladies," Lillian said, barely hiding a self-satisfied smile.

"Uhh, good evening Mrs. Hatcher," Tawny said, still surprised. "Enjoying the party?"

"Oh yes, very much, thank you," Lillian was an expert at turning on the Southern belle charm whenever needed. She hadn't won Miss Congeniality in the Miss USA pageant for nothing.

"Your husband seems to be a big hit tonight," Fox said, nodding toward where Aaron was now talking with a talk show host and the founder of the world's most popular men's magazine.

"Yes, he certainly does, doesn't he?" Lillian said, her perfect smile gleaming. "It's wonderful how the media and entertainment industry has embraced him now. I mean, I guess a love for Mother Nature can unite us all. Even people who only recently vilified my husband are welcoming him with open arms."

No one spoke for a few awkward seconds. The anchor and the writer seemed to be waiting for a shoe to drop. Lillian watched the pair from the corner of her eyes as she pretended to scan the room. She was enjoying this. She knew she was making them both uncomfortable and she had every intention of dragging it out. Who were either of these two to criticize her husband? Tawny Ray had won a TV Emmy for the writing of the sitcom in which she starred, but Lillian remained unimpressed. Rather than looking ingenious, the few episodes of the show she'd seen were filled with jokes that were at once sophomoric and tawdry. The gags were the same old school-boy locker room sex jokes and cheap laughs that comprised most of the other comedies on that network. To be certain, Tawny was no Lucy. Despite this, she had somehow become the standard-bearer for some as to who in the country was cool or intelligent or competent and who was not.

Lillian had no more regard for Seneca Fox. Fox had somehow been given the coveted anchor chair after spending eight years wearing funny hats and jabbering while some visiting chef made nachos at the crack of dawn on "The Good Morning Sunshine" show. Now all of the sudden everyone was supposed to look upon her as Edward R. Murrow. Neither of the women had the "chops" to criticize her or her husband. *Wonder if either of them graduated Suma Cum*

Laude, Lillian thought. After another minute, she finally decided to let them both know what was on her mind.

"I saw the episode where you spoofed my husband, Ms. Ray," Lillian let the "s" in Ms. drag out like a long "z" sound. "I must admit I didn't find it either funny or particularly insightful."

Tawny started to speak but Lillian wasn't finished. "Likewise, I saw your expose on my husband's supposed affair, Seneca. You should have called me. I could have told you those were lies and saved you a lot of time." Lillian expected backpedaling from at least one of these women. That's not what she got.

Seneca responded, "I'm sorry *Mizz* Hatcher if you were hurt or offended by my story. But surely, you're not that thin-skinned after all the years your husband has been in politics. And many of the rumors and accusations about your husband were never adequately refuted."

Lillian was taken aback. She was *not* intimidated. Instantly the Southern charm dial was turned down. "Why, you self important witch," Lillian hissed. "By the same token, the vicious rumors that you gave voice to were never backed up with a shred of decent evidence. And yet you have the gall to sit here and get high and mighty with me?"

Lillian locked on Seneca Fox's eyes with a laser stare, held it for a moment, and then wheeled around to Tawny Ray, who had yet to say a word and was observing this conversation with a look of shock.

"And you, Tawny—how do you think my eight-year-old daughter felt when she went to school the next day after your episode depicting my husband running down a hotel hallway in his boxer shorts aired? Do you think maybe her playmates might have made fun of her? Or did you consider that?"

"Mrs. Hatcher, please, I didn't come here to fight. I actually came here to support your husband's cause. I care as much as he does about the environment. And at no time did we say that character was supposed to be your husband."

"Oh, come on," Lillian realized she was on the verge of losing her cool. "Do you think I'm stupid, Tawny? I can assure you, I'm not."

"Oh, grow up," Seneca interrupted.

Lillian turned to face her. Now she was the one who was shocked.

"So you and your husband did your turn in the cultural crosshairs. It goes with the job. If you think you were treated unfairly, you should call some of the folks from across the aisle. Republicans get more grief from us on average in one episode than your husband got over the course of his career. Every now and then, we have to go after one of our own a little. Your husband was it for a few weeks but you can cheer up now. It'll have to be someone else's turn. Your husband is about to be the next golden boy—a regular media darling."

Fox looked over her wine glass as Aaron Hatcher approached, then took a sip. Aaron walked over and stuck out a hand. Lillian saw that tonight he was a promising young senator again. He was on top the world.

"Ms. Fox, how nice to see you again," Aaron said. "Tawny, we get a big kick out of your show. We watch it all the time. Say, I hate to interrupt your conversation but if you don't mind terribly, I would now like to dance with my wife." Aaron reached out to take Lillian's hand.

"Why, Senator Hatcher, I'd be honored," Lillian said, faking her best Scarlett O'Hara, which was actually quite good.

Tawny still hadn't regained her balance from Lillian's earlier onslaught. Seneca only smiled thinly.

"Not at all, Senator. In fact, we were just finishing up," she said standing. "Tawny, I'll call you this weekend." Then the highest paid news anchor in television history turned and made her way to the bar for a refill.

"Umm, yeah," Tawny said. "I'll see you at Martha's Vineyard this weekend."

Lillian didn't hear the end of the exchange. She was already walking toward the band, holding Aaron's hand as they weaved through the celebrities. She could feel all eyes upon her and as she walked, she thought of what Seneca Fox had told her and couldn't help but smile.

I can't believe they're playing 80s music, she thought. "There's nothing like dancing to an Air Supply song with my big man on campus," she cooed to her husband. Lillian felt like she was back in her sorority days.

22

Ian Flannery walked along Church Street toward 7th. It was the first time he'd been here in over eight years, but the old neighborhood still felt like home. He had enjoyed living here. Everything one's heart could desire was within walking distance. His apartment had only been a few blocks away. The best baklava in the world could be had at a little bakery nearby. And then there were the women. This town was home to some of the world's most beautiful women.

He shouldered past one person and then another as he made his way along the crowded sidewalk. Everyone was busy, in a hurry, behind schedule; just as they'd been the last time he'd walked along this route. The citizens were just as busy, just as oblivious. In the grand scheme of things, not much had changed. To be sure, there were some new facades, new buildings, and lots of new windows, but the overall feel of the place had changed very little.

He stopped and leaned on the edge of a concrete planter that contained a newly planted ornamental tree. As he rested his legs there, Ian took a mental snapshot of the people walking by. No one noticed that he was staring. For that matter, no one noticed him at all. It was as if he wasn't even there—they were all that busy.

Ian leaned back a little further, blew out a slow breath, and closed his eyes. He could see the faces of all those he'd looked at intently a moment before. Only now, they weren't wearing expressions of determination and a drive to succeed. Now they were wearing expressions of panic. That was the way Ian painted them in his mind's eye. That was the way he wanted to see them. He wanted to see them disoriented and terrified. He wanted a repeat of September 11. He was so proud of his role in that great victory for Allah, but now it was time for a new triumph.

This time the victory would be greater. This time the effects would be felt far beyond the confines of a single city. In fact, the entire city of New York could never contain all the victims that he would soon create. This plan was more ingenious, better organized, and would be more effective than anything that had come before it.

Ian smiled as these thoughts ran through his mind. He smiled even more broadly as he recalled how readily the citizens and leaders of America were doing all they could to assist him without even knowing it. He came to his feet quickly and looked around. A lovely young Hispanic woman, perhaps twenty-five, strode past him in a grey business suit wearing four-inch heels. Ian fell in behind her. As he walked, he thought more about what this city would look like afterwards— after the great Satan had been brought to its knees.

23

Ashley rolled up to the gate in her pickup with a huge knot in her stomach. After the party, she'd relaxed and fallen asleep with no problem, but by four that morning she was wide-awake and wondering what the day would bring. She hadn't been this nervous since her first day on the job after her graduation. In fact, she was pretty sure she'd never been this nervous.

She shut off the ignition and saw a slight puff of smoke exit the exhaust pipe. *Still don't have that carburetor adjusted right,* she thought. *Better add that to the list of things I need to do, I suppose.* She grabbed her lunchbox on the bench seat and began to walk rapidly toward the security gate. She hoped Mike wasn't working today. She didn't feel much like joking and she didn't want to be in security any longer than she absolutely had to. Security was just too darned close to the "rock house." "Rock house" was the unofficial name for SPG's management offices. Ashley was walking with her head down, determined to race right through the turnstile and head to her desk. Though she knew she couldn't hide forever, she was perfectly willing to put off any meeting with Dan or Tony for as long as possible.

She would have no such luck.

"Are you in that big a hurry to get to work?" The voice belonged to Mike. "I've seen lots of folks walk that fast getting out of here, but not many walk that fast going in," he continued.

"Not now, Mike," Ashley replied. She didn't break stride, but continued to head for the turnstile.

"Geez, what's eatin' you? By the way, you gotta go over to the other entrance. This turnstile's broken."

"Uggghhh," Ashley groaned. "Today of all days? Why today?" She brushed past Mike and headed for the other turnstile. She knew, she just knew, that this little snafu was destined to be the difference between a quiet morning and a very unpleasant meeting. As she approached turnstile 2, she heard someone call out her name.

"Hey, Ashley!" It was Tony, calling from the front porch of the rock house. He didn't say anything more. He just stood there, waiting.

Ashley turned and headed towards Tony. As she drew closer, Tony said, "Why don't you step on in here? Dan and I need to talk with you. You can set your lunch in accounting's fridge for right now."

My last meal, Ashley thought. The butterflies in her stomach were getting butterflies.

Her feet felt like lead as she walked toward Dan's office. Once inside, Tony motioned to the chair beside him in front of Dan's desk.

Ashley knew that she should just keep her mouth shut and see what they had to say first. She knew she should be careful about saying too much at any time. But she couldn't help herself.

"Tony, Dan, I swear to you, I had no idea that Shelton was affiliated with Riverguardian. Shelton and I dated for a couple of years in college. He wanted to get married. We broke up. It wasn't even a bad breakup. At least I didn't think so. He just had different goals than me. Yes, he did seem to get more and more militant in his approach to environmental activism, but he was an active, outdoorsy kind of guy.

"I just associated it with that. His activism was not why I broke up with him. It had much more to do with the fact that he treated me like I was his personal assistant rather than his potential fiancée. I have had NO, read that, ZERO," Ashley held up her right hand making a circle with her thumb and forefinger, "contact with him since the day we broke up. It never in my wildest dreams occurred to me that he was a part of this group. And I am so sorry that this happened but I had nothing to do with it." She stopped to take a much-needed deep breath.

Tony and Dan both sat staring at her. They were clearly surprised by this outburst.

After a long moment, Tony said drolly, "Well, Dan, she just cheated us out of half of the well thought-out questions we came up with." With that, he began to laugh heartily. Dan just kept staring for a few more seconds and then his stoic face crinkled into a smile and he too began to laugh.

"You really cleared the air there, didn't you, Ashley?"

Ashley looked from one man to the other, her eyes still wide for a moment. Then she let her head slump as she stared into her lap and chuckled at her own expense.

"I guess I did kind of spill my guts in a continuous stream there, huh?"

"Yes, you did," Dan said, still laughing.

That did it. The tension was broken. Ashley knew right then that, though the rest of the meeting might not be fun, she wasn't going to be fired. She felt a weight lifting from her shoulders.

"Ashley, as you might well imagine, me, Dan, and the entire management team have discussed the meeting yesterday and your role in this situation at length," Tony said. "And at the end of the day, we looked at your work history and at what we've learned about you personally in the five years you've worked here. The bottom line is, we believe you."

Dan picked it up from there. "We don't believe for a second that you've been feeding information to these folks. In fact, we believe you when you say you've not had any contact with any of them prior to yesterday."

Once again, Ashley couldn't help herself, "Thank God," she said aloud.

Both men smiled at that. "But the fact remains that you have an ex-boyfriend with an axe to grind. He didn't pick our facility by accident. He didn't just stumble on a dead fish on the bank of the river down from the plant where his former girlfriend happened to be employed," Tony added.

Ashley felt some of the butterflies coming back. *Were they going to have to let her go to protect the company?* She decided she was being paranoid.

"I have to admit," she said, "that would be a pretty unlikely coincidence.

"Highly unlikely," Dan said. "What we can't know is if he's using *you* to come after us or if he's using *us* to come after you. Whatever the case, we feel it would be in the best interest of the company to get you offsite for awhile."

Ashley looked up, now on full alert. What exactly did offsite mean? Offsite generally did *not* mean fired, that much was certain.

"What do you mean?"

Tony and Dan looked at one another, their expressions suddenly more serious.

"Ashley, we have a special assignment for you. I've been thinking about asking you to do it for a while anyway and I just couldn't decide if you had enough experience. I feel like this situation has forced my hand. In fact I am going to have to insist that you accept it," Dan said.

"What is it? I am willing to do whatever I can to help. I feel terrible but..."

"We need you to go to Washington, D.C. and testify at a Congressional hearing."

Ashley was stunned. She didn't have a ready reply for that one.

"It would require you to be in D.C. for at least a couple of weeks. Don't worry about housing—we'll set all that up for you."

"A couple of weeks?" Despite all that had transpired in the past twenty-four hours, the first thing that crossed her mind was that she'd miss the upcoming Sturgis Classic. The Classic was a road race using vintage cars like Ashley's Mustang. It was a big deal to her and her dad, and he'd be disappointed that they wouldn't get to do it this year. They were sure they had a real shot to win the whole thing. "Why me?" she continued. "I don't know the first thing about testifying before Congress." She realized that her voice was getting higher the way it always did when she got really nervous, and she made a mental note to tone it down.

"Not many people do know much about testifying before Congress," Dan said. "Don't worry, we aren't just going to throw you to the wolves. That's why it will take you a couple of weeks. When you first get there, you'll be meeting with a law firm. They'll bring you up to speed on what's going on and what you need to know."

Tony chimed in. "Basically, the Executive Branch is contemplating doing an end-run around cap and trade legislation. They know the bill will be lousy for the economy and they don't feel the public will stand for it. So instead, they're going to try and get the EPA to regulate CO_2 as a pollutant. You know how hard that would hit us? It will very nearly put us out of business."

"And it'll put several other plants out of business," Dan said. "Electric rates would skyrocket."

Tony continued, "Ashley, the regulations they're considering would mandate the closure of multiple coal-fired power plants for the sake of reducing carbon emissions. And our sources tell us that two of our units are going to be on the list."

"You're kidding me! We just spent millions on a wet scrubber and mercury reduction. We're one of the cleanest burning coal-fired plants in the world!" Ashley was growing incensed now.

Tony shook his head slowly. "None of that matters when you're talking about carbon emissions. We burn fossil fuel—there's no getting around CO_2 emissions."

"You won't just be representing us, Ashley. You'll be one of several witnesses testifying for the Utility Power Institute." Dan said. "UPI believes that this legislation will have a much greater impact on already elevated power prices than this congressional committee is anticipating. They want to defeat this before it ever comes out of committee and before it ever gets to the President's desk. You'll be testifying about some our efforts in the environmental area and trying to change the minds of one or two senators on the committee."

"I don't know how to respond," Ashley said. "It certainly sounds like a worthwhile effort, but I never even considered doing something like this."

"Under normal circumstances I wouldn't tell you this, but these aren't normal circumstances. Face it, you're young, vivacious, highly articulate, well-versed in our processes and policies, and you're persuasive. You *will* make a great spokesperson," Tony said.

Ashley looked from Tony to Dan and back again. She was trying to think of another counterpoint but wasn't coming up with anything. After a moment, Tony said, "You'll make an excellent spokesperson, right, Ashley?" Now both Tony and Dan were boring holes through her with their stare.

Ashley recalled Dan's words that he would have to insist she accept the assignment. Then, she let out a big sigh and said, "I'll certainly do my best."

"Good," Dan said, slapping his hands down on his desk. "You can have a few days to make your personal arrangements. June is already working on your flight, housing, and travel allowance. Your first meeting with the law firm is a week from today."

24

Ashley sat at a small table for two in the Nashville airport sipping a cup of Burger King coffee and munching on a croissant. She was surprised to find that the coffee wasn't half-bad. At least the airport Burger King was open. Almost every other food vendor in the place still had the steel gates pulled down in front of their entrances. One or two employees worked diligently behind the gates, readying their businesses for the coming day.

June had scheduled a flight with a 6:30 a.m. departure, so Ashley had left home at three. She'd had no choice on such short notice. The other flights from Nashville to Washington were booked and Ashley didn't like the drive to St. Louis nearly as much. As she sat waiting for a boarding call, she heard the sound of running footsteps.

She looked up over her coffee to see a man, about her age, running clumsily down the concourse. In one hand, he held an old suitcase—the old style that the gorilla threw around in that famous commercial—with no wheels. Draped over his other shoulder, and held in his other hand by the hook, was a large suit bag that he hadn't taken the time to fold over and secure for air travel. Under an arm, he held a briefcase and every few feet he kept stopping to boost it back up with his knee. The man's face looked flushed and he wore the expression of someone who was very concerned that he was going to miss his flight. Ashley raised her eyebrows in sympathy as she chuckled under her breath at the man's awkward baggage.

The concourse was empty again for a moment until Ashley saw a pretty Arabic woman holding desperately to the hand of a small boy whom she estimated was between two and three years old. The boy wore a Thomas the Tank Engine backpack and strained forward, his little legs churning like Thomas' wheels as he tried to pull his mother along much faster than she was willing to go. A good thirty feet behind walked an older Arabic woman who appeared to be the first woman's mother. Ashley was struck by how Westernized the mother and little boy were dressed. The elder woman was dressed very traditionally.

The mother wore tight designer jeans and black high-topped boots with a stiletto heel. Her black silk blouse looked designer. Ashley didn't buy designer but she liked to window shop. The woman would have looked perfectly natural walking down Rodeo drive. Before she had time to consider why the woman's manner of dress struck her as strange, both she and the boy came to a fork in the concourse.

The group was up ahead of Ashley's table by now but she continued to watch since there wasn't much else to look at. At the fork, the woman pulled the boy up short as she tried to read the signs. It was apparently of critical importance to the boy that the family walked down concourse C. However, the woman turned toward concourse B. This was most displeasing for the child who instantly threw himself on his back and began to scream.

The boy lay spread-eagled on the floor, balanced on the backpack. The backpack seemed to have provided a passable fall arrest system as the child appeared no worse for wear from his abrupt meeting with the floor tile. In fact, far from acting hurt, the boy had the energy and determination to begin flailing wildly as he screamed. The grandmother now screwed her face into a scowl and quickened her pace to catch up.

"Jeffery, please don't do this to me here," the younger woman said.

"I want to go thatwaaaaayyyy!" Jeffery screeched.

"Our plane is not that way," Jeffery's mother reasoned. "It is down here and it is going to board soon. I need you to please get up and come this way."

Ashley couldn't understand what Jeffery said next but it started with "I don't want..." and ended with more screaming and flailing. Ashley thought how much the boy resembled a very angry turtle as he rolled back and forth on his backpack. Then she came to a sinking realization that her gate would be down concourse B as well. Based on her past flight history she was certain that Jeffrey would be her seatmate.

She decided to be proactive and proceed on to her gate. Perhaps if she got there first she could strike up a quick friendship with the flight attendant and talk him or her into letting her change seats. She tossed her wrapper and Styrofoam cup into a trash can and stepped around Jeffrey, whose grandmother had now pulled up a chair and, with hands folded patiently, was waiting for the drama to play out.

At the gate, the attendant was furiously typing on a computer terminal keyboard behind the desk. All the rows of chairs were empty with the exception of one woman who slept alongside one of those folding luggage carts. Then she noticed the running man over by the water fountain drinking deeply. Ashley plopped down the one carry-on item she had—one of those knock-off light pink Louis Vuitton bags—and sat down to wait for boarding. She eyed the attendant, who had yet to look up. Whatever he was doing, he was quite enthralled by it.

In a moment, the running man walked over, sat down his suit bag, and then shoved the big suitcase under the chairs with his foot.

"They make those with wheels now, you know."

The man frowned at Ashley but it was clear that he got the sarcasm. *A sense of humor—good,* Ashley thought.

"Yes, I am aware," the man said, smiling. "I had a perfectly nice rolling suitcase a mere two days ago. Then all my luggage was lost on the way here from LA and I had to make do with some old stuff."

"Just giving you a hard time," Ashley said. "You headed to D.C.?"

"Yeah. How about you?"

"Me too. It'll be my first time since I was a kid. Do you mind if I ask why you ran all the way down here when this flight doesn't even board for another 20 minutes?"

The man laughed sheepishly. "I looked at the monitor wrong. I thought I was about to miss my flight."

"So you ran all the way down here carrying all that awkward luggage for nothing?"

"Oh no. It wasn't for nothing. It allowed me to be the first one to the water fountain. I bet I got the first drink of the whole day."

Ashley laughed. He was cute, actually. His head was covered with thick brown hair that was a bit tousled from his run. Round glasses didn't mask his blue eyes.

"How did you know I ran down here? Do I look sweaty?" he asked self-consciously, smoothing his brown hair.

"No...well, maybe a little. But actually, I was sitting in the food court and saw you run by. You were having a little trouble."

"To be honest, I thought I was in decent shape but I thought surely I'd have cardiac arrest before I got here. I felt like a real dork when I ran up to the desk. That attendant over there enjoyed pointing up to the sign and showing me that I was early."

For the first time the attendant stopped typing, looked up, and smiled broadly. A second or two later he picked up the microphone and called for boarding. Ashley breathed a sigh of relief—no sign of Jeffrey.

"Boarding rows A through E please."

Ashley frowned at the prospect of boarding a plane by row that apparently had only three people on it. Then she said, "Well that's me. Good luck in D.C. by the way."

"Yeah, um, you too," the man said. Then he turned to fumble through his jacket pocket. Ashley waved and headed for the gate.

"Oh, before you go, I uh, wanted to um, where are those darned cards? I know I had them in here, I wanted to give you a card and introduce...maybe they're in my wallet, bear with me here."

Ashley didn't hear any of this. She had already handed off her boarding pass and was half-way down the tunnel. The attendant looked up with guilty pleasure as the man continued to fumble through pockets. Finally, the man held up a business card triumphantly and looked up to see no one.

"I'm, uh, Hunt Finley by the way..."

Hunt's face fell. "Great," he said. "Smooth operator there, pal."

"Now boarding rows F through J. Rows F through J."

Hunt fumbled once again and located his already rumpled boarding pass in his hip pocket. "4A," he said aloud. He smacked himself in the forehead at the realization that he could have boarded with Ashley then stood up and gathered his things.

"My my, we do have a great big ole suitcase, don't we?" the attendant said. "Now do you really think that's going into the overhead bin? I don't think so. You should have checked that bag, sir."

"I thought I was late, sorry. Can I check it here?"

"Oh…no," the attendant was clearly feigning sympathy and was enjoying every second of this. "I am gonna need you to go all the way back up to the ticket counter and check that. If you run really fast you might just make it back before we are wheels up."

Hunt snatched his suitcase off the floor. As he took a deep breath and took a step, the attendant stopped him.

"Just kidding there, speedy. You can leave it with me. I'll check it for you." The attendant smiled again.

"Funny," Hunt said. "That's very humorous." He stuck out his boarding pass.

The attendant scanned it, and with full-wattage charm thanked him for flying the airline and returned to his desk.

Ashley was already fastening her seatbelt when she looked up and saw the screamer, Jeffery, enter the plane. The woman who'd been sleeping was five rows back and on the other side of the aisle.

"Please, no. Please. Please. Please." Ashley thought.

Jeffery stopped at her seat. "Who are you?" he demanded.

Ashley's face fell but as she tried to think of some smart aleck comeback, Jeffrey's lovely mother pushed him further down the aisle.

"Sorry ma'am," she said. "Someone is having a bad morning today."

Ashley smiled sympathetically and then breathed a big sigh of relief. At least Jeffery would be near the back. Then she raised the adjoining armrest and prepared to stretch out. As soon as she reached for a magazine, the running man came bumbling down the aisle, his briefcase bumping the back of every other seat. He kept looking at his boarding pass and then the aisle markers until he stopped at the end of Ashley's row.

"Looks like we're seatmates," he said beaming. Then he proceeded to ram and stuff and stuff and ram the suit bag into the overhead.

You've gotta be kidding me, Ashley thought. *The whole darn plane is empty and you're gonna sit here?* But she didn't want to hurt his feelings so she stayed quiet.

For his part, Hunt only had one thought, *Jackpot!*

25

Ian Flannery sat at a two hundred year-old Mahogany table across from Aaron Hatcher and his wife as the trio sipped brandy.

"So you see, Ian," Hatcher said, "we're never going to wean this country slowly off coal-fired power. We just have to go cold turkey. We have to pull the plug. We've tried sanctions and indirect taxes. We've tried for cap and trade, and some are still stonewalling us on that. We have to do the right thing. We have to just shut them down—at least these older ones. We can live with the clean coal plants for another few years until we get wind power running full force."

"Yes, I see your point, Senator," Ian said. "What is it you need from me?"

Hatcher didn't hear the question. He was still buzzing from the speech he'd made at the GreenUSA rally and he was on a roll. The stage had been surrounded by 80,000 screaming fans and behind Hatcher had stood a veritable *Who's Who* of music and entertainment. He'd made a speech in which he attempted to rally attendants to combat global warming and had received a raucous response, though the passion seemed to come more from those on stage than those in the audience. He hadn't wanted the moment to end and he tried to recapture it here.

"Ian, we are destroying our world," his voice was going up an octave. "We are destroying your children's future. The greed of this country and its insistence on having its big SUVs and its cheap electricity is poisoning Mother Nature."

Ian had already stopped listening. He was thinking about all the power plants he'd seen during his travels to India that were belching out tons of black smoke thousands of times more contaminated than the worst U.S. plant. Then he recalled that China was adding a new power plant to their grid every month—none of which would have pollution controls in place. Even if the U.S. shut down every electric plant in the country, it would not reduce pollutants globally more than one percent. With great contempt, he considered the folly of Aaron Hatcher's narcissism. *What a fool to believe that the United States has the ability to change the weather of the entire planet merely by the flexing or relaxing of its economic muscles,* he thought.

He wondered, as he had before, about Hatcher's motives. Was Hatcher really stupid enough to believe his own rhetoric? Ian didn't think so. More likely Hatcher was like most Westerners—trying to promote himself no matter what the cost to his countrymen and trying to cloak it all in demagoguery. Ian, still seeming to be completely focused on Aaron's words, smiled slightly with satisfaction that at least he fought for a cause. Hatcher was wrapping up now and Ian dialed in once again.

"Ian," Hatcher leaned in close and placed a hand on Ian's forearm just as he would have a few years ago when asking for a large campaign contribution. "We have an opportunity, an obligation, to put a stop to CO_2 emissions. There is no more time to wait and debate. We have to stop this now."

Hatcher sat back and waited for a response as Lillian looked on. She was positively glowing at her husband. Ian may as well have not been in the room. He thought he saw Lillian's chest rising and falling abnormally fast.

"I appreciate and respect your passion for this just cause, Senator," Ian said. "As you know, I too have spent much of my career fighting for environmental stewardship."

"I know that you have, Ian. That's why I asked you here today. I need your help." Hatcher leaned in again. "I need your support. Ian, you are president of one of the most effective lobbying firms in this city. I want you to catch my fever about this issue. For the good of our planet, there are some senators I want you to call upon."

26

Ashley leaned firmly against the cool window and looked out at the grays and browns of Virginia in the fall as they flew high overhead. She probably would have been content to thumb through the in-flight magazine or just sit quietly for the duration of the trip but it was clear that her newfound friend wasn't going to let that happen. She sensed him leaning on the armrest again to say something. He liked to talk.

"So, are you from Nashville or were you just flying out of there?" he asked.

"Oh no, I just like flying from there. I'm from Western Kentucky and I work in Southern Illinois. This is a work trip for me."

"Me too. I'm going to be covering the upcoming Green Commission hearings in the senate," Hunt said.

Ashley perked up at this. "Really? That's where I'm headed. I'm testifying there."

"Hey," Hunt said. "I could start working right now." He saw Ashley stiffen slightly. "Just kidding, I definitely am *not* ready to go to work yet. I live in Nashville but just got off an assignment in L.A. My luggage got lost somewhere in between."

"So I take it that you're some kind of reporter?"

"Yes, that's exactly what I am—some kind of reporter." They both chuckled.

"Sorry, I didn't mean that the way it sounded," Ashley said.

"That's okay. So who are you going to testify for?"

"UPI. That stands for Utility..."

"Power Institute—yeah, I know. I've been covering the energy sector for a few years now. I guess you guys are taking off the gloves on this one. I hear that this new EPA policy to regulate CO_2 could be devastating for coal power. The ones that this doesn't kill off, cap and trade will, if it ever passes."

"Yeah, that's kind of what I gather. To be honest, I have a lot to learn about it all. I'm going to be taking a crash course between now and the date of my testimony."

"Ahh, the old witness prep, huh?" Ashley suddenly looked uncomfortable. "Don't feel bad. The other side is doing the same thing with lots of their people," Hunt said. "It's the way these things always work. Are you excited about it? I mean testifying before a Congressional committee is a pretty big deal."

"Excited wouldn't be the right word," Ashley said. "In a way I am dreading it. I wasn't given a lot of choice."

"Well, even though this isn't a criminal trial, you'll more or less be testifying for the defense. How do you feel about that?"

"You really are a reporter, aren't you, asking me all these probing questions when we've just met," Ashley replied, smiling.

"Sorry. It's just second nature for me, I guess. I promise, I am not in reporter mode right now. I was more interested personally."

Ashley blushed at this a bit, which in turn caused Hunt to blush also. "Well, I do have a pretty strong opinion. Basically,

I work in industry. When I look back at old records we have on file from the fifties and sixties, I know things needed to change back then. There was not enough self-policing, not enough environmental stewardship. But now quite frankly, I feel like the pendulum has swung way too far."

"I don't disagree. I've been covering this long enough now that I sort of feel the same way. I mean, I am a reporter sworn to objectivity," Hunt placed his left hand in the air and his right hand over his heart, "but my personal opinion is that things like this pending policy change, cap and trade, Kyoto, and the Copenhagen conference have gone way too far."

"I wonder what this country is going to be like in ten more years," Ashley said pensively. "I work in an industry that's supposed to be the most stable of all and even they're experiencing layoffs. When you can't profit from manufacturing reliable, inexpensive energy, what industry can make a profit?"

"Yeah, it's kinda scary alright."

"And I am not just thinking of our business. I have friends—close friends—who are about to lose their house, and energy costs are a big part of the reason why," Ashley continued.

"Just wait till gasoline reaches five dollars a gallon like they're saying it will this coming spring," Hunt said. "Then your friends may not be the only one's losing their home."

Ashley finished his thought. "And then the housing market collapses again and that leads to more jobs lost..." She was rotating her left hand like a movie director signaling an actor to "wrap it up."

"This is depressing. Why don't we talk about something else?" Hunt said.

"I agree," Ashley replied. She turned to smile at Hunt and for the first time he was able to really study her face. What he saw was a young woman with near-perfect features whose soft red and auburn curls spilled down her back and across her shoulders. Her lips were full and red, seemingly without lipstick, and her milky complexion was flawless. What he noticed the most, however, were her brilliant green eyes, which sparkled with flecks of gold.

Hunt swallowed hard without meaning to and then hoped Ashley didn't notice. He knew he needed to say something quickly but his mind was blank. *Think of something funny you idiot, quick,* he thought.

"Hunt," he said.

"I'm sorry what?" Ashley said. "No, I don't hunt. I do have another hobby that I'll bet you haven't run into before, though."

"No, uh . . . I'm sorry. I didn't mean that as a question."

"Oh. Do you mean you like to hunt?"

"No, well...yes...I mean I kind of do, I haven't done it in a long time, but..."

"My Dad doesn't hunt much either, but my granddad used to love it," Ashley replied cheerily.

Hunt turned toward the aisle and grimaced. *Crashing, burning,* he thought.

Ashley rambled on, "He hunted deer some but I think he mostly hunted rabbits and quail. I think they call that small-game hunting. But then, you would know more about that than I would."

"I didn't mean that I like to hunt," Hunt blurted out.

"You just said you did," Ashley was growing incredulous. *What kind of mind games was this man playing here?*

"My *name* is Hunt. Hunt Finley. That's what I meant to say."

Ashley smiled for a second before bursting out in laughter. A snorting sound accidentally escaped from her nose.

"Sorry," she was still laughing. She didn't mean to. She actually sympathized with how awkward Hunt must feel right now. It was the fact that this was just like something that she would have expected to happen to her that made it so enjoyable. "So you were *introducing* yourself, I see now."

"Yeah, smooth operator, huh? Let's try again, Hunt Finley." This time Hunt stuck out a hand. Inside he was dying.

"Ashley Miller," She took Hunt's hand and shook it firmly, still smiling brilliantly.

I wonder if this woman realizes how beautiful she is, Hunt thought, still dazzled. *If she does, I don't have a chance.* He decided he might as well stop trying so hard.

"This is pretty much the way I roll," Hunt said. "When I am attracted to a woman, first I show off my athletic skills by running through an airport being flailed by a forty year-old, sixty pound suitcase. Then I nearly crush her while trying to get my dainty carry-on in the overhead bin. Finally, I screw up my own name really, *really* thoroughly. At that point, most women are putty in my hands. So, can I call you once we get settled in D.C.?"

Ashley, whose eyes had grown increasingly wide with delight at this tirade, now covered her mouth and nose to keep from snorting again as she was laughing even harder now. Hunt thought she had a sensuous, throaty sort of laugh.

"Well, while it is a pleasure to be wooed by one so adept at the art," Ashley said, "I really think I should focus on business while I am here." With that, she gave Hunt one of those looks that he hated—the look that said, "You don't have a snowball's chance in Hades, but thanks for playing." He thought briefly about trying a different tack, but decided against it.

"Oh, well. At least we've got that over with now," he said trying to hide his disappointment.

"Do you keep a journal?" Ashley said, changing the subject.

"No, why do you ask?" Hunt replied.

"Oh, I didn't mean to be nosy, I just thought that was

a journal sticking out of your shirt pocket," Ashley said, indicating a slender leather-bound book protruding from Hunt's pocket.

"Oh that," Hunt said. "No, that's my New Testament. I like to keep one with me. I'm a Christian and sometimes I refer to it for comfort or inspiration, or sometimes just because I like to read God's Word."

"Okay," Ashley said approvingly. "That's cool. I haven't seen one of those before. And I certainly haven't known many guys that would carry one."

Hunt only shrugged his shoulders and smiled. "Well, I can only say that I've found it a pretty wonderful thing to have by my side."

"Well, Hunt, I think that's really nice," Ashley said.

In what seemed like no time, to both Ashley and Hunt, they were being told to fasten their seatbelts for the landing. Ashley waited in her seat with her arms over her head as Hunt pulled the suit bag from the overhead bin.

Hunt laughed at her. "Funny. Well, it was nice meeting you, Ashley. You certainly made this one of the most pleasant flights I've had in a long time. And I fly a lot."

Ashley stood as she scooped her handbag smoothly onto her shoulder. "Oh, I'll bet you say that to all your seat mates."

Hunt placed his palms forward as he balanced the suit bag. "Busted," he said. "The fat guy that flew up with me from Huntsville is gonna send me a friend request on Facebook. I can't wait to get to the room and check."

Ashley shook her head and laughed again. She suddenly realized that she'd not laughed this much in a long time, but by then Hunt was already bumping down the aisle and turning left out the exit door. *Oh, what the heck*, she thought as she fished a business card from her purse. "Finally get a chance to use one of these," she said aloud.

"Hey! You go now!" Ashley felt a push right on her butt and realized that the voice belonged to Jeffery.

"Jeffery! I'm sorry, ma'am," Jeffery's mother said. Ashley turned and gave an "it's okay" smile and headed out of the plane.

By the time she found Hunt, he was attempting once again to drink from a water fountain. As he bent over with the suit bag slung over one shoulder, it slid off and simultaneously hit him in the cheek and fell into the stream of water wetting the suit bag and squirting all over his shirt.

"Well, that's just wonderful!" he exclaimed to no one in particular.

This guy's funny without even trying, Ashley thought as she approached. When she walked up behind him and stuck out her card, Hunt was trying to secure the bag and wipe off his shirt with a crumpled napkin from the plane at the same time. He looked up to see Ashley and was clearly pleasantly surprised.

"Is that for me?" he asked.

"This? No, I just thought you might use it as a squeegee."

"A thousand comedians out of work," Hunt said as he took the card before Ashley could change her mind. "Thanks."

"No, thank you for what turned out to be a very fun flight. I don't know when I've laughed that much."

"I do what I can," Hunt said.

"Just give me a couple days to get settled. Maybe we can grab that coffee."

"Great," Hunt replied. "I know a place near the Smithsonian. Maybe we can take in some exhibits while we are at it." Then to himself he thought, *Good, good, stretch out the date, maximize the time, you're making a comeback, you ol' smoothie. Now wait for the reaction...*

"Okay, that sounds nice. I'll see you then." Ashley headed for baggage claim and turned back once, catching

Hunt in the act of checking her out. He turned clumsily toward a nearby newspaper stand, but knew it was too late. A few minutes later, he would wonder why he hadn't taken the opportunity to walk with her. But for now he was too busy wishing there were someone to high five and repeating one word under his breath over and over— "Jackpot!"

27

Shelton Leonard pressed the light on his wristwatch. He was running low on time. He'd have to finish up pretty quickly. He'd planned to ride his bike out to the SPG site for their first fish-sampling event and he would need a good forty minutes for the trip. He went back into the kitchen and poured himself a Coke. It was flat, so he poured it out after one sip and decided to make a cup of tea. The steeping basket was still out on the counter from last time. He chose orange pekoe, adding an extra dash. He liked it bold. He set out a cup, placed two of those shortbread biscuits that he loved on the saucer alongside it, and waited for the kettle to boil.

As he waited, he crossed his arms in front of his chest and looked around. He needed to tidy this place up a bit but he wasn't in the mood right now. He didn't feel like doing much of anything today. He certainly didn't feel like going to this darned sampling event meeting, but it too was a means to an end. What he really felt like doing, he decided, was laying in bed all day. It was gray and gloomy outside and just one of those days.

Soon the kettle whistled and he steeped the tea, had some with the English biscuits, then washed the cup and saucer and put it away. He looked at his watch again and decided he still had plenty of time to get a shower, so he went back to the bedroom. He looked at the inviting crumpled bed sheets and without hesitating, flopped onto his back in the center of the mattress. He stared at the ceiling fan for a few minutes, telling himself not to fall back asleep. Then he reached over and pulled Ashley Miller's nightgown toward him. He held it up to his nose as he'd already done a hundred other times and inhaled. Then he held it to his chest.

Deciding that he'd surely be late, he got up, opened Ashley's top chest drawer, folded her nightgown, and placed it back where it was, two down from the top. He'd picked this one because it was black silk--the others were cotton. It fit better with the image he had of Ashley. Finally, he got up and headed for the shower in Ashley's bathroom. From the bathroom, he took a peek through the venetian blind at the neighbor's house. He knew both parents worked and the kids were with a sitter. For the past two days, he'd left his bike in the woods behind the house and entered through the rear door. He was long gone by the time the neighbors started arriving home, though he'd cut it close a time or two. He had the neighbors pretty well patterned but it never hurt to be cautious.

After a good look around, Shelton closed the blind and got into the shower. He had to hurry so that he'd have the bath wiped down prior to leaving. That would be one less job to do when he came back tonight long after midnight to do his housework. Once he tidied up, he could finish going through Ashley's emails.

28

Shelton pumped the pedals with abandon. He'd pulled out of the woods and onto the highway about a half-mile down from Ashley's house. The road was empty and he wanted to make his turn, about a half-mile ahead, before anyone drove by. He didn't think he'd be recognized anyway with his sunglasses and his helmet on, but why take chances?

Shelton leaned the bike hard and made the turn. Once on the next straightaway, he eased back to a more leisurely pace. He rode daily and had the aerobic fitness to ride at near maximum speed all the way to the plant, but he didn't want to show up for the meeting wet with sweat. He liked to bike as much as possible because it was environmentally friendly and it gave him time to think. Today he was thinking about Professor Michael Chandler. Shelton supposed he'd always cared about Mother Nature, but it was Professor Chandler who inspired him to realize that whom modern man called Mother Nature was, in fact, a deity. The ancient Greeks had called her Gaia. Shelton determined that he would dedicate his life to her preservation.

During invertebrate zoology class—Shelton's first with Prof. Chandler—the lectures had frequently deviated into condemnations of the capitalist mindset and how that mindset had led to the destruction of so many species and to the loss of so much pristine wilderness. Man was so incredibly shortsighted, it sickened him. He recalled the imagery of the gold rush of the early 1800s. Miners had used hydraulic drills to completely level entire mountains, all for a few nuggets of gold. Professor Chandler had shown slides of such activity, and his words still rang in Shelton's ears.

"This is the perfect metaphor for what corporate America wants to do and is doing today. The only difference is that yesterday's greedy miners are today's CEO's. No matter what you may have to do to stop these barons, remember this—the end justifies the means," Chandler had said. Shelton figured he had a bead on some greedy miners at SPG and today would be the beginning of the end for them.

29

Leroy Allen reached over the tailgate of his old pickup and gave Elmo a scratch between his ears. Elmo looked at him, eyes pleading, until Leroy finally rolled his eyes, broke off a chunk of his breakfast biscuit and fed it to the pig. "Dang it, Elmo! Don't look at me like that," he pleaded. "All you're doin' is hurtin' yourself. You're just too darned fat now, boy. You gotta let me cut you back some. I'll see ya at lunch." With that, he scratched Elmo again and took a few steps toward the plant, when he was nearly run over by Shelton Leonard on his bicycle.

"Hey! Watch where you're goin' with that thing. I been workin' thirty five years around machinery, now you gonna kill me with a bicycle?"

"Sorry," Shelton said. "I was trying to hurry to a meeting."

"Well you don't hafta kill me just cause you're in a hurry."

"Sorry," Shelton said again, growing impatient. "Is that a pig in the back of your truck?"

"No genius, it's a Chihuahua with a rare growth hormone disorder. Yes it's a danged pig, what does it look like?"

"Why are you bringing him to work?"

"Well because, ya numbskull, that's where he lives."

"He lives in the back of your truck?"

"Yeah, I got 'im last year. Wife got mad at me about it. Won't let me unload him. Says he'll root up the yard." Leroy leaned in close to whisper, "I was gonna fatten him up and eat 'im but I kinda got fond of 'im." He then began to speak in a normal tone once again. "He goes everywhere with me now. He loves this 'ol truck. I let him out at the carwash a few times a week when I wash the bed out. He don't roam far. Say, ain't you that fella that's gonna come in and watch me sample fish?"

"Yeah," Shelton said, unsure now of whom or what he was dealing with. "I thought I was supposed to work with a lab technician."

"What's that supposed to mean?" Leroy asked. "I am a lab technician. I went down here to Shawnee and got an Associates in chemistry ten years ago. Straight A's. Bet I can balance any equation you can, boy."

"I'm sure you can. I didn't mean it like it sounded, okay? I don't want to get off on the wrong foot."

"Too late for that," Leroy quipped.

"You go on in the rock house and check in. They'll get your visitor pass fixed up and you'll need to complete some safety training. I'll catch up with ya later."

Leroy held his large metal lunch box in front of him and passed through the turnstile. Shelton looked on with disdain. Leroy wore denim overalls and work boots. Hardly the image Shelton had of what a lab tech looked like. If this was what these people passed off as a laboratory technician, Shelton wasn't sure what to expect next. He locked up his bike and headed for Security. He didn't know it then, but he was making a grievous error underestimating Leroy Allen.

30

Ashley had never thought of herself as a small town girl. In fact, she always thought she was pretty darned cosmopolitan. After her confusion over the cab ride to her hotel, however, she had had an epiphany. This was really the first time she'd ever traveled to a major city without her parents or a group of friends. She wasn't the least bit intimidated by that fact but she was self-conscious. She thought back to her cab ride and smiled at her naïveté.

She had first upset the cabbie by opening his trunk for him after he had hit the button from inside the car so that she could set her own bags inside. Apparently, that was encroaching on his territory. Then she had gone all white knuckles on his driving style. It wasn't the speed or close proximity to the other cars she'd minded—she was used to that and more on the racecourse. It was more a question of technique. The cabbie had not appreciated her driving tips in the least.

She was now schlepping her bags down the hall of the hotel. After what seemed like a very long walk, she finally arrived at her room. She laughed at herself, as she was actually excited to open the door and see what her room looked like. She reckoned they would have the good soap in this place. "Country comes to town," Ashley said, blowing her bangs out of her eyes.

The room was even nicer than the website pictures had indicated when June made the reservation. She opened her curtain on her 17th floor window and gasped at a great view of the Pentagon and the Air Force Memorial. The sun was setting and as Ashley watched, the memorial was suddenly illuminated. The lights shone on the Washington Monument in the distance and Ashley stared for a long moment, still feeling it was a bit surreal that she was actually in Washington. She picked up the phone and dialed her Mom, who answered on the first ring.

"Hi! You still at the airport?"

"Do you keep that thing glued to your hand? How do you always answer so fast?"

"The phone makes that little ringy sound, I push the little button and say hello. There's not that much to it really."

"You are not gonna believe the view. I'm about to send a pic to your phone."

"I don't have that, send it to my email."

"I thought you were getting an I-Phone," Ashley said.

"No, you thought I *should* get an I-Phone. That's way too much technology for me."

"Well anyway, you should see it here. Think Daddy would let you come up for a long weekend? The room's free."

"I know you mentioned that before you left but your father and I haven't even talked about it. I don't suppose I had better leave him for that long. He might starve. Better let you go for now, I'm driving. You know they say not to be on the cell phone when you're driving."

"Okay. Talk to you soon."

Ashley hung up and began unpacking her suitcase. When she opened up her bag, she found a surprise. *Aw,* Ashley thought. *This is so incredibly sweet.* Emma had come over briefly while Ashley was packing for her trip. She'd been carrying a Raggedy Ann doll with her and had looked suspiciously like she was up to something the whole time she was there. Unbeknownst to Ashley, she'd placed the doll in the suitcase under some clothes with a picture she'd drawn. The picture had two stick figures holding hands in front of what was apparently a house. In the foreground was another stick figure kitty cat. Tears came to her eyes and she made a mental note to buy Emma something while she was in town.

After unpacking, she hit the whirlpool bath, where she spent more time than she intended to, thinking about Shelton. She really wasn't sure how she felt about all that had transpired. One thing that the meeting had affirmed for her, she didn't love Shelton anymore. There had been some recent lonely Friday nights where she'd struggled with that question.

That struggle would never surface again. In fact, she was now at a point where she was pretty certain that she'd never actually loved him. It was almost as if their relationship had just gathered momentum somewhere along the line and begun to move from one stage to another. In retrospect, she never felt that she'd taken time to come to grips with her true feelings for him. At the time she'd met Shelton, she subconsciously believed that she'd reached an age where she felt that she should have a serious relationship, so she'd had one. She'd never felt swept off her feet or any of that other princess/prince stuff. Still, even after accepting that reality here in her hotel room, she was deeply hurt that he would turn on her this way. It hurt a lot.

She shook her head and decided to stop thinking about men and love and relationships. "Oh, the folly of it all," she said aloud, imitating Scarlett O'Hara. "I simply refuse to think of it anymore today."

She finished up, and started to call room service. Then she decided she didn't feel much like an in-room movie and decided to head to the lobby. There'd been a nice looking restaurant there. She reapplied her make-up and after her thoughts about Shelton, the mood suddenly struck her to just go all out. It was a Monday night and the clubs might be dead but she was thinking seriously about checking out the Washington social scene.

She slid into that perfect "little black dress" with ankle-strap stilettos she'd bought three years ago and had never gotten to wear. She rifled through her handbag and finally withdrew an expensive looking leather case. She'd only allowed this to leave her house one other time, back when she was dating Shelton. Inside was a sparkling diamond necklace. She stepped over to the mirror and, for the first time since college, put the necklace on. "This thing is worth more than my house," she said. She checked herself in the mirror, decided she looked great and wondered if she'd overshot it for a hotel restaurant. "What the heck," she said aloud. "Like they say on the cruise ships, I'll never see any of these people again as long as I live."

Satisfied, she headed for the elevator. The regular elevator was closer to her room but she walked well out of her way to take the glass elevator that emptied in the center of the lobby. *For once in my life, I am making an entrance,* she thought.

31

Ian Flannery was sipping burgundy in the Coach and Six Lounge, watching the front doors. His contact would be arriving any second now, and for the first time that he could remember he was scared. The man he was about to meet was a well-skilled killer and a consummate perfectionist who was intolerant of mistakes. Ian was certain that he had covered every angle in setting up the pending operation but he was intimidated nonetheless.

It was at that moment, when he needed to be completely dialed in to the conversation that he was about to have, that an absolutely stunning redhead in a sexy black cocktail dress came down in the glass elevator. The doors opened right in front of him and the woman stepped out, looked around briefly and walked to the restaurant in the hotel. Her walk was confident and her legs were gorgeous, but he had locked in on her eyes. Her eyes darted about uneasily. This woman was a fish out of water; she wasn't used to this environment or this town.

Ian's breathing sped up in that now-familiar way, but as was his habit, he quickly regained control. Coolly, he stood with his drink and stepped to the edge of the bar until he could clearly see that Ashley was being seated at a table for two near the lobby. He hoped she wasn't there to meet anyone. That would make it more difficult for him—not impossible, just more difficult.

"Don't make me wait for you."

Ian jumped at the sound of the voice and the thick Russian accent. His contact had walked right by him while he'd been staring at Ashley. Now Ian's heart truly began to race. If he had been seen being distracted at a time like this...

"Let's sit," the contact said abruptly.

The two men sat on either side of a round table near the dark paneled corner of the Coach and Six Lounge. They barely looked at one another. Ian had communicated with this man many times in the past two years. This was only the second time they'd met face to face. The barrel-chested, powerful looking man across the table from him was known throughout the clandestine world simply as "The Russian." As he waited for Ian to speak, he sat with one meaty hand covering a large portion of the table. The knuckles were misshapen and covered with scars. Ian was surprised at how nervous he was. He steeled himself, determined to take the initiative in the conversation.

"I've admired your work over the years, even going all the way back to your country's war with Afghanistan," he said.

"Vodka martini, Absolut. He doesn't want anything," the Russian said. His tone was firm, unyielding.

Ian looked over his shoulder to see a waiter scurrying back to the bar. He hadn't even heard the waiter coming.

"I don't know what you are talking about—my work. And I was never in Afghanistan. Never bring either of those subjects up again. I'm not your damned friend," The Russian leaned in close as he spoke. He smelled of Lysol or some other disinfectant. His expression was nothing short of menacing and even Ian recoiled slightly, despite himself.

Such an unprovoked precautionary maneuver on his part embarrassed him. "The group wants to know if you have the Senator, uh, Hatcher."

"Yes, I think we do."

The Russian leaned in even closer, raising his voice. "You *think* we do?" As the Martini arrived, he lowered it again and continued. "If I tell my group that we are going forward and you don't have Hatcher, then they could be exposed. If they are exposed, they may be tied back to me. I won't like that."

"Hatcher will do what he is told. Don't worry." Ian wanted to follow that up with "don't threaten me," but he simply didn't have the nerve.

"I wanted to look you in the eye when you answered that. Good. Now there's something else."

Ian stiffened, then he caught himself and a relaxed smile returned to his face. "What is it?" he asked.

"It has come to my attention that you may be planning something on your own. I am getting chatter that you may be working on some sort of strike."

Ian sat back, looking puzzled. "That's ridiculous. I don't have time to work on…"

"I have seen your house in Sri Lanka as well as the one in Pakistan and even the lovely little apartment in Viet Nam. You won't be able to hide. You should know, Muhammad, if you forget our agreement, if you make any attempt to double-cross me, I will kill you very slowly."

Ian's blood ran cold. The Russian had used his Muslim name. A name he had kept secret from everyone outside of his inner circle. And he knew about hiding places that Ian was relying on for his escape when all was completed. Ian could hear his own pulse beating in his head. He had to calm down. He needed to find out how much this man knew. Ian's entire operation could be compromised.

The Russian smiled and sat back in his chair. He knew duress when he saw it, despite Ian's best efforts to hide it. He had pushed the buttons he wanted to push. He had to be careful now. He mustn't let Ian know that the location of the apartments and the name was all he had. He picked up his glass and drank the martini in two large swallows, holding the olive spear with one thick finger.

Ian gathered himself and began to think of all his plans unraveling. The Russian had only named three locations. There were dozens under multiple names. The Russian couldn't know much about the strike or he would have already killed him and his men. He decided he was fishing.

Ian's anger flared. "So how is it an issue with you that I like to have somewhere to stay when I travel? It has no bearing on our work whatsoever. I developed the plan. My people and I are flawlessly executing the plan. I certainly have no intention of causing an upset when we are this close to the money. You should get new sources. The ones you have now are sending you on wild goose chases."

The Russian held the martini glass in one hand and stared hard at Ian. "Yes, of course," he said. "I thought I had a good read on you, Muhammad. You like western life, don't you? I certainly know that you like nice apartments and beautiful women. No, no. You are no ideologue or religious zealot. You and I are very much alike in that way." With that, he popped the olive into his mouth, brushed his hands together quickly, and stood.

Ian wished at that moment that he were clutching his favorite ceremonial sword. He would love to cut this infidel's head off right here at the table. The Russian had no idea how deeply he had just insulted him. He didn't look up. He didn't speak. He only gripped his glass of burgundy so tightly that he thought it might shatter in his hand. Without another word, the Russian turned and walked out the front door of the hotel, disappearing into the crowd.

Ian sat for several minutes and gathered himself. He signaled the waiter and downed another burgundy. He knew at that moment that he would need to kill the Russian very soon. He shook his head to clear it. He would plan that later. For now, he needed to escape for a few hours. That's when he turned his gaze back toward the restaurant where Ashley was sitting.

32

Ashley had ordered a white zinfandel. She didn't usually drink, but tonight she was celebrating. What exactly she was celebrating she wasn't sure, but that was beside the point. She was the better part of the way through her second glass before her salad arrived and she was embarrassed to be feeling a bit of a buzz. "Teetotalers shouldn't drink on an empty stomach, I suppose," she thought. She had another sip, then set the glass down and ran her finger around the rim. She saw the man's reflection in the glass briefly before he came and stood right beside her. The first thing she noticed was that he was on the verge of being uncomfortably close. That was before she looked into his face.

She looked up into the dark complexion of the best-looking man she'd ever seen in her life. He was smiling a pearly white smile that made her stomach do a flip.

"Hello," he said, sticking out his hand to take hers. "I'm Charles Fagan."

Ashley was taken aback, unsure why this man had approached her. "Hello."

"I hope you won't think me terribly forward," Charles Fagan, aka Ian Flannery, aka Muhammad, began. "But I just moved here to Washington on business and I barely know anyone. I was wondering..." Flannery feigned awkwardness. "I was wondering if...well, I just hate eating alone. Would you do me the honor of allowing me to join you? I would be happy to take care of your meal."

To say that Ashley was caught off guard would have been a colossal understatement. She realized that she was being hit on but she really didn't mind. From where she sat right now, there wasn't a downside.

"Sure." She surprised even herself by blurting that out without thinking it through as she waved a hand toward the other chair. *That certainly was a snappy comeback*, she thought. *Really cosmopolitan.*

"You're too kind." In one smooth motion, Ian then grasped Ashley's hand and kissed it. Ashley blushed, but was flattered. If this guy was playing her, she would give him only a few more hours to knock it off.

As he pulled out a chair and sat, Ashley took a quick inventory. He wore a tan Cashmere blazer, an oatmeal-colored sweater, and dark blue slacks. His watch was a Rolex but other than that, he wore no jewelry. Ashley realized she was staring and looked away. He seemed more handsome than he had been a moment before.

"And what might your name be?"

"Gretchen. Gretchen Collins," Ashley shocked herself with how easily she lied and then wondered why she'd done it.

"And what brings you to Washington, Ms. Collins?"

Ashley decided to go for broke. She still didn't know what she was doing, why she was doing it, or where she was headed. "I'm scheduled to do a photo shoot for a modeling agency here. They wanted some of the memorials as a backdrop." She waited. She wondered if Fagan would burst out in laughter any second. He didn't.

"Ahhh, a model. I should have known."

Ashley mentally patted herself on the back for pulling

that one off. This was getting fun.

"What do you mean you should have known?" she asked.

"Well, a woman of your stunning beauty surely had to be a model or an actress or something of that nature."

Ashley's eyes sparkled as she took another sip of the wine. *This guy is completely full of it,* she thought, *and right this minute I think I love him for it.*

After dinner, Ashley sipped a glass of port that Ian had ordered for her as she watched him finish a Crème Brule. Even after a full meal, Ashley was still feeling a buzz from the three glasses of wine she'd had before and during dinner. Now with the port, she was feeling quite warm all over. She hadn't had to utilize her modeling cover very much. So far, Charles Fagan was primarily interested in talking about himself. All that she had needed to do was to lie about where she had flown in from and her hometown. That was okay with Ashley. She could sit and watch this guy talk all night as long as he kept wowing her with his British accent.

"So, I left Oxford," Ian went on. "And I had an opportunity to work for an exporter, art work, and artifacts for collectors mostly. I gained an appreciation and ended up in New York as an importer."

"So what brings you to D.C. from there?" Ashley asked. "This doesn't seem like an import kind of town."

"Oh, but you're wrong," Ian held up a finger. "You forget about the Smithsonian. They are constantly interested. I am focusing now on artifacts from the Ottoman Empire. I never knew my birth parents, but that is my heritage, after all."

"So are you Arabic?" As soon as Ashley spoke the words, she wondered if it would be perceived as racist and she regretted asking. Ian, however, didn't seem to notice at all.

"No, Turkish," he lied. "So who are you modeling for?"

Suddenly he wants to talk about me. Ashley wasn't ready for the question but recovered quickly and blurted an answer.

"It's just a clothing shoot for Ladies Home Journal," Ashley had no idea what she was talking about and hoped Ian knew less than she did. It occurred to her how abruptly he'd changed the subject once the conversation turned to his heritage. Ashley immediately felt guilty for thinking that.

"So do you have plans for the rest of the evening?" he asked.

Ah, Ashley thought. *That was quite a commentary. He is clearly fascinated by my modeling career. Hey, there buddy. Don't be getting all up in my business.* She was getting sarcastic and silly now, a sure sign that she'd had too much to drink.

"Really, I just flew in today and I really was just going to get some rest," she said to Ian, wishing she'd not said "really" twice in the same sentence.

"Now, Gretchen," Ian said, a tone of mock scolding in his voice. "Beautiful women like you don't put on a beautiful dress like that only to have dinner alone in a hotel restaurant."

Ashley blushed again, and Ian's confidence that the night would go according to his plan grew.

"Let's do this. Let me take you for a drive, a quick tour around the city. Then we can have a coffee at a little shop I recently found and I will have you back before eleven."

Ashley knew better. She'd never gone anywhere with a stranger in her life. Still, the warning bells that she'd relied on to get her safely through college were strangely muted. She didn't feel alarm. She wasn't sure if it was the wine, or the fact that this guy was clearly rich and classy, or just his looks. Perhaps it was all three.

"Gretchen, please. Don't make me go down the street to my empty apartment to stare out the window." Ian pouted provocatively. If it had been just about any other man, she'd known the maneuver would have made her sick. This one however, pulled it off beautifully.

"Okay," Ashley heard herself saying almost as if it were another woman talking. "Let's go for a drive."

33

Shelton had once lain on his back in the woods and watched overhead as two desperate songbirds had harassed a hawk that flew too close to their nest. Those two tiny songbirds had taken on a fierce predator. Shelton's plan from day one had been to be to SPG what those songbirds had been to the hawk. He'd planned to create a media circus that would harass the company into financial concessions.

Shelton had hoped he could get SPG to fund research projects and make large donations to Riverguardian. On the day that Ashley had been responding to the oil spill, Shelton had been hiding here collecting samples just as he had almost every day prior to that for months. Long ago, he'd set up his own crude sampling system at the plant's discharge canal. The centerpiece of his strategy at that time was to collect a large volume of dead, or better yet, wounded fish, which he would place on the banks near the plant's water discharge. The flopping cripples and their dead counterparts would make a devastating photographic report in an environmentalist journal and on the evening news.

The meeting he'd demanded of SPG officials had been a feeling-out process, nothing more. He'd wanted to see how SPG responded to being pushed. Dan and Tony pushed back, but at the same time they had given him the keys to the kingdom. He'd been certain after that meeting that with direct access to the plant, and proper sampling equipment, so many fish would be collected that he'd be able to shut the whole place down. At the same time, he intended to collect a much greater financial reward.

However, things were not playing out according to his plan. So far, day after day spent sampling at the intake with Leroy hadn't yielded much. After many days of sampling, they'd only collected a handful of gizzard shad, a few measly juvenile sunfish, and a single freshwater eel. The gizzard shad was a baitfish that existed in the river by the millions, there weren't enough sunfish to make any kind of PR impact, and he wasn't likely to generate much sympathy for an eel.

So on this night, while Ashley was leaving her D.C. hotel for a drive with Ian Flannery, a man that Shelton knew nothing about, he sentenced himself once again to a night of sampling. It would be a night of creeping around in the bulrushes between the riverbank and the SPG discharge canal.

He was confident that the sampling equipment that was being used by Leroy was viable and accurate. Therefore, he couldn't understand why more fish weren't being collected. He felt it had to be due to some slight-of-hand by SPG. At no time did he consider that perhaps Leroy was right and SPG truly wasn't having a large impact on river fish. At this point, Shelton was blinded by his desire to create a public relations nightmare for SPG, which would allow him to manipulate the company into doing his bidding, up to and including taking units offline.

This, however, was going to be his last night of covert sampling. Despite all his suspicions, he simply could find no evidence that fish were being trapped and killed at SPG. Then, when he was pulling in his net one last time, everything changed. He couldn't believe what he was seeing even after he saw it.

There in his net lay a madtom catfish. The madtom was a tiny three-inch fish that was considered endangered in this state. This specimen was still breathing and viable, though it was wounded. It had survived its trip on the traveling screen and was within a few feet of making it back to the river where nature could take its course. Instead of allowing that to happen, he rapidly slid the fish into a jar of formaldehyde, killing it instantly.

Once the fish was secure in the sample jar, Shelton set it down gently and lay prostrate on the ground. He kissed the earth and thanked Gaia, for she was the goddess of the earth, for providing this sample for him. This was as close as Shelton allowed himself to get to ever worshiping any entity. Next, he asked Gaia's forgiveness for taking the little madtom's life. Shelton felt certain that Gaia understood. This little one had to die. The ends justified the means.

34

Charles Fagan/Ian rested a hand on the Jaguar's tan, saddle leather gearshift knob and cruised around the loop at a silky smooth eighty-five mph. Ashley was growing increasingly nervous. Being alone with a total stranger this far from the city was one thing. The fact that Ashley had stolen property now in her purse was another.

Back in the restaurant, Ian had been anxious to leave and had grown impatient while waiting for the waiter. As he'd stood to go and find someone to take his money, a white business card had fluttered out of the attaché he pulled from his inside blazer pocket. Ashley had picked it up with every intention of simply giving it back to him. At least that had been her original intent. At the last moment, before Charles/Ian had returned to the table, Ashley had simply thrust the card into her purse. She realized a few moments later that she was being sneaky and nosy. She felt bad about it, but the more time that passed, the more difficult it became to return the card, until finally she decided that the best thing to do was to keep quiet about it.

She decided to relax and enjoy the ride. It was her first ride in a Jaguar and she loved the sound of the twelve-cylinder engine. She didn't tell Ian it was her first time. She figured models were supposed to be used to Jaguars.

They'd been driving for nearly an hour when Ian lifted his palm off the top of the steering wheel and glanced at the gauges. He had half a tank of gas but needed a reason to get off at the next exit. He exited off a ramp into a very depressed looking neighborhood without saying a word to Ashley.

"Where are we going?" Ashley asked. "It doesn't look like there would be any sights here." For the first time she felt a twinge of fear. The tour had been quite pleasant up until now, but the wine was wearing off and her instincts were growing sharper.

"I am sorry, Gretchen. I didn't realize I was so low on petrol. We can zip in to a station and be back on our way in no time." Ian didn't care for her tone. He had her in his car now and he always had trouble keeping his domineering side in check when he had one this close.

Ashley leaned over toward her left a little, annoying Ian even further. "It looks like you've got half a tank to me. I don't see why you have to stop in an area like this."

Ian didn't like that either. He wasn't used to bossy women and it made him even more determined to break Ashley's spirit before this night was over. "Yes, well, that's a funny thing about the twelve-cylinder version of the Jag. It simply doesn't run well at less than half a tank," Ian lied.

"Well, Charles," Ashley said. "I hate to tell you, but you sure have lousy taste in filling stations."

Typical western woman, she had no idea of her place. He flexed his jaw muscles and decided to let it go. They drove down a boulevard that ran perpendicular to some residential streets. Gang graffiti covered several buildings. When they occasionally came to a streetlight that worked, Ian's face was illuminated. He didn't look like a new guy in town who was searching. He looked like he knew right where he was going. Ashley reached for a GPS unit that was plugged into the lighter and sitting on the console.

"Maybe we can have this thing look for a station," she said. She didn't like it here. She didn't like that he had brought her here in a fifty thousand-dollar car making them both a potential target.

"We don't need that," Ian slapped her hand away hard enough that it stung. Then he gathered himself. "I know where I am going. It's fine. I will have us out of here in a moment, I promise." He flashed the smile again but it wasn't the same this time. Something was different. Ashley was getting downright scared, and when that happened she became increasingly sarcastic.

"Well, you certainly do know how to show a lady the town, dontchya, Charles?" They passed another streetlight just in time for Ashley to see Ian snap his head toward her. There was a look in his eyes that gave her a cold chill.

Who does this infidel whore think she is? Ian thought. Then he gathered himself once more. It was too soon. He needed to stay with his cover. It was only a few more blocks to yet another one of his "love nests." He hadn't killed in this one since last year.

"Here we are right here." He pulled the Jag into a run-down station. "Gretchen, I promise I will only be a moment and then we'll be back on the interstate and we'll get that coffee."

Ashley started to protest, then thought better of it. Let *him get out of the car so you can think.* Her heart was starting to pound now. *This was all wrong. What had she been thinking? That look. She hadn't imagined it, had she? No. There was something very unnerving about this guy. What on earth had she been thinking?*

She looked around, not sure what to do.

35

Ian swiped his card for the third time. The pump reader wouldn't work; he would have to go in. He was growing more impatient by the second. He had been fiddling around with this skank too long already. He wanted to get her to the room and get things over with. He took a breath, then tapped on the passenger window.

Ashley acted as if she couldn't find the button, couldn't get the window down.

"I'll be right back. Card reader won't work. Right back." Ian held up a finger. Mr. Friendly. Mr. Charming.

"Yeah, why dontchya grab me a Slurpy while you are in there, you jerk," Ashley said aloud as he walked away. "Let's just see what we have here, shall we?" she said. She tried to open both the console and the walnut embossed glove box. Both were locked. *That was more than a little snoopy anyway, shame on me*, she thought. Her guilt quickly faded, however, and she grabbed the GPS.

Miller, I can't believe you're being this nosy. You're watching way too much CSI, she thought. Then she said aloud, "Well, well, nothing in Washington. That's odd for a guy who claims to have just moved here. And he sure found this place in a hurry. Kind of like he knew where he was going. Hmm, couple of addresses in Maryland. Oh, why, lookie here...the Pink Pony, probably a gallery for fine artwork or something. Yeah, right."

Ashley looked up, nervously realizing she had been careless to be so enamored by what was on the screen.

She could just see Ian in profile still in line, now behind a man who was being very choosy about some lottery scratch-off tickets he was buying. She scrolled further down the list. She thought about writing down an address or two and doing a MapQuest later but didn't have a pen. None of this was any of her business anyway and besides, no matter what it took, she was going to tell this guy to take her back to her hotel immediately.

36

Ian/Charles looked out towards his car but couldn't see Ashley for all the junk displayed in the grimy window. He'd already waited behind an Asian man buying cigars and a man who was on break from his security guard job who took a long time to select a lottery scratch-off ticket. Ian was livid.

He seemed to be getting sloppier each time. He'd brought this woman down this street to get her closer to his nearby apartment. Then when she had raised such a ruckus, he decided he had better pretend to get gas just to calm her down. He didn't need a big scene getting her into the apartment. If he didn't hurry up and get out of here, he felt he would kill someone in this store. He only had one more person in front of him after the security guard, a chunky lady dressed mostly in white.

Ashley looked toward the store. He was waiting impatiently behind two more people. She had some time. Her feelings of guilt over snooping didn't last long as she began to feel under the car seats. Nothing under her seat, so she leaned over toward his. She could feel something. Her heart began to beat faster and then her eyes widened as she pulled a fourteen-inch sheath knife from beneath the seat. It was a military-style knife like one might see in a commando movie.

What the heck is an art importer doing with this? She thrust the knife back and sat upright in her seat. She checked the store again. She could just see him in profile. He looked very irritated. Then she thought of the business card in her purse. Not wanting to attract Charles Fagan's attention by flipping on the dome light, she held the card up alongside the window.

Karen Turner
Crystal Moon Foundation
"So that your kids can look up and see the same crystal moon that we grew up with."

Ashley frowned. "As far as I can tell you can see the moon more clearly now than you could when I was a kid, pollution controls on everything from cars to power plants are so much better....Okay, I'm talking to myself here." She took a deep breath. She was nervous and more than a little scared. Her babbling was just a form of whistling in the proverbial graveyard. She checked the store once more. He was still waiting. She flipped the card over to see if anything was written on back.

Holiday Inn
Vidalia, Georgia

Ashley froze. Her heart began to race. Ashley knew someone in Vidalia, Georgia. She couldn't think of who it was, but she remembered seeing it or talking about it somewhere or something. She thought she had a postcard or picture from there that someone had given her as sort of a gag, a testament to small town, USA. She didn't know how she knew of this place—she just knew it. She looked up at Ian again.

He was paying. She only had seconds. Alarms began to go off inside her head. Something was terribly wrong. For a moment, it was sensory overload. How could this total stranger have an address written on a card that seemed so familiar?

What had been a little voice in her head when Charles had given her "the look" now became a cacophony of warning buzzers. Suddenly all other thoughts were crowded out of Ashley's mind by a new one, "GET OUT!" She had to get out of here. There was not another second to think it through. Ashley unbuckled the seatbelt and stepped out of the car. She pushed the door closed lightly so as not to attract attention. Everything seemed to slow down for her. Through some sort of sixth sense, she could see a stout woman in a white dress cutting line in front of Charles just when he was sticking out his money. If he turned toward the window, he would see her leaving and surely come after her.

The shortest route to get out of his sight was to go to the left of the small building and dash behind the station. After that, she didn't have any ideas. Her heart was pounding. *Don't panic, Ashley. Just keep thinking.* She ran to the corner of the building in her heels expecting any minute to hear him call after her. There was a bathroom on this side! That would be the first place he would look for her. She couldn't walk down the sidewalk either. He would spot her in seconds.

She ran up on her toes, her feet moving in a sliding motion so as not to click her heels on the pavement. As she reached the back of the building, she heard a chime on the front door. Charles might be walking out. How long did she have before he came here looking for her? Had he already seen her walking this way? *There, a dumpster.* She stepped behind it and squatted down. She still didn't like it. She was a sitting duck here. She could feel her pulse beating in her throat. The she heard Charles' voice.

"Gretchen! Gretchen!" It wasn't a voice of concern. Instead, it was demanding. He sounded angry. Then there was silence. Ashley strained to hear any sounds of his approach. She felt around for something to use for a weapon. Then she heard something else. There was a growling sound. She squinted hard in the darkness and saw the outline of a large cat less than two feet away. If he made a sound…

Ashley jumped despite herself as she heard the bathroom door being rattled against its lock. Then a fist pounded the door. "Gretchen! Gretchen! Are you in there?"

She tried to slow her breathing. She was certain he would hear her heart pounding almost out of her chest, or that the cat would yowl at any moment. *My pepper spray,* she thought. She had bought it years ago and never even considered using it. She only hoped it still worked.

"Gretchen, I know you are in there," Ian rattled the door impatiently. Then he said under his breath through clenched teeth, "Why couldn't you wait till we got out of here you filthy…" His voice tapered off.

This guy has got problems, Ashley thought. *I wasn't being paranoid about that look This guy is violent.* She was now in a nearly full-on panic. She grasped her pepper spray firmly, placed her thumb on the trigger and slowly eased it toward the area that she thought Charles's face would surely appear any second.

It was quiet again but Ashley was afraid to stand. She'd never heard a sound as he'd approached the bathroom, so how could she be sure he'd walked away? The cat growled again. She had to do something. She couldn't stay here. The combination of fear and the smells from the dumpster, the bathroom, and the cat was making her nauseous. If she got sick, he would surely find her. Just then, she thought she heard the door chime again, faintly. He was probably going after a key.

Holding her breath, she stood. He was gone. Ashley, still grasping the pepper spray, looked for somewhere to run without exposing herself. There, a few feet in front of her, was a broken gate in the old chain link fence surrounding the back of the station. She ran toward it and sucked in her breath as she squeezed beneath the chain and padlock and through a small opening. Even under these circumstances, she couldn't help but laugh nervously at herself. *I cannot believe I am doing this in this outfit,* she thought. She emerged into an alley between two row houses. At the end of the alley was a street.

She began to run. She thought about kicking off her high heels, but was too scared to stop that long. She felt as if Charles Fagan would grab her any second. The hairs on her neck stood up. She had intended to run to the edge of the buildings, hide and check the street. But she was awkward in the heels and she nearly fell, stumbling out into the street. Headlights washed over her and the driver of an oncoming car braked hard—luckily the tires didn't squeal. Ashley's eyes flew open wide, thinking it was Charles' Jag. Then she saw the "taxi" light on the roof. She ran toward the passenger door waving frantically.

"Girl, what in the world you doin' runnin' 'round out here this time a night dressed like that? I told y'all girls I don't take them kinda fares." Ashley looked into a face that was as black as the night.

Ashley couldn't help but roll her eyes at his comment before blurting breathlessly. "I'm an engineer, not a hooker, and I've got a hundred bucks here for you if you'll just get me out of here and not ask any questions." She held up the crisp hundred that she'd drawn from petty cash before she left the plant and placed in her small clutch at the hotel. She didn't concern herself with what would go on the expense report. The driver looked her over for a brief second.

"Why you still standin out there? Les get outta here." As Ashley got into the car and pulled the door closed, the driver smoothly took the hundred out of her left hand and stepped on the accelerator.

37

Ian was livid. No woman made him look foolish. He would first make this one wish she were dead and then kill her. He had checked the bathroom, found it empty and left the key in the lock. He thought about where she might have gone and why she might have left. She would never dare walk further into this neighborhood. She would head back toward the loop and try to flag someone down. He screeched the tires of the Jag and slid the back end around as he took a hard left out of the station, which took him back the way he had driven in and parallel to the street Ashley's cab was currently heading down.

"Don't go fast," Ashley told the cabbie. "Let's just cruise along slowly and hope we don't see him."

"First of all, don't tell me how ta drive my cab. And second of all whos's 'he'? A hunnerd dollar bill don't buy you no chase scene now. If we're gonna have that kinda trouble, you best find yourself another ride."

"He's some guy I met at a restaurant and like an idiot I got in a car with him and then he started acting really creepy. I can't believe I did this."

"I can't believe you done it neither. I ain't never met the dude and I can tell you he's creepy, else he wouldn't of brung a lady like you down here. And by the way, I wish you hadn't a got me in on it. I can retire in six more months."

"Just please don't put me out. Oh God, there he is. There goes his car."

The cabbie went through an intersection just in time for Ashley to see Ian's Jag speed toward the loop only one block away.

"You shoulda spoke to God when you was in that restaurant 'fore you made all them dumb decisions. It's a little late to be callin' Him now. Though it can't hurt neither one of us, that for sure."

It was only then that Ashley took a second to look around the cab and see the wooden cross dangling from the mirror and a small, wallet-sized painting of the face of Jesus glued to the dashboard.

"That's right. You done gone from running from Mr. Creepy to ridin' in a cab wit one a them fundamentalist religious nuts. Dadgum the luck you havin', huh?"

Ashley smiled a genuine smile. For the first time since she left her hotel room, she felt completely safe.

***

Ian lifted his hand from the steering wheel and checked his speed. In his fury, he was driving over a hundred. He lifted his foot off thc accelerator and took a deep breath to collect himself. He had been lost in mental images of how he would make this idiot model suffer for her disrespect. Now he nearly shot past the exit that would take him back to her hotel so that he had to brake sharply. The tires squealed as he jerked the car across two lanes and onto the ramp.

He knew he had to calm down. The last thing he needed right now was to be stopped by some D.C. cop. He rode the brake down the ramp and brought the car's speed down just enough, but he still made the light. He turned right and within two blocks, he was turning into the circular drive in front of her hotel. He paid the valet and decided to head back to the Coach and Six. He had no idea how long it might take her to return here, but she would return. And he would be waiting. He couldn't have his men do it. This was his mess. He would clean it up.

***

"Name's Walter. by the way, Walter, not Walt. This ain't 'Leave it to Beaver'." Ashley smiled again. She had gone from abject terror to doing a lot of smiling since she'd climbed into Walter's cab. Walter had suggested they take a longer route back to her hotel since Charles—she had told Walter the name Ian had given her—was possibly heading to her hotel to wait for her.

"I'm Ashley," she said as she stuck out her hand. "Thanks for saving me. Maybe he won't go back to my hotel. Maybe he'll just get frustrated and go home, thinking he's left me to fend for myself."

"Naw, I'm afraid he won't do that. From what you tol me, he'll be waitin'. His type always do."

"How do you know so much about it?" Ashley asked.

"You know back there when I asked if you was a hooker? Well, I don't take them kind of fares where they are plying their trade. But I give them rides all the time to try to keep 'em safe. To try to get 'em away from some john or some crazy pimp. You don't wanna know some of the things I've seen, Miss Lady."

"I guess I really messed up this time, huh? All I did was take a ride in a car with a very handsome, very nicely dressed gentleman. Other women my age have been a lot more foolish. Why does it have to turn out to be Attila the Hun when I do it?"

Ashley's face fell and her shoulders slumped. The stress of the day was starting to take its toll on her. The two rode for several minutes without speaking. Then Walter broke the silence.

"Can I ask you something, Miss Lady?"

"Yes, but don't call me that—please call me Ashley."

Walter seemed not to hear that. Instead, he went on with his question. "Look at you. You a beautiful young lady. I can already tell from talkin' to you that you're smart. Why in the world would you ever want to go take a ride with some strange man you just met? You know what you done when you done that? You give up a part o' yourself that you should keep…always.

"See, the trouble with young ladies like you these days is you forgot what you are. Just like what I just called you. You're a lady. Women today haven't been brought up respected enough to remember they're ladies. They turn on every TV program, look in every magazine, look on that Billboard right there," Walter motioned toward a billboard with a very scantily clad model caressing herself under a headline for a spa that read "Indulge Yourself." "Everywhere you look, folks are telling you that you're a stripper, a hooker, a sex object. When really you wasn't meant to be none of those things. Them girls on those programs and on these streets weren't meant to be that neither."

Ashley looked up, surprised by the fire with which Walter spoke. "So what were we meant to be?"

Just as Ashley asked the question, Walter's cab pulled up to a red light. It gave him the opportunity to lean his right forearm on the stack of logbooks between them and draw a little closer.

"You is a treasure," he said quietly but definitely. "You God's treasure. Yeah…yeah…" He pursed his mouth and squinted slightly to emphasize his point. Ashley felt herself tearing up and turned to look out the passenger window.

She felt the car start to move again and said, "You sound sort of like my dad. I'll bet he would be ashamed of me right now," Ashley choked up.

"No, Ma'am. No, Ma'am, I don't believe he would."

"Do you have a daughter?"

"Got two, Martha's a doctor and Mary's a teacher over at Georgetown. My son Gideon is about to graduate from "West Point." Ashley could sense the pride in Walter's voice, particularly when he said 'West Point'.

"Wow! That's great. They probably did so well because they have a pretty great dad."

Walter kept looking straight ahead but Ashley could see a slight smile crease the corners of his mouth.

"You gonna be all right, Miss Lady. You gonna be just fine." He looked over at her again now, that squint of intensity still in his eyes. Then he reached over, patted her arm and said, "Yeah... yeah."

38

Ian was getting a little tipsy and a whole lot tired of waiting. He had downed three Cognacs and rebuffed the advances of two bleached blondes who were in town on vacation. He was starting to regret that choice now after spending nearly an hour watching the lobby. The Cognac was taking the edge off his anger but it had done nothing to deter him from his mission for the night, the mission to torture and kill "Gretchen Collins."

Walter drove right past the main entrance to the Sheraton and took a left around the corner and another into the parking deck. He pulled the cab up parallel to the valet station and rolled down the window.

"Walter, my man!" the young Asian valet exclaimed.

"All right now, Won. How you doing? That wedding still on for next week or has she done come to her senses?" Walter held out a hand, Won slapped it instead of shaking it and laughed more heartily.

"That wedding's going down, Walter. We got the honeymoon suite booked right here." He jerked a thumb toward the revolving door of the hotel.

"Gonna let some of these folk give you the royal treatment for a change, huh?" Walter said.

"You got it. Will I see you at the ceremony?"

"I ain't gonna blow no smoke, Won. I probably won't make it. That's a pretty rough haul back into the city on my off day. But I will promise this. I'll say a prayer for y'all that day—ask the Lord to bless you with a whole houseful of children." With that, Walter's face broke into a bright smile and both men laughed as Won patted Walter on the back.

"Listen Won, I got to help this lady for a minute. There ain't no problem with me parking in the Security spot a few minutes, is there? She's gonna wait here for me."

"Well, Walter you know I ain't supposed to do that, but for you I'll make an exception."

"I knew that you would," Walter winked and jabbed the younger man playfully in the ribs. Both men laughed and Walter turned, placed Ashley's room key in his hip pocket, and stepped through the hotel door. He didn't take the lobby elevators but instead jumped into the service elevator with a bellman. Ashley couldn't hear him talking anymore, but it was obvious from the behavior of the bellman that Walter was on a first-name basis with him as well.

Ian couldn't see the rear door of the hotel from his vantage point, and even if he had been able to, he would never have noticed Walter. He fully expected Ashley, or Gretchen, as he knew her, to naively walk right through the front door after hitching a ride back.

After what seemed like only a few minutes, Walter came off the service elevator with all of Ashley's possessions neatly placed on a luggage cart. He rolled the cart up to the trunk and Ashley heard the lid pop. She started to step out to help him but then recalled his instructions to remain in the car no matter what.

In another five minutes, they were back on the boulevard and heading across town to a Hilton. Ashley made a reservation by cell phone, then called the Sheraton and agreed to pay a one-day penalty for canceling the room early, which she placed on her own credit card. She would have enough to explain to accounting about her expense report as it was.

"I can't tell you how much I appreciate all you've done for me. If you take credit cards, I want to pay you some more."

"I take credit cards but you keep it in your pocketbook. I would want somebody to do the same for my daughters if they got in a bad way." Then Walter looked at her and winked as he had with the valet, "You've paid me enough."

Ashley smiled before saying, "So do you know every valet and bellman in Washington?"

"Know a heap of 'em. Don't know that I know all of 'em. Say, I'll tell you what you can do. You say you're gonna be in town a couple weeks, how about, you need a cab, you call old Walter?" He reached up to his visor, pulled a business card from a strap on a visor pouch, and handed it to Ashley.

"Can't think of anybody I would rather use. I sure am glad you were on tonight."

"That's just it. I was supposed to take off today and go see my wife's family down in Maryland. But her aunt took sick so we didn't go. I almost wouldn't have been rolling down that street when you ran out. I'm telling you, Miss Lady, you a treasure. Somebody looking out for you." Then he squinted at her, pursed his mouth and said. "Lord, looking out for you...yeah....yeah."

39

The next morning was the first day that Ashley was to report to the law firm to begin preparations for her testimony. Walter wasn't working so she walked to a nearby Metro station that took her to within three blocks of the law offices of Claiborne, Claiborne, and Couch. Ashley hadn't had time to do much research on them but she had called Annette, who did a Lexus Nexus search and found out that they were a 100-year-old corporate firm. They had an excellent reputation in defending against frivolous lawsuits. Despite that, they became infamous in legal circles by losing a lawsuit brought by an obese man who claimed that he didn't know donuts were fattening.

As Ashley walked into the lobby, she immediately knew she was in another world. Expensive looking art pieces sat on clear glass tables and hung on the walls. A circular-shaped desk was at the center of the lobby. Ashley hesitated for a moment, looking at a painting of Washington crossing the Delaware, before heading toward the desk where a pleasant looking young woman sat. After only a few steps, she was intercepted by an attractive woman whose piercing blue eyes were accentuated by flowing, possibly premature, gray hair.

"Ashley Miller?"

"Well, uh, yes," Ashley answered with surprise.

"I'm Martha Claiborne." The woman held out her hand and Ashley shook it. "We've been looking forward to working with you. Would you follow me?"

Ashley followed the woman into a large paneled office that contained a breathtaking mahogany desk.

"It was my great grandfather's desk. He started the firm." *She must have noticed me staring,* Ashley thought.

"It's beautiful. So are you a partner here?" As she asked this, she looked at the license and diplomas on the wall. One was from Harvard law class of '81, which made Ms. Claiborne a good ten years older than she looked.

"Yes, I'm senior partner. Let's get right to work, shall we?"

No small talk here, Ashley thought.

"How much have you been told about why you're here?"

"Not that much, really. I know I'm supposed to testify before Congress."

"That's true," Claiborne said. "And no matter how big a deal you think testifying before Congress on a matter like this is, it's bigger than that. Put quite simply, if the EPA succeeds in what they're attempting to do, the cost of energy—all energy—in this country will quadruple. It will make cap and trade legislation irrelevant. It will be a very effective end-run by the executive branch around the legislative branch. No one, and that includes the congressmen who are hearing this testimony, fully understands the ripple effect this will have."

"And you do?" Ashley blurted out her question without thinking about how accusatory it might sound. She held her breath as she waited for an answer. Martha Claiborne only stared at her for a long moment, her blue eyes vivid over the top of her reading glasses.

"Yes, I do," she finally answered. "I've specialized in environmental law for over thirty years. I'm not shy about saying that I probably understand more about environmental legislation than the Supreme Court and the director of EPA combined. I've seen its benefits and its unintended consequences. I can tell you unequivocally that if the policy to regulate CO_2 as a hazardous pollutant goes forward it will adversely affect the economy of the entire world."

"So what you're telling me is there's no pressure at all about this testimony thing?" Ashley laughed awkwardly at her own joke before realizing that Claiborne had her locked in an icy stare. She cut her laughter short.

"No. That's not what I'm saying. What I'm saying is that you may go the rest of your career without doing something of this much importance and that will have an effect on this many people."

Ashley took a deep breath. She didn't know what to say. She'd not asked for this assignment and still didn't fully understand how she'd ended up here. Finally, she raised her eyebrows, sighed deeply and said, "Wow."

"Wow is right." Claiborne answered. "You will be spending eight hours a day—ten if needed—with some of our staff drilling on every possible question that might come up. We'll tap into your expertise but we'll enhance that expertise with intensified training of our own. You won't be testifying to make yourself look important and you won't be just representing your company. As far as the committee is concerned, you will be representing power plant environmental compliance professionals throughout the entire generation industry.

"So then there's no pressure?"

Martha Claiborne smiled slightly. Like most people, she'd taken one look at Ashley and jumped to conclusions. She'd immediately assumed that some good old boy executive was giving his eye candy underling what he thought would be a cherry gig in D.C. and that, in so doing, he was wasting a great deal of her firm's time. Now she was beginning to see Ashley differently.

"Okay," she let out a little breath. "Maybe I came on a little strong at first but I do need you to understand the magnitude of what we're doing here. If you're like most people, all you know about testifying before Congress is what you have seen on C-Span—some poor guy sitting behind a table talking to two or three senators and a whole lot of empty chairs where other committee members should be sitting. This one is not going to go down like that. Global warming and carbon emissions reduction is the hot topic in town this month. All the players are going to want to be front and center once the hearings start. They won't want to miss that photo op."

"I was happier when I thought I was going to be the poor schmo behind the table talking to one or two bored senators," Ashley quipped.

Claiborne smiled again. This kid was going to be all right.

After talking for another twenty minutes and giving Ashley an overview of what to expect, Claiborne buzzed a legal clerk to her office and instructed him to take Ashley down to a small conference room for her first day of training. The bespectacled clerk now walked rapidly down a long hallway. He talked to Ashley over his shoulder just as fast as he walked.

"Don't expect to see her again until the day before you go up on the hill. Partners don't have time to spend with little fish like you. That's what they pay us for. My name is Zachary Dillon. Call me Zach. Just don't call me every five minutes—I have work of my own to do. Julie, this is Ashley Miller, she's the UPI girl."

Zach introduced her to a pretty blonde who was a few years younger than Ashley and who looked all too ready to help at a moment's notice. She reminded Ashley of one of those super friendly kids who worked at Disney, but before they could exchange pleasantries, Zach was off once again, motioning for Ashley to follow.

"Here's the thing. You're going to need coffee, lots of it. The first several days of this are going to be excruciatingly boring. Then you'll have about three or four days of testimony rehearsals which can be kind of exciting for a while. Then Martha or one of the other partners will come and grill you, at which time you'll feel like you haven't prepared at all, and they'll just generally treat you like you're a blubbering idiot. Sitting in with the partners is like pre-op for major invasive surgery, with your trip to the Hill being like the surgery. Yes, pre-op is excruciatingly unpleasant, but it's oh so necessary to do before having your colon removed the next day. So boredom, boredom, boredom, followed by chaos, and then abject terror."

Zach stopped at the doorway to a windowless conference room and leaned against the doorjamb as he waved Ashley into the room as if he was a flight attendant pointing to the plane's exit. Ashley looked in the room at a foot-tall stack of what looked to be ledger books sitting neatly on the table. Along one wall were two banker's boxes marked "Cap and Trade" in black marker.

"Thus beginneth the boring part," Zach said, as he followed Ashley into the room.

"I have to read all this?"

"No. You just have to read the pages with words on them. Probably five percent of the pages have graphs on them—you can just look at those," Zach answered.

Ashley blew out her cheeks in disbelief and continued standing alongside the table.

"There's a Coke room down the hall to the left and a ladies' room straight across the hall from that. You'll be tempted to just skim half this stuff and not actually read it. Don't do that. You'll end up very embarrassed."

Like a whirlwind, Zach whisked from the room and left Ashley there alone. As she pulled out her chair, he stuck his head back in the door.

"And no, I was not kidding about the chaos and terror stuff." Then he was gone again.

40

Shelton turned up his nose at the smell of dead fish and river mud as Leroy struggled to lower the sample basket into place with a hoist.

"You folks can actually make yerselves useful, you know. You don't just *have* to stand there like bumps on a log," Leroy said.

Reluctantly, Summer, who was there with Shelton, along with a college kid who was working as a summer intern with Riverguardian, stepped forward.

"What do you want us to do?" she asked.

"Well, grab the danged basket, dumb bunny. I can't control the hoist and maneuver the basket at the same time. I only got two hands," Leroy was beginning to raise his voice as the heavy sample basket swung out of control on its cable.

"Well, you don't have to insult me," Summer said, as she barely clasped the sides of the basket with her fingers.

"What you got them brand-new work gloves for, missy? Grab the thing like you want to hold onto it 'fore it swings around and hurts ya. And you two guys, get your tails up here and help her instead a' standin' there with your arms crossed."

Actually, none of the group was supposed to be doing any work on SPG property. They were not employees or contractors and there were liability issues. But Leroy was all about practicality. He needed help and three able-bodied people—the same people that wanted this fish sampling done in the first place—were standing nearby. Why should he not utilize the resources at his disposal?

Everyone wore high rubber boots, work gloves, and heavy Carhartt overalls. Leroy's coveralls were faded and threadbare from years of wear, while the trio from Riverguardian wore brand new coveralls that were stiff from the store. As the basket lowered into place, Leroy had everyone let go so as not to pinch their hands or fingers. Then, once they were clear of the basket, Leroy lowered it rapidly, splashing river water well up onto the rubber boots of Summer and Shelton. Shelton shot him a look, but Leroy turned his back as if looking out at the river and suppressed a chuckle.

"All right, now let's gather up our stuff and we'll put out the other sample baskets. Then I'll get the screens rotating and we'll start the sample time," Leroy instructed.

Protocol for proper representative sampling was for the plant to place screens in strategic locations in their discharge canal. Then when the rotating screens were turned on, trapped fish would be washed off into the canal and would be collected in the baskets. The fish could then be preserved as specimens and shipped to a biologist for identification. Finally, all the fish in the basket would be counted. This would be done once per week for several months. In addition, electrofishing—a process where fish are stunned prior to capture—would be conducted in the river itself. This would provide data as to the type of fish in the waterway. This data would then be compared to the data from the screens to determine how damaging SPG was to the overall river fish population. Leroy had conducted this type of sampling twenty years prior when it was mandated by the clean water act, so he'd been chosen to head up the current test.

By the time the four of them got the baskets in place, started the screens, and got the electrofishing boat on the river, with Leroy doing 90 percent of the work, it was nearly lunchtime. Leroy reached around for his black metal lunch box.

"Hope y'all brought somethin' with ya ta eat 'cause I ain't got enough in here to share," he said.

"Your lunch box looks like something off a Fred Flintstone cartoon," Summer said.

Leroy stared over his glasses for several seconds. Then without saying another word, he took a bite out of his sandwich and looked out toward the river as he chewed.

"You don't like us much, do you, Mr. Allen?" Shelton asked as the boat rocked gently in the current.

"'Bout as much as you like me, I'd guess," Leroy said.

"There's nothing personal going on here, Mr. Allen. We're only trying to stand up for something we believe in. We're trying to accomplish something for the good of the environment."

Leroy shook his head and took a sip from his Thermos cup.

"I take it by your reaction that you don't approve. Don't you care about the environment, Mr. Allen?"

"I was gonna let it go, boy. But now I don't think I will. Son, I was on this river before you were born. I've fished it, swam in it, I've even drank out of it. I brought my kids here and I still bring my grandkids. I would say I care about this river just as much as any of you do."

"Well, then you should be excited about what we're trying to accomplish."

"What you gonna accomplish? You gonna shut that plant down and save all the fish? Is that what you gonna do?"

"I don't have the power to shut anything down and hopefully that won't happen, but if that's what it takes to save some of these river species, then so be it." Shelton was lying. He had every hope that the plant would be shut down before he was through.

Leroy was getting a little more irritated now. "Boy, look out there at that river. You see how fast that current is? Look. Look there. You see how fast that tree limb is floatin' by? I can tell you from experience that is at least a 30 percent faster current than we create with our pumps by pullin' river water into that plant. Any self-respectin' fish that can swim against that current can dang sure swim away from our intake."

"What's your point?" Shelton asked.

"My point is that the only fish we're trappin' on them screens were already wounded or dyin' before they ever got there. And most of those that do get trapped are gizzard shad. I could throw a three-foot net out anywhere in this river and catch hundreds of gizzard shad. We ain't hurtin' the fish population in this river one bit. If we were, there wouldn't be fishermen sittin' in their boats right off plant property almost 24 hours a day for the past fifty years."

"I don't believe that to be the case, Mr. Allen. And if it is the case, then you won't mind taking some samples to prove that."

"I do mind," Leroy said. "I mind a whole heck of a lot. The whole lot of ya ain't nothin but a botheration to me. Not to mention the money this is all gonna cost my company just to prove what we already know."

Shelton was growing impatient with the lecture. "Look, Leroy. You've made your opinion clear. Unfortunately, your opinion doesn't count for much in all this. The data is what will count. The science will count."

"Science, my hindquarters," Leroy said. "You ain't gonna find enough fish to fill up your hat in them baskets. And what if you do? Is it worth shuttin' this plant down to save those few fish?"

"Yes it is. There are some things more important in this world than your job security.

"Job security," Leroy scoffed. "Job security is a small part of it, boy. Look over there on that far bank. You see them houses? Now you see our transmission lines crossin' that river. Them houses got lights in 'em. And it's getting cold so they're also gonna need their heat. On down those power lines is a school, after that is a hospital. I'm a whole lot more worried about somebody's grandma on a heart/lung machine in that hospital having the electricity she needs to keep her alive than I am about some danged fish. These people ya see around here, they don't just rely on electricity. They rely on electricity they can *afford*. You people gonna bring all that down and for what? So you can get all puffed up and feel like you done somethin'. And half this environmental stuff added together don't make up to a hill of beans. It's just another way for somebody to stick it to the workin' man. That's all in the world it is."

Leroy finished his speech and then threw the rest of his sandwich into the river. He abruptly snapped the lid down on his lunch box and tossed down the dregs of his cold coffee.

"You can write me a ticket for samwich pollutin'," Leroy said. "Lunch break is over kiddies. Let's get to sampling fish."

41

At the time that Leroy was starting the boat motor, Muhammad Raschi—he wasn't thinking as Ian Flannery just now—was pushing his fists into the sides of his head so hard that it made his arms quiver. He had to learn to control his weakness for women. Suddenly he slapped the computer monitor in front of him so hard that it nearly toppled off the desk. He'd been at the computer all night, searching the name Gretchen Collins—the alias Ashley had given him. He'd looked through site after site of models and had not seen her face. He now had to admit to himself that he'd been duped by a woman.

"What did she see?" he said aloud, his fist now pressed against his lips. What had made her run from his car in a neighborhood like that? Why did he choose to stop for gas when he did? In a few more blocks, he would've had her at the apartment he had used to kill the others. Within a couple of hours after that, she would have been dead and no threat to compromise his mission. Now he had no idea who she was, where she might be, or how he could find her.

He'd slipped the desk clerk at the hotel where he'd met Ashley a hundred dollar bill, but the records showed no one by the name Gretchen or Collins had been registered there.

Then he had a thought: *maybe he could have his new friend at the hotel check on anyone who checked out within two hours of this so-called "Gretchen" disappearing.* Perhaps he could utilize that to find out her real name.

Muhammad forgot about how tired he was and headed to the bathroom to shave and change. Whatever he had to pay, he had to have a name. He had to find this woman. And he had to kill her. He told himself what he always did: she would have to die for the good of the mission. Yet, like always, in the dark recesses of his mind, he was nearly sick with anticipation.

and she felt she now had a better understanding of at least one root cause for this phenomenon. The country, with the help of compliant political leaders, had developed a real propensity for shooting itself in the foot economically.

43

The act of forcing herself to focus on her required reading and the political ramifications of them helped take her mind off Charles Fagan. She was once again rubbing her eyes and shaking her head at invading thoughts of the man when she heard the door open.

"Okay, take a break. I need you to step down the hall and put this on."

It was Martha and she was holding a hanger containing a black business suit in one hand and a pair of black pumps in the other.

"What do you mean put that on? Where are we going?" Ashley was asked. She'd been locked in this tiny conference room for three days eating take-out, been allowed almost no time to see any of the city, and now was being ordered around like a summer intern. Martha didn't seem to notice.

"You've got an appointment in forty minutes with Keitha Dobbs."

Ashley recognized the name from some of the articles she'd been reading.

"You mean the senator from Seattle who chairs the committee?"

"That very one," Martha said as she brushed a fleck of lint from the suit.

"I didn't know anything about any one-on-one meeting," Ashley protested. "And how do you know if that stuff will fit me or not?"

"I'm telling you now," Martha replied unsympathetically. "These meetings don't come easily and you take them when you can get a few minutes. The window of opportunity just opened so there you go. My driver will take us and I'll brief you on the drive over to the hill. Oh, and the clothes will fit. We do this all the time for clients. I have people."

"You mean people that guess clients' sizes so that they won't have to wear their prison jumpsuits to court?" Ashley asked dryly.

"Cute. Now go get dressed."

She took the clothes brusquely, unhappy with this unexpected surprise. Keitha Dobbs was no friend of industry. Ashley would be entering hostile waters.

Five minutes later, she stepped back into the hall where Martha was waiting with Zach and Julie, the two clerks she'd met on her first morning at the firm. They all stared at her for what Ashley felt was a long moment.

"Sharp-dressed gal," Julie said. Then she turned to Martha and held up a palm, "Told you she'd be a six and you were going to try to put her in an eight. It would have swallowed her."

Martha handed Julie a twenty-dollar bill.

"Never doubt me, Martha," Julie said smugly as Zach rolled his eyes.

"You do look nice," Zach confessed. "Julie knows her fashion."

Moments later, she was in the backseat of a limo rolling down I-395 toward Capitol Hill.

44

Martha didn't waste any time getting into the briefing. "Keitha Dobbs is a genuine flower child of the sixties. She cut her liberal teeth following Abby Hoffman around Chicago in '68 for a short time and was involved in what he labeled as the yippies or Youth International Party. Then she fell in with a band from Seattle for a while. One of those one-hit wonders, I don't recall the name."

"Somewhere around 1974, she actually had to get a job and began working for a Seattle attorney who specialized in bringing environmental lawsuits. He was instrumental in getting a ban on DDT, even though the science of that was very thin. The results of the ban have been millions dying from what would have been avoidable malaria cases—one of those unintended consequences I was telling you about. Rumor has it that the two were dating, though our guy has never been able to confirm that. The lawyer was thirty years her senior and married at the time.

"It was through that movement that she got interested in politics. She ended up marrying a congressman from the 5th district, which includes Seattle, in '83. He was elected to the senate in '89 but died unexpectedly of coronary disease before he finished out his second term. Dobbs was appointed to his seat by the governor and had never really been challenged in ensuing elections.

"I probably shouldn't even consider a meeting between the two of you but I've decided that the risk is worth the reward. You are pretty charming. If you can win her over, at least show her that you are not blatantly anti-environment, it would be a big coup for you during your testimony. I'll sit in with you and try to direct the conversation as much as I can."

All too soon, the limo pulled up to a secure entrance at the Richard B. Russell senate office building, the building where the infamous Watergate hearings were held. Before she knew it, Ashley was sitting in Senator Dobbs' office.

She'd assumed that the senator's office would be in the Capitol building and she would thus get a behind the scenes view of the historic halls. However, no senators had offices there. Instead, they were housed here or in another office building.

Now, inside the receptionist's office, Ashley couldn't help being struck by how much this looked like any other office of perhaps a mid-level executive. Senator Dobbs' receptionist first greeted Ashley as though she were reuniting with an old and dear friend. The room cooled noticeably when Martha stepped in.

"Hello, Counselor Claiborne," the receptionist said as the bright smile slowly left her face.

"Hello Katherine. How wonderful to see you again," Martha said. Ashley couldn't be sure but Martha's tongue seemed to be firmly in-cheek.

"The pleasure's all mine," Katherine said with a slight scowl. "And this is?" she asked, indicating Ashley.

"This is Ashley Miller. I believe she's on the senator's schedule for eleven?"

"Yes, please have a seat. The senator should be finishing up another meeting any moment."

Ashley and Martha both sat down but Martha seemed to be intent on watching Katherine sit. Once Katherine scooted her chair under her desk and began working on her computer, Martha said, "Katherine, would we be too terribly much trouble if we were to ask for a cup of coffee, please."

"That's okay..." Ashley's sentence was cut off by a quick elbow from Martha.

Katherine glared in Martha's direction but then forced a smile and stood.

"With cream and two sugars for both of us would be wonderful," Martha said.

After she left the room, Martha leaned over to Ashley and whispered. "I don't want coffee either, especially from her. The witch will probably spit in it. But since I know how much she hates me, I just thought I'd give her a little jab. Our history is a long story but..."

Katherine came back in to the room bearing two coffees in black mugs with the seal of the State of Washington on them. The coffee was unstirred and large clumps of powdered creamer were still floating on the top. Martha didn't even reach for hers, so neither did Ashley.

Ashley looked around the room at the memorabilia from countries around the world. There were photos with foreign dignitaries and hardhat-clad union workers. There was a photo of Senator Dobbs and the two most recent Democratic Presidents. There were books on the shelves, but not that many. She couldn't help but notice that none had anything to do with U.S. government or history.

The senator's office door opened.

45

"Thanks so much, Senator," a man's voice said just before he stepped out of the inner office door. He wore an expensive looking suit and Ashley thought he looked familiar. She wondered if he were famous. He barely looked at her or Martha.

"You keep me posted on how much you're willing to participate, Kevin. I'm excited about the prospect of you all working alongside us in this."

Senator Dobbs, dressed in a distinguished cream-colored suit, stepped into the reception area. Gray streaks ran through her once black hair and her makeup was heavy. Ashley could feel butterflies dancing in her stomach again.

The senator smiled thinly at her and Martha and then followed the man out into the hall.

Martha leaned closer to Ashley. "That's Kevin Knowles. He's CEO of one of the largest utilities in the country. His and a few other companies have decided to play ball. Rather than join us in fighting draconian CO_2 regulations, they're going to roll over. Try to save themselves that way. I have a big time problem with that."

Now she understood why the man had looked familiar. She'd seen him give the keynote address at an environmental conference she'd attended a year prior. Before she could tell Martha that however, Dobbs walked back in.

Martha stood and held out her hand. Dobbs folded her arms across her chest.

"So this must be Ms. Miller. I understand you'll be speaking with our committee next week," Dobbs said.

"Yes ma'am," Ashley answered. As she did so, she cringed inside, realizing how much she'd just sounded like a star-struck child.

"Well, it's nice to meet you," Senator Dobbs held her hand out and Ashley shook it. The senator's hand was cold and limp and she took it back quickly.

"Why don't we step in my office," the senator said.

Martha picked up her portfolio and took a step to follow. Senator Dobbs held up a hand.

"That's all right Martha. You can relax out here. We're merely going to have a little chat."

Martha stiffened ever so briefly. She hadn't expected this but she should have anticipated it. She could keep Ashley, who was the personification of her client, from going in but then she lost all advantage she'd hoped to gain from the meeting. She'd be put on the defensive while making it look as though Ashley had something to hide, which she didn't. Of course, Dobbs knew all of this.

"Certainly, Senator. I'll just sit right here with Katherine."

Katherine looked up with a wry smile as Dobbs closed the door.

"Ms. Miller, what exactly was it you wanted to see me about? I'm sure you understand that I don't have a lot of time."

Ashley had no idea what she wanted to see Keitha Dobbs about. In fact, she didn't want to see her at all. She'd been ordered here.

"I just wanted to take this opportunity to meet you face-to-face and introduce myself to you," she replied. It sounded so good that she almost believed it herself. It didn't satisfy the senator. She was clearly looking for more.

"I wanted you to know that UPI would love to work with you and your committee to come up with a workable solution that we can both embrace." As soon as the words left her mouth, Ashley immediately thought, *What the heck did I just say? What am I talking about? Wonder if I can climb out there a little farther on that limb?*

"And what kind of solution might that be, Ms. Miller? One that costs utilities nothing and benefits the environment even less?"

Ashley wasn't sure how things got contentious so fast but they had. She felt like saying that it would be hard to be less beneficial to the environment than the cap and trade proposals that Dobbs was so high on.

"No, not at all, I was just trying…"

"I'm sorry, Ms. Miller," Dobbs said leaning her hips back on the front of her desk. "You've been placed in an awkward position. Martha has dragged you all the way up here to glad-hand me and I'm not interested. She's been inside the beltway long enough to know better."

Something in the senator's body language made it blatantly obvious to her that Martha's hope of softening up Dobbs was hopeless. Ashley was about to decide that she may as well use the opportunity to make a point. Still, she held back. She didn't want to turn this woman into more of an enemy than she already appeared to be.

"I'm sure I don't know what you mean," she said, although she knew exactly what Dobbs meant.

"I don't believe you have any new ideas to share with me, Ms. Miller, because the mantra from your industry has not changed in ten years. You never want to do anything to benefit the environment and now you're a group of 'deniers.' You deny that global warming exists even though many scientists are in agreement that it does."

Ashley knew that statement was patently false. The coal-fired power industry had already spent hundreds of millions of dollars to insure good environmental stewardship. Manmade warming was not even a well-demonstrated theory, much less a proven fact. She resented the use of the term "denier" as though she was being grouped with holocaust deniers. She realized, however, that she could learn something here. She had to participate in the conversation, get Dobbs on a roll. It was clear Dobbs wanted to vent. She just needed a nudge.

"I'm sorry. I disagree with your assessment."

"You disagree? Young lady, how long have you worked in the power generation industry?"

"Five years now, ma'am." Ashley purposely wanted to appear naive.

"Five years. That long? I've been on this committee and in close negotiations with your industry for twenty-four years. And in that entire time I've not received one ounce of cooperation in trying to make this planet safer for our nation's children as well as the children that perhaps you'll have someday. In fact now, thanks to all the greenhouse gases your industry emits, we must ask ourselves if there will even be a planet left for your children."

46

Dobbs had just lost all credibility with Ashley. She'd read enough in the past days to now know that even the worst-case scenario models didn't propose things were that bad or that problems of that magnitude would occur within this generation.

"Did you see that man that just left my office?" Dobbs went on. "That man is a person who's willing to sacrifice his own selfish goals for the good of the planet. He's the president of a large utility company and all he talked about was how he wanted to help curb his company's greenhouse gases. He wants to join me at the Copenhagen conference. He wants to show solidarity to the world and let them know that we must all solve this crisis together."

"What crisis?" Ashley blurted out. "There is no demonstrable crisis. The science is so thin, the so-called data so subjective, that it's proven nothing. Far from being a consensus scientific opinion—an oxymoron if there ever was one—this is not even a settled hypothesis yet."

Dobbs looked at Ashley as if she had just committed blasphemy.

"I think that right now would be an excellent time for you to leave my office, young lady. There's no reason for us to waste one another's time, is there? I'm sure I'll have lots of questions for you on the day of the hearing. For now we have nothing further to discuss."

"I'm sorry you feel that way," she said, as she stood. She thought about really giving Dobbs a piece of her mind. She considered educating her on all that SPG had already done on behalf of the environment. She paused on her way out the door.

"Is there something else?"

"No" Ashley said. "I'm sorry that we couldn't speak longer, that's all."

"And I am sorry that you aren't interested in discussing substantive issues," Dobbs replied. "Counselor, your client and I have concluded our meeting. Have a lovely afternoon."

The door slammed loudly, which irritated Ashley more than anything else that had occurred. "What the heck is her...?"

Martha held up a hand and Ashley clamped her mouth shut.

"'Bye now, Kat," Martha said. "Perhaps we'll see you at Ford's sometime. Do you still have your tickets?"

"Why of course I do, Martha," Katherine replied. "All the best people are going to the theater these days. So I guess you won't be able to make it?"

Martha ignored the jibe and placed a hand on the small of Ashley's back and ushered her out the door. As the door snapped closed behind them, she spoke in a semi-whisper. "She once told me that she hates it when anyone calls her Kat."

"Senator Dobbs didn't like me any better than Katherine liked you, Martha, and I just met her. She kept hurling all these bogus, random accusations, never let me speak or make any kind of a case, and then had the nerve to tell *me* that *I* didn't want to discuss substantive issues."

"That's not surprising. The last comment of hers you mentioned is familiar to me. She does it all the time. It's classic psychological projection—she's the one that had no intention of discussing substantive issues."

"Well, if this is what you expected, do you mind telling me why you dragged me down here in the first place?"

"We had to try. There was an even chance that she would have let me go in with you. If she had, we could have probably taken a little more control of the conversation. If I could have just gotten her to see that you're a reasonable person, we would've been ahead of the game. Still, we learned something."

"What's that?"

"We learned that the deck is more stacked than we thought. We learned that this committee is going to be the toughest I've ever had to deal with and that they likely do not intend to give us a fair hearing. Their minds are already made up," Martha said.

47

Julie, Martha's blonde haired, blue-eyed clerk, had been nice enough to give Ashley a ride to her hotel. She was beyond tired and stressed and had planned to head straight for her room. It wasn't until she stepped into the lobby and Julie drove off that she realized she really didn't feel like eating alone. She tried to catch Julie on her cell but it rolled straight to voice mail. She closed her phone and breathed a reluctant sigh as she stepped toward the hotel restaurant where she'd eaten half a dozen times before.

Before she could place her phone in her purse, it began to vibrate. She didn't recognize the caller and her first thought was that Charles Fagan had gotten her number. She was still far from over the fear she'd experienced a few nights before. The phone vibrated again as she debated whether to answer. She decided that she at least needed to know if they guy had her phone number. With her heart beginning to race, she pressed the answer key.

"Hello," she said tentatively.

"Hi there."

She didn't recognize the voice but it definitely wasn't Charles. There was no British accent.

"Please let me take you to dinner so I can be delivered from the hotel from hell."

Silence.

"You have no idea who this is, do you?"

"No, I'm sorry. The voice seems familiar, but I…"

"It's Hunt Finley. The guy you met on the plane."

Ashley felt the tension ease from her shoulders.

"Yes, of course I remember. I just didn't recognize your voice on the phone. How are you?"

"I'm fine except that I desperately need to get out of my hotel. I would love to buy you a nice dinner and tell you a good story about my experiences here. How about it? I promise to make you laugh."

Ashley smiled. Actually, this was just what she needed and she was more than a little impressed with Hunt's sense of timing.

"Okay. I'm in."

"Great," Hunt said and blushed at the sound of exuberance in his voice. "Now let's see how we should do this. I still haven't rented a car so…"

"I don't mind taking a cab and meeting you somewhere," Ashley said.

"No, no please," Hunt said. "I can just get one myself and pick you up."

"I've got an idea," Ashley replied. "I met the nicest man my first night here. He has his own cab and gave me his card. Why don't I call him and we can pick you up? You get dinner, I'll get the cab."

"Well, I really don't want you to have to pay for anything but you call your guy and I'll pay you back."

Ashley started to argue, decided against it and said, "Okay. What's the name of your hotel? If you don't hear back from me, expect us to pick you up at eight. That will give me an hour, which should be plenty of time."

"Great," Hunt answered, still thinking his tone was a bit over the top. "I look forward to seeing you then." He hung up. "I look forward to seeing you then," he said smacking his forehead. "Why didn't you just say, 'Thank you so much for going out with me because I am a needy freak who hasn't had a date in six months. Well, I'm not needy and I have had dates in the last six months.' Plenty of them. And they were both quite pleasant outings, thank you very much."

While Hunt was beating himself up, Ashley was dialing Walter's number. He answered on the second ring.

"Ranger Cab." Ashley was struck by how comforting the sound of the elderly man's voice was.

"Hi Walter. It's me, Ashley Miller."

"Miss Lady," he responded enthusiastically. "I'm bettin' you need a ride someplace."

"As a matter of fact, I do. I was hoping you would sort of chaperone me. I've accepted a dinner invitation."

"Glad to, glad to, long as it ain't with that fella from the other night. I don't feel like doin' no chase scenes tonight." Walter chuckled.

"No, this guy is different."

"Well then, that do sound nice. Be at your hotel in 'bout twenty minutes."

Ashley closed her phone, marveling at the depth of her final comment to Walter. She barely knew Hunt. Yet, her intuition told her that he was more than just a different individual from Charles. He was a different kind of man.

48

Shelton surprised himself with how nervous he was. He wasn't expecting this to be all that challenging. Still, if he were caught…

As he waited for Leroy, he lightly touched the packet in his pants pocket. He would need to remove it discreetly, smoothly.

"Another day of fun and games in paradise," Leroy said. "How you folks doin' this fine mornin'?"

"We're fine, Leroy. How are you?" Summer answered. Despite themselves, both Summer and Stacey had grown to like Leroy. They saw him as a lovable curmudgeon. Shelton was ambivalent. Frankly, he was equally ambivalent about Summer and Stacey.

"The ends justify the means," he repeated to himself, quoting his former professor. "The ends justify the means."

"Okay, lessee what we got here," Leroy said. As he spoke, he was holding down the button on the remote control hoist that would lift the large stainless basket from the discharge canal. "Looks like another light day folks. Sorry to disappoint ya."

Summer and Stacey looked at one another and rolled their eyes before both broke into a grin.

"Leroy, you're just loving proving us wrong, aren't you?" Stacey said.

"Well, it do make the day go by a little quicker, I'll say that," Leroy replied, still looking into the basket. "Got some algae and river grass bound up in there. Lemme clean that out."

The girls, both wearing heavy rubber-coated work gloves, leaned into the basket as Leroy sat it on the deck and began to help pull the vegetation carefully away. The three of them were each being careful not to discard fish with the weeds. As soon as Shelton saw that they were occupied he turned his back on them.

"Oh, what am I thinking? I need to get my gloves on," he said.

Shelton fumbled clumsily with the packet in his pocket. He was certain that any second Leroy was going to lay a hand on his shoulder and say, "Gotcha!" He couldn't get the package opened. If he didn't hurry, they were going to have the basket cleaned out before he could do anything. He held it in one hand as he slid a glove on. *Rats!* he thought. He'd dropped it. Had they seen? He quickly dropped the other glove on top of it. Then he stooped down, took a deep but ragged breath and placed it in the palm of one gloved hand. He turned back to the basket. Leroy shot him a look.

"You may as well keep your hands clean now, princess. The three of us nearly got this job knocked out."

"Nice, Leroy. Excuse me for not having my gloves on sooner. I came here to help"

Shelton knelt at one end of the basket where there was still a little pile of grass. He scooted his hand as far underneath as he could reach and released the madtom. He then began grabbing grass half-heartedly from the basket, acting as though the smell of it made him squeamish.

"Ugh. This grass smells like dead fish."

"That's 'cause it's been at the bottom of a river, twinkletoes. Probably full of fish pee," Leroy laughed at his own joke, but Shelton's heart was racing.

"Okay, lessee what we caught today," Leroy said.

Summer turned to reach for a jar of formaldehyde. Any fish species that was caught in the sample basket for the first time was to be preserved. So far, all they had were two or three species from earlier sampling events.

"Threadfin shad," Leroy held a dead three-inch shad out in his palm for the others to see. Once they nodded agreement, he tossed the fish into a trash bag.

"Gizzard shad, another threadfin," Leroy continued to count through the ten or so captured fish. Shelton stood behind him, his gloves off. He held the gloves in one hand, with his fists on his hips.

"Say, Leroy, what's that one?" Shelton asked.

"What is what one?" Leroy said, looking around the basket.

"Over there, under your hand."

Leroy finally saw it. It was a tiny fish not even as large as the shad. One dorsal fin was damaged as if from a bite.

"Huh," Leroy remarked. "Never saw one of these before. Looks like some kind of juvenile cat. But he's colored up different than any catfish I ever saw."

Shelton stared into the basket, waiting. *Come on Stacey, come on!* He thought. *Either you or Summer has to recognize what this is.*

"Oh, my gosh," Stacey exclaimed.

Summer must have realized it at the same instant because she pulled off one glove, threw it aside, and covered her mouth.

"What is it?" Leroy asked, rising to one knee. "What are you two getting all upset about?"

"That's a madtom," Summer said. "A madtom catfish."

"Okay, so?" Leroy said, still holding the little fish in his palm. The madtom was stiff and Shelton hoped that Leroy couldn't smell the formaldehyde.

"So that's an endangered species, that's what." Stacey's tone had completely changed. She was very vehement now.

"You gotta be kiddin' me," Leroy stared down at the fish in unbelief.

"Shelton, get over here now. Look at this. Can you believe this?" Summer looked around for Shelton who by now had eased over to the nearby worktable that they used to weigh and measure new species.

"Oh, crap!" Shelton feigned shocked. He looked at Summer. "What are you doing?"

Summer had dug her cell phone out of her pocket and was furiously dialing numbers with her thumb. Leroy noticed tears beginning to stream down her cheeks. "I'm calling a marine biologist," she said. "Maybe we can save him."

Secretly Shelton wanted to slap her across the back of her head. He never dreamed of this reaction but he knew he at least had to seem sympathetic.

"No, baby, no…he's already gone."

"NO!" she was screaming now. "I'm gonna at least try."

"On my Lord above," Leroy was standing now. "What the heck are you cryin' about, girl? It's a two-inch catfish. I'll bet a thousand people died in wars somewhere today. I don't see you cryin' for them none."

"You shut up, you fat redneck," Summer shouted. "You with all your down-home talk and your cutesy nicknames. You knew this was going on before we ever came out here the first time."

Leroy looked genuinely hurt by the comment. He'd grown to enjoy being around these young people, despite their ideological differences.

"I don't think there's nothin' funny about it. I just think it's just a fish." Leroy spoke very quietly now. Then he looked around and shuffled uncomfortably from one foot to the other. He didn't really want to hold the fish any longer but he didn't know what to do with it. He didn't want to be there anymore. He felt ashamed and he resented that because he'd done nothing wrong.

"Summer!" Shelton grasped both of her shoulders and spoke emphatically. "The best thing we can do for him now is get him preserved so that we can get his family some help."

Summer raised the phone to her ear. Shelton wanted to snatch it and throw it into the river. This was going to screw up all his plans, but he kept his composure. Then he heard someone's outgoing voice message on the other end of the line.

"No!" Stacey exclaimed softly as she let her hands drop to her side.

"Summer, hand me the phone." Shelton ran his hand down Summer's forearm almost sensually. He pulled her to him with his other arm and bent around to kiss her cheek. Summer spun around as Shelton took her phone and buried her head in his chest.

"We need to do something with this before he drops it or eats it on a sandwich or something," Stacey said as she jerked her head to indicate Leroy. Then she snatched the fish out of his palm.

"Hey, careful!" Shelton exclaimed. He hadn't wanted anyone else handling the madtom. He didn't need them sensing the formaldehyde already present in its flesh. Before he even had time to step towards her, however, Stacey slid the madtom into the specimen jar. *Perfect.*

Stacey put the lid on the jar and said, "I'm so sorry, little guy. But you did not die in vain."

With that, she looked disgustedly at Leroy and walked angrily towards the gate. Shelton, his arm around Summer, shot Leroy a judgmental look.

"She didn't have to talk about me like I wasn't standin' right here," Leroy said softly. He didn't think about the fact that Stacey actually had no right to take the specimen. He wouldn't think of that until he was reminded much later. For now, he just felt blindsided. He suddenly realized that at his age he should have known better than to assume these young people were becoming his friends. Now that was all he could think of. Shelton escorted Summer towards the parking lot and within minutes, Riverguardian and the madtom were gone. Neither would ever be seen at the plant by Leroy again.

49

Aaron Hatcher sat at the "House of Ginger" tearoom in a red leather wingback chair. His cup of tea was growing tepid on the walnut table to his left. He never was much on hot tea. He was staring out the window at the people walking by on the street in Georgetown. Everyone that passed by was so lovely, all fit and outdoorsy looking in their fall Eddie Bauer collections. Aaron found it ironic that these were the type of people that U.S. Senator Keitha Dobbs was living near.

They certainly weren't the type of people she used to associate with. Aaron had first met Keitha as a thirteen-year-old boy standing alongside his father, a very powerful committee chair himself in those days. She would have been in her early twenties. Aaron chuckled as he recalled that at the time he'd found her kind of hot. Of course, he'd been at an age when he found almost every female kind of hot.

His dad had been attending the very first Earth Day protests, April 22, 1970. The day had been billed as an environmental "teach-in." The senior Hatcher hadn't wanted to attend and had complained about the "long hairs" all the way to the event. However, he'd needed to bolster his standing with the twenty-somethings, so he showed up. Keitha was there with her husband. All Aaron could remember now was that she wore denim bell-bottoms, leather sandals, and a black choker. At the time, Aaron had never seen anyone like her except on the nightly news. The girls around his father's horse farm still dressed like it was the 50s.

Despite her somewhat eclectic charm, Aaron sensed that Keitha Dobbs found him and his dad repugnant, and deep down he'd felt the same about her. She didn't look clean and she spoke to his father with an air of contempt. Looking back on it, Aaron figured she'd seen his father as part of the establishment, as someone who was only there for his own political gain. She'd been at least partially right.

Now Hatcher couldn't help but think of Dobbs as a hypocrite. She was chair of one of the most powerful committees in Congress. He'd seen with his own eyes the way in which she milked the position for every perk and every bit of lobbyist graft she could get. No matter. Whether or not he would have ever bothered speaking to the woman under other conditions, he needed her now.

50

Ashley was doing a quick job of freshening up in her room. Walter would be here to pick her up in another ten minutes and she didn't want to keep him waiting. As she reached for her toothbrush, her cell phone rang. She picked up without looking at caller ID. "Hello," she said, trying not to sound as though she had toothpaste in her mouth.

"Hey Ashley. It's Annette, from work."

"I know who you are, Annette. You don't have to say 'from work'"

"Oh, sorry," Annette said. "Listen, I've been doing some checking on your boyfriend's group, Riverguardian."

"Please don't call him my boyfriend, but thanks for checking." She couldn't help but think that it was a little bit late since the meeting was over and she was in D.C.

"I just got into it and I kept digging. Listen, none of this goes past you and me, okay? I am really, really bending the rules here."

"What do you mean?"

"Let's just say that your boyfriend doesn't keep very good security software on his computer. He was easy to hack. And I can tell you that his group has been getting some pretty large checks. He's received these checks six times so far this year. It's apparently what he and those other two are living on, as well as providing the funding for their web page and lawyers' fees."

"Sounds like they are big checks."

"Ten thousand in the first payment. Fifteen on the next two. The last one was over twenty. I don't remember the exact amount."

"I wonder who's giving him that kind of money?"

"All it says for payee in his computer is CMF. I'm still doing some checking."

"I appreciate it. But you really don't need to do this on my account at this point. I was only trying to prepare for the meeting down there. Then they snuck up on me and I had to meet them cold turkey. I don't want you getting in trouble for me."

"I know. If I keep pursuing it, it'll be for my own curiosity at this point."

The two talked a moment more and then Ashley had to go. She had less than five minutes before meeting Walter.

51

"Take 5th Jimmy, it'll be faster. The loop will be packed today. I think there's a ball game," Keitha Dobbs said to her limo driver.

"Yes ma'am," Jimmy said aloud as he thought: *You silly twit. How many times do you think I've driven this route, before, during, and after ball games, Inaugural Addresses, every other traffic-choking event?*

Dobbs looked back down at some files on her lap. She scanned them quickly. She wasn't in the mood to read them. She was never in the mood to read the legalese in these stupid bills. That's why she had a staff. She tossed the files back in her briefcase. She didn't know exactly what Aaron Hatcher wanted to meet about but she had a pretty good idea it would turn out good for her personally. That was a bonus. Dobbs still believed that she had a higher calling.

She'd long ago lost focus on exactly what that original calling was. Somewhere along the line, it had morphed from a desire to facilitate a greater awareness of the environment, into a deep-seated distrust, even a hatred, of corporate America. Dobbs was never happier than when she had some Brooks Brothers-clad CEO squirming in his chair before her committee. Deep in her heart of hearts, she was convinced that each of them had gotten filthy rich while standing on the backs of people like her, her old man, and her deceased husband's family, and while running roughshod over Mother Nature.

Day after day, she'd watched her father come in from the factory where he worked, sit down with his black steel lunch box and eat a bite before heading out again to work a second job as a plumber. Sure, he'd done it for her and her sisters. He'd sent them all to prep schools and private universities for their master's degrees. But Keitha always resented the students on campus who were dropped off in shiny cars or who wore the best clothes. Why should they have what she didn't?

Now, as the senator leaned forward to change the channel on the small TV in the console of the limo, she didn't grasp the irony. All her father's hard work had prepared her to achieve heights he'd never dreamed were possible. The success of corporate America had provided a tax base with which to subsidize the endowments at state universities that she'd benefited from. She was living proof that the American dream was more than just a vision—it was very much a reality. Keitha Dobbs simply didn't see it that way.

52

Ian Flannery scratched desperately at his shin. The Jag swerved slightly as he weaved through traffic while trying to smooth the crease on his dress slacks. The itching was driving him crazy. Twenty-four hours ago, he'd been in a hellish swamp in southern Georgia doing paramilitary training maneuvers. He and his team were getting close to mission-ready. It appeared that the strike would go off with razor-sharp precision.

Unfortunately, none of them had been forewarned about Georgia ticks. The cottonmouths and wild hogs were bad enough, but the entire team had come back covered in ticks and tick bites. Ian marveled that now, only a few hours later, he would go from those conditions to sipping tea in some pretentious tearoom in Georgetown with two Washington power brokers. "America—what a country!" Ian laughed.

He was relieved to be back in town. He would now have time once again to search for the woman who'd gone by the name Gretchen Collins. He'd been forced to abandon his search in order to make the training rendezvous. The search had proven to be both frustrating and fruitless so far, but he would not give up.

He pulled the Jag to a stop in front of the valet stand just in time to see a senate limo pulling out. Perfect timing. His most important contact was already here. He handed the keys to the valet and walked straight back to the meeting room where he knew Aaron Hatcher would be waiting.

53

"Ian! Great to see you again," Hatcher lit up like a Christmas tree at his approach.

"Senator Hatcher. So nice to see you as well." Ian took Hatcher's hand in a warm handshake and looked toward Keitha Dobbs expectantly.

"This is the former senate colleague I was telling you about—Senator Keitha Dobbs. Senator Dobbs, this is Ian Flannery." Ian bowed gallantly, took Dobbs' hand and kissed it lightly. As he did so, he longed for a day when he could crush that same hand with a rifle butt. Dobbs blushed slightly. Ian noted this and knew immediately he would control the meeting.

Tea was ordered with accompanying tiny sandwiches and then Hatcher began, "I asked you both here today because we all have something in common. We all care very deeply about our environment and about this nation's culpability in its demise. I know that you, like me, embrace the Kyoto protocol, the United Nations Framework Convention on Climate Change, and the Intergovernmental Panel on Climate Change Report. I also know that I'll be seeing both of you in Cancun. As such, I don't have to tell the two of you that something must be done right now. The truth is there is a level of greed in this country that continues to block us from doing the right thing."

Hatcher leaned in close and placed a hand on Flannery's and Dobbs' forearms.

"I want the three of us to form a domestic coalition to force this nation to do the right thing…"

And sweep you right into the White House, Ian thought. As he so often did, Ian soon tuned Hatcher out. As he watched Hatcher's mouth move, his thoughts went to the former senator's true motives. Ian was certain that Hatcher cared about as much about the environment as he himself did—not at all. Flannery suppressed a smile as he thought, *If you think greenhouse gas warms the planet too much, I wonder how you will like the temperature after the thermonuclear incineration of Israel and your United States?* That would come later, however. Flannery knew that dream would have to become a reality in small steps.

54

Keitha Dobbs listened to Hatcher's pitch with only slightly more interest than Ian. She knew before she arrived what Aaron Hatcher was really interested in—he needed a signature issue that he'd eventually use as a cornerstone of a presidential campaign. That was fine with her—it dovetailed quite nicely with what she intended to gain from this meeting.

Dobbs assumed as well that the very handsome Mr. Flannery was likely to have some type of ulterior motive. She'd been inside the environmental movement since its inception. She knew a true believer when she saw one. Neither of these men fit that mold. What Ian Flannery's motives were, she couldn't be sure and she didn't particularly care. What she was sure of was that the environmental movement could benefit from their involvement. She was also sure of her own passionate belief in the need to clip the wings of the U.S. industrial giants.

For far too long the U.S. corporations and utilities had been allowed to pursue obscene profits with an almost total disregard for ecology. If she could use Aaron Hatcher as a point man to hurl wild accusations that she dare not make as a senator, she would. And to whatever extent she could influence Mr. Flannery to bankroll the effort, she would do that too.

55

Aaron Hatcher took a long breath and sat back with a twinkle in his eye. He knew when he was on, and he was on tonight. He considered himself an expert at reading people's faces and he liked what he saw in the faces of Ian Flannery and Keitha Dobbs right now. He'd dazzled them. Though he wasn't particularly passionate about global warming, he had managed to make a very passionate case for it and had clearly made believers out of his small audience. He smiled to himself as he recalled an old fraternity buddy once saying, "Hatcher, you could sell ice to an Eskimo." Well, he certainly had sold 'em tonight. Just as he was preparing to set the hook, Flannery spoke up.

"Senator Hatcher, I have been authorized to speak on behalf of my coalition of concerned parties. And after listening to your very eloquent presentation, I can assure you of their financial support."

"I assume your coalition consists of private citizens from several of the UNFCCC nations?" Dobbs asked. She knew she was better off not knowing exactly who the individuals were by name or what specific countries they represented. That could be politically quite dangerous. Suffice it to say they had money and they were willing to spend it for a cause she believed in.

"Yes, Senator Dobbs. That is a safe assumption, at least partially." Ian flashed his most dazzling smile and watched with delight as Dobbs, twenty years his senior, drank it in. Flannery wasn't lying this time. His understanding was that at least one of the coalition members was on the UN committee.

"Well then, Senator Hatcher, you can count on the support of the Democrats on the committee. Obviously, we mustn't be too overt about our support but you can count on periodic press statements and mentions in speeches supporting your efforts. Didn't you tell me when you called the other day that you'd begin with an outdoor concert in Rio?"

"Yes, that will more or less kick things off," Hatcher said. He was practically buzzing. He wanted to leap from the chair and pump his fist. He was back in the game, baby! For now, however, he had to keep a lid on his emotions. As for the coalition that Ian Flannery spoke of, Hatcher had no idea who they were either. A contact of his who'd retired from the CIA a couple of years ago thought it might be some socialists from Europe and a couple of progressive-minded Russians. Hatcher assumed they wanted to be certain their countries had a seat at the table when a treaty was written for carbon reduction, but he didn't know for sure what they were after.

"Well, I can't be there," Dobbs said. "But I can probably get a couple of our governors to show up. Plus I know a junior senator who owes me big. He can step out on stage, wave to the crowd and what-not. That should lend an air of patriotism, don't you think? It will sort of be a de facto endorsement of the United States government."

"That's precisely the kind of endorsement I'm looking for," Hatcher said. "With those endorsements, and with your support," he raised his cup to indicate Ian, "I am certain that we can finish what others have started. We can force the removal of at least a few coal-fired units from the electrical grid. The purpose of the program I'm proposing is to show the world, and particularly spoiled Americans, that we can do without many of these coal-fired plants. We *can* make up the difference with things like wind and solar power. Yes, we can! Sure, it will drive costs for replacement power up but that's partly the point. When demand for power gets high enough, people will be more than willing to pay the premium for wind and solar. In addition, they'll be forced to change their lifestyle, forced to conserve."

Flannery had been waiting for this opportunity. "When do you plan on having the units off-line? Do you have a date in mind?"

"I haven't thought out all those details but I was assuming sometime in the spring when temperatures are mild and demand will be lower."

"Forgive me for saying so, Senator Hatcher, but that is too small-minded for a man of grand ideas such as you. You would make a much bolder statement by taking these units off in a highly publicized manner in say...February. If you are going to make a point, make it with emphasis. When your country sees that they can live without coal power when everyone's heat is running, then you will have the public relations homerun you are seeking."

Hatcher pursed his lips and shrugged. "I like your line of thinking there,Flannery. See, this is why I brought these great minds together for this meeting." Everyone laughed self-effacingly.

"Have you come up with a name for your program *former* Senator Hatcher?" Dobbs asked.

Aaron Hatcher caught the insult from Dobbs but knew he had to let it go. "Yes, Senator, I have. I am calling it Smartpower USA.

"Very patriotic," Dobbs said.

Before they could talk further, the second round of tea arrived. It was another very rare variety imported from China. They each took a sip and had another sandwich. Only Ian considered the irony involved in two senators with such anti-capitalist bents smiling broadly as they sipped four hundred dollars worth of hot tea.

56

"Miss Lady, you do look lovely this fine evenin'! This young man gonna be on cloud nine while he eatin' dinner." Walter spoke to Ashley's reflection in the rearview mirror of the cab as he drove.

"Walter, please stop calling me that."

"What, you don't like me to call you a lady?"

"It's not that," Ashley said. "It's not that at all. It's just that..." Ashley hesitated.

"It's just that what?" Walter asked.

"It's just that, well, it makes me seem racist."

"Oh Lawd a mercy," Walter smacked the steering wheel lightly. "Aw, not you too, Ashley." It was the first time he had used her actual name. Walter pulled the cab over, threw the transmission into park and turned around, resting an arm on the front seatback.

"Young lady, lemme tell you a couple things. I done fought in two wars for this country. I got the Distinguished Service Cross in Korea and the Silver Star in Vietnam. I've had the love of the best woman in this world my whole life. We just celebrated our fiftieth wedding anniversary. I got three very accomplished children. Two doctors and a teacher, and me and this cab and my army retirement paid for every penny of their education. Now do you really think I need some guilt-ridden little white girl to make me feel like I'm worth somethin'? Like I'm a man? Don't answer that, 'cause I don't. It don't hurt my feelins one dang bit to call you Miss Lady. I hope somebody somewhere is callin' my daughter somethin' to show just as much respect. Now are we gonna have to have this talk again, 'cause I sure hope not."

"No, sir," she said meekly.

Walter's face creased into a broad smile. "Well, awright den, Miss Lady. Let's get you to that date."

"It's not a date. We're just having a little dinner, that's all."

"What is it with yo generation? My daughters was the same way. Never want to admit they's on a date when they's on a date."

"We just don't consider the same things a date as your generation did."

"What you consider don't mean nothin'. A date was a date long before y'all was born and this here thing you doin' tonight is a date."

Ashley rolled her eyes and smiled as the cab pulled up to Hunt's hotel. Ashley put her hand on the door handle to step out and into the lobby to call Hunt's room, but before she could get out, she looked up to see Hunt jogging toward the cab.

"Somebody sho' is anxious," Walter smiled into the rearview, having feigned a bit stronger accent than usual as he tended to do when teasing Ashley.

Ashley blushed. "Oh, stop it!"

Hunt opened the front door and Walter shook his head disapprovingly.

"Young man, what you doin' up here. I ain't going to dinner with ya, if that's what you thinkin'."

"Oh, no, I didn't mean…I mean, I was just thinking it would be…"

"Young man, get in back there where you suppose to be and don't you come up here in da front of my cab no more," Walter scolded. He actually let people ride up front all the time, just as Ashley had done a few nights before. But he acted perturbed about it now for Ashley's sake.

Soon the cab was rolling toward The Pine, one of Washington's landmark restaurants. Hunt had suggested it. Once they were underway, Hunt appeared to relax and began to act like himself.

"Well, I want to thank you both for getting me out of that place," he said.

"You mean your hotel," Ashley replied.

"Yeah. My hotel."

"Why is that?"

"You aren't going to believe this one, but this is the kind of stuff that just happens to me. I don't go looking for it; it just follows me wherever I go. Okay, I go in the other day to register for my room and who should walk up to the desk clerk beside me but these two guys with tails!"

"What do you mean tails?" Ashley asked.

"I mean *tails.* One of them had a tiger's tail and one of them had a zebra's tail. And the zebra one had little hoof things over his shoes and the tiger one had little tiger paw shoes on. Oh, and they both had ears attached to a headband on their heads."

Ashley covered her mouth and tried unsuccessfully to suppress a laugh. Walter was watching the road but he was shaking his head and smiling.

"Lawd, Lawd, it take all kinds, don't it," he said.

"You haven't heard anything yet," Hunt said. "I did some asking around and a Google search or two. Turns out these folks like to dress up like animals and have conventions. Their called *furvies* or something like that. The ears and tails are just their daytime costume. These guys have the whole entire get up. Like a college mascot or something."

"Oh, brother," Ashley rolled her eyes. "What do they do at a convention?"

"I am not sure what all they do. And I am not sure I want to know all of it, but get this, as I was leaving my room a few minutes ago, I passed by the ice machine. There stands this giant raccoon. A giant raccoon is getting ice out of the ice machine! I couldn't help but stare for a minute. All of a sudden he looks over at me, takes his paw off the ice button and waves, 'Hey, how you doin'?' he says in this Bronx accent. I just waved and came down to meet you guys."

"So, let me get this straight," Ashley said while laughing out loud. "You chose to come to this hotel while they were holding a furry convention or furbie or whatever you said it was called."

"No, no, heck no. I didn't know they were having it. I use this hotel every time I come to D. C. I never saw anything like this before in my life."

Even Walter was laughing now. "Remind me not to use yo travel agent," he scoffed.

"I resent that," Hunt said mockingly. "I happen to have a pretty good track record. Well, except for that time that I came back to my room from dinner and there was this family of gypsies in my room."

"You mean that actually happened to you, too?" Ashley was starting to tear up.

"Yeah, it was a small motel in Alabama. I was doing a story down there. It was before digital keys. Apparently, they'd stayed there before and had a key made. They were going to try to cop a freebie and didn't realize I had already checked in."

"I don't mean to sound judgmental," Ashley said. "But I've only known you a few hours and it seems that you have lots of funny and...well...weird things happen to you."

"You're not being judgmental—you're being mildly observant. Yes, weird things happen to me on a regular, nay, a near daily basis. I don't go looking for this stuff. It's just a special blessing God laid on me, I suppose."

Hunt assured that there was frequent laughter for the remainder of the trip. Both Ashley and Walter found him quite entertaining and without a pretentious bone in his body.

After a raucous ride to The Pine, Ashley and Hunt enjoyed a much quieter dinner. It didn't take Ashley long to realize that she'd had more fun and more thoroughly pleasant conversation with Hunt in a couple of hours than she'd had with Shelton during their entire relationship.

Put that out of your head, Miller, she thought. *This is just one dinner, that's all. It's a good alternative to eating alone, nothing more.*

Still, she couldn't help but notice that Hunt was a lot cuter than she remembered from the airport. For his part, Hunt was completely blown away by the sight of Ashley in the candlelight. He really couldn't believe he was out with someone this beautiful. And nothing about their evening seemed forced. She was easy to talk to and he genuinely liked her.

Earlier he'd insisted that they share a dessert called "death by chocolate." When Ashley had protested that she was too full, he assured her that he'd ordered one before and there would only be a small portion for each of them if they shared.

"Just enough to satisfy the sweet tooth," he said.

Ashley noticed that the waiter walked away smiling after the order but she didn't give it any importance—that is, until the desert showed up in a portion adequate for an entire NFL football team. The pewter bowl held an entire cake and the top was brimming over with chocolate ice cream, whipped cream, and chocolate syrup.

"I thought about warning you about the portions, but you mentioned you'd had this before. You seem like a man who knows what he wants," the waiter said as he sat two plates on the table with the gargantuan dessert.

"Apparently…I…um…ordered this at a different restaurant," Hunt said, his face reddening.

"Wow, that's a big dessert we have there, Hunt," Ashley said, shielding herself from view with a hand at the side of her face. She began to laugh as she noticed that other diners were staring. Hunt began to recover his footing.

"Well, I certainly hope John and Marsha and their friends get here soon before all this ice cream melts," he said loud enough for those nearby to hear. Ashley was laughing harder now and shaking her head.

"We may as well go ahead and have some while we wait," he said at the same volume.

As he scooped what he assumed was an appropriately ladylike portion onto one of the plates and handed it to Ashley, he noticed the sparkle in her eyes. She reached out for the plate but he held it for an extra second. In that moment, Hunt forgot that he was nervous.

"You know," he said, "you really are very beautiful."

Ashley froze, still holding the plate in mid-air. All her life she'd been hit on or heard borderline lewd comments from guys about her looks. Yet, she'd never in her life been told that she was beautiful. Not like this. Not with this level of sincerity.

She blushed and then hoped Hunt hadn't noticed.

"I've embarrassed you," Hunt said. "I'm sorry. I didn't mean…"

"You didn't embarrass me at all," Ashley said. There was a slightly awkward silence but Hunt wasn't ready to let go of the moment yet.

"I've really enjoyed our time together," he said simply.

"So have I," Ashley replied, taking a small bite of the ice cream. And then she realized Walter had been right. This was a date. And she was glad.

57

Toward the end of dinner, they called Walter and after he'd dropped off another fare, he picked them up. Hunt decided he wasn't ready for the evening to be over and he took what was for him a bold step.

"Ashley, I don't drink, but I would love to buy you a coffee at your hotel bar. It would give me a few more minutes away from the *furvies*."

Walter spoke next. "You need to know, I'm 'bout to head home. You won't have a ride back to your hotel," Walter said. There was an air of warning in the statement. Walter was getting protective.

"That's okay. I can get the bellman to call one for me. Not that I wouldn't use you if you were available, Walter."

"Uh-huh," Walter said doubtfully.

"Well, if you don't mind taking your chances with a D.C. cabbie that's not Walter then, sure, I'll take you up on that coffee," Ashley said.

Hunt held the door for Ashley, who turned to head into her hotel lobby, assuming that Hunt was right behind her. As he leaned in the window to pay the fare, Walter stopped him with a firm grasp on his forearm.

"Young fella," Walter said. There was intensity in his eyes and clarity in his speech that Hunt had not noticed earlier. "You treat this lady with respect. I've done taken a liking to her. I consider her my friend. And I look out for my friends."

Hunt met Walter's gaze and didn't speak for a moment. Then he said, "And I appreciate that about you. Walter, I know you don't know me but I will not only *treat* her with respect—I do respect her."

Their eyes locked for a moment more, studying, reading, until finally Walter winked and said, "You know. I'm thinking you all right, son. We gonna get along real fine, real fine."

58

Once inside both of them ordered coffee. It was the first night since Ashley had come to Washington that the temperature had been cool instead of cold. The sky was clear and windless so they decided to sit on the patio. With their coats on and the hot coffee, they were comfortable and had complete privacy. They sat and sipped coffee for a time and stared at the stars. Hunt broke the silence first.

"I love crisp evenings like this one. This is the way Fall is supposed to feel," he said.

"Yes, it's quite nice," Ashley replied. She glanced up at the moon, which looked close enough to reach out and touch. For the first time since she'd picked up the business card that had fallen from Charles Fagan's pocket, Ashley thought of the name of the organization printed on the front side. She made a mental note to Google it when she got back to her room. "Well, it doesn't look so bad, does it?" she asked.

"What doesn't look bad?"

"The moon," Ashley said. "I mean it doesn't look like it is being covered over by clouds of toxins created by greedy people like me that work at power plants or in industry.

Although, I suppose I am just ignorant since I'm trying to judge the atmosphere by its appearance rather than the rings in one tree in one forest somewhere." She regretted her sarcastic comment almost as soon as the words left her mouth.

"Where did that come from?" Hunt asked.

"I'm sorry. I guess I'm just frustrated. I mean, they've had me locked up in that darned room reading one article after another, one report after another, that accuses my industry of basically destroying the planet. I never realized I was a part of such a vile group. I guess it's got me feeling a little super sensitive."

"Ashley, I report on environmental issues but that doesn't mean that my personal opinion is automatically going to be that industry is bad or even that global warming is the bane of our existence. In fact, I'll bet you'd be surprised at my viewpoint on some of these issues. But before I say too much, I'd like to know where you stand."

"I work for industry, don't I?" she asked.

"Lots of people join the military, that doesn't mean they favor all foreign policy in the same way. Some are interested in learning a trade or gaining skills, not all of them are hungry for combat," Hunt countered. "You might only be working for industry because you have to."

"No, I don't have to. I chose this job. I had options. I actually had an offer from the Sierra Club. I initially took the job I have now because it paid better and was close to my parents, but now I'm genuinely proud of what I do and of my company. I gave industry a try and I like it. So does that make me a mercenary?"

"No, I would say that makes you pragmatic at worst and a highly productive contributing member of society at best. There's nothing at all dishonorable in having taken the best job, but we've ended up back at my original question. How do you personally feel about things like carbon reduction and cap and trade?"

"I really can't say that I've had that strong of an opinion up until the last few days. Because of my job responsibilities, I've seen some excesses from the environmental movement, so naturally I've been a little skeptical of all global warming talk. Still, I mostly gave the pro-global warming scientists the benefit of the doubt. I assumed they knew a great deal that I didn't know. I thought that with all the hype there must be something to the theory. But after this past week or so, after having spent hours reading articles, technical papers, and reviewing data, I've moved squarely into the category of skeptic."

Hunt raised his eyebrows. "You'd better be careful; you'll be labeled as a 'denier'."

Ashley wasn't finished. "I've seen some of the most bogus data this week. I mean the so-called 'scientific consensus' is laughable. I took enough science courses to have a good understanding of the scientific method. I can tell you that many of the studies that global warming assumptions are based on make a mockery of that method. Data sets are not representative, sample populations are entirely too small to be conclusive, some of these so-called studies wouldn't pass a freshman level science class."

Hunt was pleasantly surprised. He'd heard this before. Some of it from the mouths of researchers who didn't agree with manmade global warming or climate change theory. Still, Hunt enjoyed hearing Ashley's manner of presenting it. She was on a roll and Hunt let her go.

"That's not to mention the most obvious fraud—the hockey stick graph. That's a graph of a supposed drastic increase in temperatures in the past few years. The only problem is the scientists fraudulently left out the medieval period when it was much warmer than it is now. They did that in order to make their graph more dramatic. It also makes the graph and the contention that the earth is suffering unprecedented warming a complete fallacy. But hey, it *is* a very dramatic looking graph."

"And one can't overestimate the usefulness of a dramatic, albeit totally inaccurate, graph," Hunt said.

"Oh, absolutely not," Ashley said, smiling now. The smile left her face as she continued. "Now I'm starting to think that more and more of the global warming movement and the drive for carbon reductions don't have that much to do with benefiting the environment. And believe me, after this past week, I'll bet I'm as well-read as anyone on this topic."

"Research huh? Getting ready for your testimony, I suppose?"

"I guess that's what they call it," Ashley answered. "I'm not sure how much good it will do me. I've read so many articles and documents that I'm reaching information overload. What's more, at this point I still don't know what purpose I'm supposed to serve. I mean, anything I say before the committee they're just going to discount because I work in a power plant."

"You're the face," Hunt said.

"'The face'? What do you mean 'the face'?"

"You're the face of industry. You're the face of industry that the law firm wants the committee to see and want the news reports to show. I wouldn't be surprised if you're their star witness."

"So I'm up here because of my looks? Is that what you are saying?"

"No, it's more complicated than that. You're clearly very smart, very competent in your field; but yes, you're also very pretty."

Hunt tried to read her expression in the light from the coffee shop window. "You shouldn't be offended or feel used. They'd be crazy if they didn't let you testify. I'm sure there are plenty of other attractive women in the industry but they probably don't have your unique knowledge base."

The two sat quietly once again. Occasionally a patron

from inside the coffee shop would walk up to the glass doors and look out at the brilliant moon. Each time it was clear that they weren't seeing Ashley and Hunt because of the reflection in the glass. Ashley subconsciously realized that she liked being hidden in plain sight with Hunt. She reached out and gripped her hot coffee mug in both hands and drew her feet up into her chair. The air was beginning to feel cooler.

"Okay, so your turn," Ashley said.

59

Hunt didn't want to mess up a lovely first date by showing how opinionated he really was. "My turn what?" he asked.

"You never told me where you stand. You're the environmental reporter. What do you think of global warming, cap and trade, carbon footprints and all that stuff?" Ashley asked.

"I didn't start out to be a reporter who only does environmental stories—it just worked out that way. I am a journalist. I pride myself on being able to separate my personal beliefs from the facts of a story. And the facts of this story all lead me to believe that global warming theory is about many things, none of which have to do with any real threat to the environment. And as far as being a reporter, I may have to find another line of work someday. Old fashioned objective reporting is not very welcomed by editors nowadays, especially on this topic."

"What do you mean?" she asked.

"Almost every editor I know suddenly has an agenda on the subject of global warming, or climate change as they're currently calling it."

"Yeah, what happened there? "

"The hardcore believers in global warming—the ones who think the planet is doomed because of it—didn't want to deal with the fact that what's actually happening in nature didn't fit their models. As you already alluded to, the planet is actually cooling right now and it has been for ten years. So they had to change the name of the supposed threat. And that's always a good indicator of the merit of a set of beliefs. If something fundamental in those beliefs has to change because of changing conditions, then the belief was probably misguided from the start. But rather than admit that the theory of global warming may in fact be overblown or perhaps even flat-out wrong, the believers in it just changed the name of the theory."

Ashley shook her head. "That dovetails quite well with what I've been reading. I mean the global warming/cap and trade crowd doesn't seem too anxious to debate their theory on its merits."

"Just the opposite is true, I'm afraid," Hunt said.

"I notice that you keep using the term 'beliefs.' You talk about all this like it's a religion or something. You started sounding like a preacher just then yourself," Ashley said.

Hunt smiled. "Yeah, I suppose I did. So do you hear a lot of preachers, go to church, believe in God, all that kind of thing?"

"Oh, no," Ashley said. "I mean...yes...well...I go to church a couple times a month. And I definitely believe in God. But no, I wouldn't say I hear a lot of preachers. Just the preacher I grew up with when I went to church with my grandma."

"Some people would call me a religious fanatic, I guess," Hunt replied. He was watching Ashley out of the corner of his eye, wondering if he was about to end any chance he had at a relationship with this woman. "I don't mind the label. I'm a devout believer in the Bible and in Christ. I don't apologize for that. I'm proud of what Christianity has done for mankind. Almost all the great medieval universities were Christian in origin. The printing press was created so that more people could have Bibles. Missionaries built hospitals and taught agricultural techniques all over the world, but the only missionaries they make movies about are the few who were misguided or who actually distorted the Christian message and ended up doing harm. They were very much in the minority."

"Hey, you don't have to convince me," Ashley said. "I'm Christian too, but I couldn't call myself anything like devout. So how did we go from talking about global warming to Christianity, anyway?"

Hunt laughed. "It's funny that we did that but the two aren't that far apart really," he said. "In fact, in my opinion, they're closely related," Hunt said. "Do you mind if I give you a little history lesson? I promise to keep it short and it might help you in your preparations for testifying."

Ashley looked at her watch, sighed deeply, and rolled her eyes. "Well, I was really itching to get up to my room and watch some "People's Court" reruns—but if you insist."

Hunt smiled and started the lesson. "In 1957, the Navy was studying potential effects on the ocean from World War II nuclear testing. They hired an oceanographer, who in turn hired a chemist. They got interested in monitoring CO_2 levels. Eventually the pair came up with the greenhouse effect theory, even though, according to scientists I've interviewed, they never offered any proof that CO_2 was, in fact, a greenhouse gas. This was well beyond the scope of what the Navy was interested in, so they didn't want to keep funding the research. So the oceanographer and his team came up with global warming. Now if these rising CO_2 levels are a dire threat, then these guys can keep getting funds and justify their jobs. Incidentally, one of the guys ends up as a college professor who taught Senator Aaron

Hatcher. Hatcher has been going around recently getting celebrities on-board the global warming bandwagon."

Ashley was intrigued.

"It gets better. In the sixties, there were some legitimate concerns about the pollution in our cities. Combustion engines and factories were inefficient and heavy polluters. The environmental movement gained momentum. The first Earth Day was held in 1970. These global warming guys jumped on the wave. They ended up working with the UN to form the International Committee on Climate Change."

"The IPCC. Yeah, I've seen them quoted hundreds of times in the research materials I'm reading," Ashley said.

"Right, well, that's the same group, only it's not anything like the purely scientific body it's portrayed to be. It's primarily political. It's also extremely effective at PR. Next thing you know, Hatcher does some propaganda piece for the news wires, he writes a book filled with errors on the topic, the book becomes a bestseller, celebrities galore start buying in, and suddenly global warming becomes the *in* cause on Rodeo Drive..."

"And we end up with the cultural tsunami we have today."

"Exactly, and it's a tsunami that sweeps innocent people up and propels them toward economically devastating legislation like cap and trade."

"Celebrities live in a dream world," Ashley said. "I can see why *they* might buy in, but what about everybody else? Why don't people rise up against this stuff when it's going to end up costing them so much?"

"Like you said, it's not just celebrities. I've sat down to dinner with politicians, celebrities and plenty of scientists, sometimes all at the same table, and everyone at the table except me believed passionately that increasing CO_2 levels are dooming the planet. After a number of these meetings,

I finally realized that all of these people have something in common in addition to their belief."

"What's that?"

"Unapologetic passion and nearly blind allegiance to what is essentially a weakly supported scientific theory. There's a fervor underlying their belief in this theory that can only be likened to religious zeal."

"Are you saying that you think climate change has become like a substitute religion for them?" Ashley asked.

"No, I think that it has gone beyond that. It is not *like* a religion. It is a religion. Keep in mind; many of these people are equally passionate in their refusal of the Judeo-Christian ethic. So instead of demonstrating faith in God, they've substituted faith in climate change theory. What's more, in the science community many believed in this new religion before they ever took a single science course."

"So are you saying that their ideology drove their research?"

"Yes. I believe so. I believe there's a great deal of 'square peg into round hole' stuff going on out there. Some researchers have stopped being scientists and have started trying to force the science to fit the assumption."

Hunt got up and went inside for refills for them both. He came back in a minute with both mugs and a saucer of beignets.

"You know, that's all quite depressing when you think about it," Ashley said. "How can otherwise intelligent, good people get so caught up?"

"'Claiming to be wise, they became fools...they exchanged the truth about God for a lie and worshiped and served the creature rather than the creator,'" Hunt said.

Ashley set her mug back down on the table and looked at Hunt. "A quote from the Bible, I suppose," she said.

"Paul's letter to the church at Rome, chapter one."

Hunt answered. "So many in this country don't believe in the Bible, don't believe in God. People need something to believe in. In the absence of God, they will find something larger than themselves to worship. We humans were made to worship. I'm afraid we have a society that is bowing at the altar of a fictitious Mother Nature."

"Don't you believe in taking care of nature, in taking care of the Earth God gave us?" Ashley asked.

"Absolutely, and I want legislation in place to help take care of the Earth. But I believe that the most precious thing to God is human life. *We* were created in the image of God—not the snails and not the trees. God's creation is yet another way that He reveals Himself and His love to his children. Somewhere else in the Bible, it says that the Sabbath was created for man. Not man for the Sabbath. I believe the same holds true of nature. We have a duty to be good stewards and caretakers of nature. But we should never sacrifice humans in order to honor nature."

"Well, I don't think anyone is proposing that, are they?"

"Tragically, yes, they are. And some that are suggesting things like population control to reduce carbon emissions are in positions of power. Many believe that the best way to lower our carbon emissions is to have fewer people exhaling and using energy."

Hunt saw that Ashley had a stricken look on her face. He quickly moved to her side, knelt down, and leaned in close.

"Say," he said, "do I know how to show a gal a rip-roarin', knee-slappin' good time or what?"

Ashley leaned in towards Hunt until their faces were almost close enough for a kiss.

"Yes, sirree," she said. "You are one ginormous ray of sunshine. Maybe next time we can talk about famine or pestilence or something cheery like that, you know, the topics that really melt a woman's heart. So did you have to attend charm school for terribly long to master the art of conversation?"

Hunt smiled broadly. She was both beautiful and funny. He really liked this woman. "No, no," he said. "It's a gift really. Just comes naturally. I don't take it for granted though. I have nothing but pity for lesser men. How about we go back inside? It's getting cold out here."

60

Shelton threw his cordless phone against the far wall of his Airstream. He'd just been turned down by the local television station and he was running out of options. With the exception of a reporter from the county paper who interviewed him briefly over the phone, no one was the least bit interested in Shelton's dead madtom. Nobody cared. One reporter had said those exact words to him. This wasn't the way it was supposed to go. He thought he'd make a handful of phone calls and have the parking lot filled with media in half an hour. Now he realized that wasn't going to happen.

He took his Blackberry off his hip as Summer walked through the room without speaking. It was two in the afternoon and she was just waking up. She still looked a little high from the night before. He scrolled through his contact list and when he didn't find anyone he thought could help, tossed it on the table in front of him.

"Say, babe?" he called toward Summer's back. She was pouring stale cereal into a bowl.

"The milk's expired," she croaked through a dry throat.

"Summer, focus please. What was that guy's name that you dated for a while sophomore year? The journalism major."

"I don't remember. We only went out a couple times."

"Yeah, I know. Didn't I hear that he ended up at one of the networks?"

"Bobby. Bobby Jones. That was his name. Did you buy Pop Tarts?"

"That stuff is crap. I told you I don't want you eating that. There's wheat berry bread in there, toast a slice of that. You're still half-asleep. Bobby Jones was a famous golfer."

"No, that's his name. They used to tease him about golf all the time because he stunk at it. Last I heard he was an intern at NBC."

A Google search and a couple of wrong numbers later and Shelton was standing outside the trailer talking to Bobby Jones—not the golfer and not the intern anymore. Jones had made it all the way up to producer. He didn't remember Shelton but he remembered Summer quite well.

"I could probably get a crew out there tomorrow but I don't think it is worth my time. It really doesn't seem like a big story."

"That's why I'm calling you. You can make it a big story." There was silence on the other end of the line. Shelton thought for a moment. He didn't want to say what he was about to say but he had to do something bold. He was going to have to share. He took a deep breath and blew it out into the phone. "And I can make it worth your time."

"What's that supposed to mean?"

"It means what it sounds like it means. It means that if you can make this story big enough, then I will have access to some money, a lot of money. And I could see my way clear to give you a cut."

"First of all we don't take bribes to air stories, and..."

"I know, I know, it's all about the public's right to know for you. I get that. Listen, what did your anchor make last year, huh? What did you make? Seventy grand, maybe eighty? And you have to pay cost of living in New York?

Are you kidding me? Help me get this story national and I can pay you one hundred and fifty thousand dollars."

"Where are you gonna get that kind of money?"

"Let me worry about that, all you need to know is that the money depends on the story breaking big. The bigger the better," Shelton said.

"Look, you're talking about something that could cost me my job." Jones hesitated. Neither man spoke for at least a minute. "I'll need to talk to some people. Get some approvals. I'll call you in the morning." The line went dead.

Shelton took a well-worn Post-it note out of his wallet. He dialed the number he'd written down ten months prior. He'd received funding from this organization for years but it was only a year ago that he was able to make a high-level contact. He'd met her during a networking opportunity at last year's Earth Day celebration in Chicago. He punched in the number.

"Yes, this is Shelton Leonard. I met someone from your organization during Earth Day. I'm calling to see if anyone has claimed the reward you were offering at that time. Well, it was my understanding that, as part of Crystal Moon's goals, you were offering a significant reward to the first group that managed to force at least a partial shutdown... Yes. Yes, I do. I feel confident that we'll be able to create a significant amount of public relations pressure to...What do you mean what's the name of my group? We've been getting funding from you for years. Well, I appreciate the fact that you support a large number of organizations but...My group is called Riverguardian and we're currently involved in an action in Illinois...Well, I'm certain that dozens of other groups have tried and failed. Riverguardian is not like dozens of other groups."

Shelton listened to the woman on the other end of the line for a moment. Then he said, "Yes, email me the application and I'll give you all of that kind of information in writing.

I'll try to call you back and give you an airdate but suffice it to say that you might want to be watching the NBC news very closely in the next couple of days. And get your checkbook ready. I predict that within a week this story will be worldwide."

61

George Fuller was eating a microwave burrito with one hand and furiously clicking on a mouse with the other. George was the only employee of Crystal Moon who actually worked out of an "office." The office was a rundown building that had been abandoned by a drive-thru-only burger chain. It still smelled like old grease, the ventilation system barely worked, and George felt like he should be flipping burgers instead of running a bank of computers, but the boss wanted him here. The building was unassuming and unnoticeable and it was located in a very out of the way section of Pittsburgh.

He'd been hired by Karen Turner, whom he'd never seen again after the interview. He rarely talked to her or the CEO of Crystal Moon, a man named Ian Flannery, whom he'd also never met. This was all perfectly acceptable to him since Crystal Moon paid him more money than he'd ever dreamed he'd make in his life. His job was straightforward—he was to maintain the various websites under various names that Crystal Moon used to spread its message. At the same time, he was to keep the parent organization itself well out of the reach of search engines and hyperlinks. The boss wanted publicity for the web pages and the pseudo organizations, not for Crystal Moon itself.

George didn't handle any of the money. He did know from the computer database he maintained that Crystal Moon had money in dozens of accounts. They periodically deposited money from those accounts into the accounts of people like Shelton Leonard. The handling of the money was mostly Karen's area. He didn't ask questions about any of that.

As George was working diligently on a website upgrade, the phone rang. It was Karen Turner. She didn't say hello. She never said hello.

"George, within the next couple of days you'll receive a cell phone number via text message. I'm authorizing you to speak with Ian Flannery. When you speak with him, you're to tell him that an organization is attempting to make a claim on the reward money. The organization is called Riverguardian and is run by Shelton Leonard. Do you understand what I've said?"

"Yeah, I mean, yes, ma'am. Say, do you want me to..."

George heard a click. The line was dead.

62

Ambassador Pan ran a finger along the rim of his glass of cognac, his face filled with distrust. The Korean ambassador knew of the man simply called "The Russian." His bloodthirsty reputation preceded him, but he didn't expect him to show up at this meeting and he didn't want him here. He also didn't like being kept waiting by some two-bit Bolshevik. Finally, his Russian counterpart walked in, ten minutes late.

"Ambassador Pan, thank you for coming," the Russian ambassador said through an interpreter.

"Spare the niceties, Markov," Pan said. "You know perfectly well that I had no choice but to come. Now I've been sitting here being stared at by this ape… this butcher, for twenty minutes while I wait for you."

"The Russian" raised his glass toward Pan and flashed a gap-toothed smile at the ambassador's description of him.

"I'm terribly sorry," Ambassador Markov lied. "There were problems with the traffic."

In reality, Markov had been sitting in the back of his limo for nearly half an hour sipping vodka and reading *The Wall Street Journal* online. He'd wanted Pan and the others to have ample time to enjoy the company of his ex-KGB counterpart. As expected, his strategy had worked beautifully. Even now, everyone's eyes kept darting nervously from him back to "The Russian." They seemed adequately intimidated. It was time to proceed.

"Gentlemen, thank you for coming. This will be our final meeting. I trust that you have each had time to look at our model. It is based upon the European Emissions Trading System. As you saw in the package of information we prepared for you, that small market has already done 3.5 billion Euros in trading thus far in 2010. Our system will do ten times that volume. It will strangle the other markets out of existence. Our market will use the carbon financial instrument or CFT as the Chicago Climate Exchange already calls their unit. That will be more palatable to the Americans."

"You're very presumptuous as usual, Markov." The delegate from Venezuela said. He wore a three thousand dollar Italian suit and his hair was artfully slicked back. He looked like an older version of a Calvin Klein model. As he spoke, he glanced nervously at "The Russian."

"You assume we are all going to sign on to this," he continued. "Do you really think that we don't know where the leaked emails came from? You cannot even control your own KGB. How do you expect us to believe that you will control a world market? Even without the emails, we know your intentions. Russia will end up bullying us in this endeavor in the same way you bully the other oil marketers in the Eastern bloc. Perhaps we do not *want* the market that your people have designed to favor them."

"Victor, we are giving you an opportunity to make a significant amount of money on a product that previously did not exist and that costs you nothing to produce. We have done all the groundwork. We have spent tens of millions to soften and prepare the Americans. We have all but created the American market and we will manipulate it to our advantage. We are being very gracious in including you at all. Why would you even consider turning us down?"

Markov continued. "And as for the emails that were leaked—Climategate, as the conservative media is calling it—that was most unfortunate. It seems that some of my comrades' loyalties are still to our petroleum industry. That is outdated thinking." Markov looked to "The Russian" who leaned forward in his seat. "My colleague here will insure that they see the error of what they have done."

Victor continued his argument. "Even if you can eliminate this blatant security breach, how can you be so sure that the American financiers will not revolt? How do you know that they will not utilize this carbon emissions trading you have modeled to have increased economic leverage over us?"

"Victor, Victor," Markov said placatingly, "We have been over all of this numerous times. Within two years of signing the UN treaty on carbon emissions, the Americans will come to us with their hats in their hands. *Why* you ask? Because we will stifle all development in the third world countries. We already have economic control of those countries. We will bank the CFT's that are intended for development in those countries. By that method, we will rapidly accumulate huge numbers of credits.

"The American environmentalists will refuse to allow the building of enough clean coal or nuclear generation plants. No one will want a power plant near their community. Before the Americans know what has happened, they will find themselves with nothing but their antiquated, and by then internationally illegal, plants to produce electricity.

"They will become desperate for credits and they will have no choice but to turn to us. The treaty they will soon sign will demand it. The CFT market will then skyrocket. When the Americans finally realize that wind and solar can never satisfy their demands, it will already be too late. We will have transferred massive amounts of their wealth to our countries and, in turn, we will have altered the world economic landscape for generations."

"There is no assurance that any of this will occur," Pan spoke once again. "You're basing all our hopes on some lobbyist none of us has ever met and on the activities of environmentalist groups that you likely have no control over whatsoever."

"Don't you read the papers?" Markov snapped. "The lobbyist has done a phenomenal job. His and his staff's work is nearly done. And as for the activists, we don't need to control them any further. They have already exceeded our expectations. After years and years of media-assisted berating of the American public, the emotional gallows of guilt is complete. Thanks to our most recent lobbying efforts, compliant leaders and a very helpful media and entertainment industry, we will soon hear the trapdoor open. The American economy will voluntarily take 'the drop.'"

"What on earth are you talking about?" Victor asked.

"My dear Victor, must I connect all the dots for you? Our people have been infiltrating the education system for decades. Americans have been told for years that they are destroying the environment. The current workforce has been steeped in that mindset since they were in grade school. They are ready. They are nearly ready to jump off a cliff if that will save some turtle or a shrub somewhere. The activist groups, having brought lawsuit on top of lawsuit, have pushed politicians, who have been equally well conditioned, to create laws that at least pretend to protect the environment no matter what the cost.

"The public is finally accustomed to that type of legislation. They expect it. All we need the activist groups for now is to provide a slight nudge of the populace. Once that is provided, then they will do the *right* thing. They will step forward and place their heads through the noose. They will practically demand that their leaders sign a treaty that both creates a global carbon credit market and unwittingly cedes control of their economy to us."

Markov smiled, raised his glass, and downed the rest of his vodka. As he continued, he pouted mockingly and feigned a voice that sounded as if he were about to sob. "They will see it as their pittance, as the least that they can do for being such horrible global citizens." He smiled again as he looked around the room at the faces representing six different countries. When his gaze stopped on "The Russian," the two began to laugh heartily.

Ambassador Pan still didn't look pleased. "We have each invested over a hundred million dollars and allowed you to do with that money as you saw fit," he said. "Now you are telling us that the entire plan hinges on this lobbyist who goes by the name of Flannery but whom our intelligence sources tell us is actually connected to the highest levels of Al Qaeda. Yes, Markov, don't look so surprised. We have our intelligence people in North Korea and they have been doing their own checking. I don't mind telling you, Flannery's connections do not bring the Prime Minister comfort. He doesn't trust religious fanatics."

Markov spoke through clenched teeth. "I will repeat my previous vow. I can assure you that this man is in my control." His eyes shone with a black anger that no one in the room besides "The Russian" had ever seen before. Markov looked toward "The Russian," who spoke for the first time.

"This man is no ideologue. He has a penchant for strippers and prostitutes. Money and power motivate him just as they do most of you. A man like that, I can easily manipulate."

"The Russian" sat back with a self-satisfied grin. He reveled as he watched the men come to the realization that they had just been insulted. "The treaty will be signed, gentlemen. Your investment will be returned a thousand-fold. The momentum toward a global carbon emissions market treaty is now unstoppable."

"Well, I certainly am pleased to hear that you have so much trust in your contact," Victor said. "I only wish I could share your optimism."

Markov stood up and walked to the front of the room. "Gentlemen, we are sorry if you thought you were coming here to enter into a negotiation. Negotiations are over. It is now time for you each to agree to our plan. Don't look so gloomy, comrades. Remember this day. This is the day that you took the first step toward bringing the capitalists begging at your doorstep."

63

Hunt and Ashley had spent most of Friday in the Smithsonian on their second date in one week. Now with evening approaching, they walked along the Mall toward the Lincoln Memorial. Martha had given Ashley the afternoon off. Research and study time was over. She would spend Monday and Tuesday in a mock hearing while Martha grilled her, as she knew the senators would. Almost as soon as Ashley had walked out the door of Martha's firm yesterday, she'd called Hunt. She had been gratified at how he had instantly agreed to ignore his latest deadline and spend the day with her. The weather was rapidly moving from crisp to cold as night approached.

Hunt was nearly exhausted. It was tiring spending so much time arguing with one's self. All afternoon his head had been filled with thoughts such as, *Do something...make a move...now, now, reach for her hand... oh, great, now you missed the opportunity.* He was always a little nervous on a first date but he was positively intimidated by Ashley. He wasn't sure if it was her stunning looks, or her confident personality that had affected him so. He only knew he'd been bonkers all afternoon. Finally, by the time they headed for the Memorial, he'd begun to relax.

"I'm starting to get hungry," Ashley said. "What are you doing for dinner?"

"Oh, you mean I gotta hang out with you for dinner, too," Hunt said. "Gee whiz, I didn't know you were looking for this level of commitment. I had some socks to iron tonight back in the room."

"Yeah, you can forget that, buster. I'm not going to be dragged all around points of interest in the greater D.C. area and then let you get away without feeding me."

They looked into one another's eyes and smiled. Hunt thought that Ashley looked even more beautiful in this setting. She seemed more like herself. She wore suede boots with the legs of her jeans tucked in and a waist-length, corduroy jacket. Her cheeks were tinged with red from the cold and freckles were more apparent across her nose as she wore only light makeup.

"Wow, Ashley look at that."

As they looked, the sun was setting behind the Washington Monument as if a giant orange ball were landing on its point.

"Okay, now that is a Kodak moment if there ever was one." Ashley reached into her pocket and pulled out her small digital camera.

"Haven't the batteries gone dead in that thing yet? You must have taken a million pictures already."

"One can never have too great a photographic record of one's adventures," Ashley replied. "My ultimate goal is to end up with a humongous shopping cart full of unlabeled, seemingly random pictures that I can bore people with at the park once I become a doddering old bag lady."

They continued their slow walk towards the Lincoln Memorial. By the time they reached it, the lights were all on and night had fallen on the Mall.

"You know, I've never actually seen this in person," Hunt said.

"Me either," Ashley replied.

No one was around as they climbed the steps. They stood at the feet of Lincoln for a long while, still not speaking. Though both of them had seen the Memorial dozens of times in books and on television, there was something very different about being this close.

They stood close to one another and Hunt could feel the warmth from Ashley as she pressed against his shoulder. He let his hand run gently down her forearm and she took her hand from her coat pocket in time to meet his. Their fingers intertwined as they read the words of Lincoln's Gettysburg Address. They finished reading at nearly the same moment and then looked at one another. Both had tears in their eyes.

Hunt pulled her gently towards the inscription of the second Inaugural Address and they held hands as they read it silently.

"...urgent agents were in the city seeking to *destroy* it without war—seeking to dissolve the Union and divide effects by negotiation. Both parties deprecated war, but one of them would *make* war rather than let the nation survive, and the other would *accept* war rather than let it perish, and the war came...of the people, by the people and for the people shall not perish from the earth," Hunt read aloud.

"Yeah, those lines really grabbed me too. Sort of reminds you of what's happening to our country now," Ashley said.

"Yes, it does, doesn't it? It seems like half the people would sacrifice our country, our economy, and our way of life over some misguided beliefs."

"Do you think people will still see the wisdom in these words a hundred years from now? Do you think America will still be here?"

"I hope so," Hunt said. "But some days I really wonder."

"Me too," Ashley replied.

They walked back towards the Smithsonian and the Metro station there. They alternated between hand holding and locking arms as they walked. Soon they arrived at a stand of large oaks to the right of the Reflecting Pool. The area was at once romantic and spooky in the impending darkness.

Hunt noticed how Ashley's red hair shimmered in the silvery starlight. She turned now and leaned her back against one of the massive tree trunks. She looked up at Hunt as he stepped closer to her. He cupped Ashley's face in his hands. The warmth of his palms was in stark contrast to her cold skin. He pulled her gently toward him. Ashley closed her eyes and let him kiss her. A slow and incredibly gentle kiss.

Hunt pulled back and looked into her eyes again. She smiled and he kissed her again, more firmly this time and longer. They held one another close and, in that moment, there were no worries about the world or the politics that they couldn't control. In that moment, they felt like the only two people on earth.

64

Later, as they arrived at the Mall's center they paused and took a last look around. All the monuments were beautifully illuminated. Hunt looked toward the Capitol. "How does it feel to know you'll be up there in a few days in an official capacity?"

"Daunting," Ashley answered. "I already didn't feel worthy to be testifying, but after what you said the other night at the coffee shop and while walking around here, I almost feel like I'm participating in something even bigger. Just my luck to end up in this spot. I can't for the life of me figure out how I ended up pulling this duty."

"First of all, luck had nothing to do with it," Hunt said, still looking toward the Capitol building.

Ashley looked over at him, "What do you mean? Do you think I wanted to come up here and do this?"

"No, I think God wanted you to."

"Whoa now! Wait just a minute. I'm a Christian but I'm not quite ready to be an instrument of God or something."

"Maybe you are and maybe you aren't. Either way, it's not your call. It's His. Look Ashley, I don't hear voices and I'm not some weirdo who does bizarre things because I think God told me to. But I've had a lot of stuff going on in my own life the last couple of years. Some of it was very tragic and difficult but God used those things to strengthen my faith and draw me closer to Him.

"One thing I've learned through all of that is that even in difficult times, God is sovereign and He's at work. He likes to use His people in that work. He especially uses those of us who believe in Him and in His Son, as you do. I don't know why, but I just have this feeling that God has you up here in D.C. for a reason. He's going to use you somehow. And maybe it isn't even going to be through your testimony. Maybe your testimony is just an aside to something bigger."

"Well, I did get to meet you on this trip," Ashley said. *Oh no, did I say that out loud?* There was an awkward silence. Ashley was glad it was dark because her face felt like it was on fire. *Just great, Miller. Why don't you just go ahead and add, 'Oh, darling, after one and a half dates I'm certain we're meant to be together for the rest of our natural lives!'*

Hunt was still silent and Ashley was about to try an apology, when he said, "I would be honored to think that was true." He drew her closer to his side.

Great response, Ashley thought.

65

Hunt walked Ashley back to her hotel and he gave her what she felt was the best kiss of her life outside the door of her room. She walked into her room, threw the bolt closed, and leaned against the inside of the door, catching her breath and allowing her head to stop spinning. After a few moments, she walked over to the bed and picked up Emma's stowaway Raggedy Ann that the maid had kindly propped up on the pillows. She held the doll out at arm's length.

"Raggedy, this guy may be a keeper. I gotta tell ya, I'm really likin' him. And he's a perfect gentleman, wouldn't you know it. Just my luck, huh," she said. She tucked Raggedy Ann under one arm and stared for a moment at the far wall. She began to recall how just a few short days before she'd been hurt, as she had so many times in their past, by Shelton. She thought of how stark the contrast was between time spent with Hunt and the time she used to spend with Shelton. She smiled and released a deep sigh.

66

Ashley's eyes popped open. She looked at the clock. Three a.m.! She'd fallen asleep in her clothes still clutching Raggedy Ann. The curtains in the large window looking out over Washington were open. She rubbed the sleep from her eyes and, still lying on her back, turned to look out. Once again, her focus was drawn toward the full moon. Suddenly she remembered the business card from Charles Fagan's pocket. She'd been either too tired, or too enamored with Hunt, to remember to search the name Crystal Moon. Though she hadn't thought of it at all in the past couple of days, her thoughts went back to her attempted rendezvous with Charles Fagan.

She wondered how Hunt would view that in light of his theory that God was using her. She thought again about what could've happened to her and that look in Fagan's eyes. Every time she recalled that evening, she couldn't get that look out of her head. Something within assured her that Charles Fagan would've killed her that night. She shuddered beneath the covers at the thought. Certainly, her going off in the night and being chased by some whacko was not in God's grand plan.

Thus far, she'd blocked out thoughts about who Charles Fagan really was. Allowing her mind to go there had proven too frightening, so she chose not to think about it. Now however, in the clarity of the very early morning, she began to focus on what had happened that night.

She felt certain Charles Fagan was not his real name. He certainly hadn't looked English and, considering his ability to find an obscure filling station, he clearly was not new to Washington, as he'd said. So who was he? She recalled her fruitless Google search on the small Georgia town written on the back of that card.

Charles Fagan, alias psycho freak man, drives down to Georgia for a little two thousand-mile jaunt to get some onions. Doesn't make sense. She knew she was missing something. She was missing a bunch of somethings. She looked out at the moon once again and thought of the name on the card.

She sat up, threw back the covers, and reached her laptop without turning on the light. It was time to look into Mr. Fagan a little more deeply. She "Googled" Crystal Moon and came back with eighteen million hits. She narrowed the search by adding "environmental." That got her down to ninety thousand, but there was nothing on the first two pages that looked remotely like it was related to the environment.

She scrolled through page after page. Finally, she found something at the end of page twenty. It was a link to a blog called "Bringing in the Green." The description was the same as the inscription on the card,

"So that your kids can look up and see the same crystal moon that we grew up with."

This was getting exciting. Ashley felt like a private detective. She went to the web page but all it said was that Crystal Moon had donated money to the National Educators Coalition to promote education on the crisis of climate change. There was nothing else about the organization, no names, no ribbon-cutting picture, no nothing.

Ashley continued searching using various search strings, hoping that something would pop up about the group's activities. Nothing. Then, she remembered the moon-shaped logo on the card.

She typed in "crescent moon." The very first hit made her heart begin to pound. The crescent moon logo was the logo of Islam. Charles Fagan had said he was Turkish. *Wasn't Turkey a strong Muslim country? So what did that mean?*

"Easy there, Miller, easy," Ashley said aloud. "Talk about profiling. The guy looks a little mean, may be Muslim, and has some card with a moon and some woman's name on it in his pocket. Now there is an ironclad body of evidence if there ever was one. The guy is clearly Osama Bin Laden's right-hand man."

I can hear the headline now, she thought. *A cell of Islamic terrorists was uncovered today by one Ashley Miller. Seems they were planning to hurl onions during the President's next speech. I still don't know why the name of that town seemed familiar, though. I don't even like onions. The cards probably aren't even his. Maybe they belong to a girlfriend or something. Go back to bed.*

She slipped into the frumpy-looking flannel gown that she loved. She picked up Raggedy Ann and then caught her reflection in the mirror. She thought about Hunt. "If you could see me now, baby, I'll bet that gentleman stuff would go right out the window." She struck a pose like a Victoria's Secret model with Raggedy propped on one hip. *Wouldn't be able to keep his mitts off me.*

She lay down and pulled the covers up to her chin. It didn't take long before she was drifting in and out of a light sleep. Suddenly she had a mental image from three years before. She was sitting at a long table about to partake of a box lunch. It had been a working lunch at an environmental conference. She was in a conference room with a group of about twenty environmental engineers. They were doing a breakout session on the new Mercury rule and compliance strategies. She heard the repeat of a taunt she'd heard that day.

"We figured you'd bring onions for your sandwich. Don't you folks from Hatch pack onions with you wherever you go?"

Ashley's eyes flew open again. That was it! That was why Vidalia was familiar. One guy who had been in the working group that day lived there. But it wasn't where he lived that made Ashley's heart skip a beat. She'd finally recalled that Vidalia was home to a great deal more than onions. On the outskirts of this sleepy Georgia town was one of the largest nuclear power plants in the world.

67

"Oh my gosh…oh my gosh," Ashley was walking around her room, her fingers laced over the top of her head, talking to herself.

"I have to call the police," she said. "But what will I tell them? Let me think. Okay, what do I have? I meet this guy who probably gives me a fake name. He is Turkish or Arabic. He looks like he wants to strangle me for making one smart aleck comment. He chases me and beats his fist at the bathroom door where he thinks I'm hiding. He follows me back to my hotel. He has a business card in his pocket with a crescent moon on it and written on the back of the card is the name of a town that's home to the biggest nuke plant in the world. Man, is that thin. If I go to the cops with that, they're going to laugh me out of their precinct. But it's not that thin. This is a whole lotta smoke for there not to be some fire."

She remembered something President Bush said a few years earlier. "Be on alert. Even if you don't think something is worth reporting, report suspicious behavior." But that was then. The current environment was quite a bit different. Nowadays what she had was thin—really thin. She needed to call somebody else and bounce this off them. But it was now four thirty in the morning. She looked at her cell phone and thought about Hunt.

Oh, that'd be just peachy. Just peachy, she thought. *Hi Hunt, it's me Ashley. Listen, I know it's four thirty in the morning and I know you think I am a real nice girl and all, but I just wanted to call and tell you about how just a few nights ago I decided to hit the bars and try to get jiggy with one of Bin Laden's boys.*

She determined then and there that she wasn't going to talk to Hunt about this, at least not until she had a little more to go on. She opened up the laptop once again. She got over her embarrassment and went to Facebook and sent a message to Connie, summarizing for her all that had come to mind. Annette Boone wasn't on Facebook and she didn't have any contact info for her, other than her cell phone, and she wasn't about to wake her up at this hour. She asked Connie, through Facebook, to find Annette and elicit her help in finding out something about Crystal Moon.

Once that was done, she got up and took a shower. There was no way she was going to fall back to sleep tonight. She couldn't stop trying to connect dots but she didn't have all that many dots to connect. Tomorrow was Saturday. She and Hunt had a brunch planned.

I'm not going to obsess over all this and let it affect my day. I'll think about it some more when I get back, she thought.

68

Annette didn't need a message from Ashley to prompt her about The Crystal Moon Foundation. On the night before Ashley sent her message to Connie, she'd found that organization through Riverguardian. She'd hacked Shelton's website—getting through his encryption and security had been child's play—and discovered that most, if not all, of his funding was coming from an organization by that name. Trying to hack any accounts used by Crystal Moon was another matter entirely. Their security was extremely sophisticated and tight. She'd used hacking skills in the previous few days that she swore she'd never use again. Somewhere along the line, this had become a personal challenge.

She hadn't been able to get directly into any data belonging to Crystal Moon, however. What she had done was hack into other environmentalist groups' websites. She targeted groups that were similar to Shelton's. What she found there was very interesting indeed.

At least ten out of the approximately thirty organizations she'd checked were receiving funds from Crystal Moon. It was clear that Crystal Moon had an agenda. She'd only had time to do a modicum of research on a few of them but she'd already seen a common thread. They were all involved in protesting against the energy industry in one form or another. Before she could do much more research though, her husband had insisted that they go into town for supplies.

He felt they should rush out to the stores because it was time for the annual winter panic. Forecasters were predicting a devastating winter storm as they did every year. Annette was sure that just as in every other year, no storm would come. This did not discourage virtually every citizen in the county from descending on the local Wal-Mart. The place had already been buzzing, as everyone was in the pre-storm panic typical of Southerners not used to frozen precipitation. She thought the whole thing was a gross overreaction. People would buy a couple hundred dollars worth of groceries and then even if snow did come, the next morning the temperature would rise, everything would melt, and everyone would go out to eat at restaurants. Nonetheless, Bill had wanted to be prepared just in case.

Now that they were home, Annette could barely wait until the groceries were put away to get back to work. She was far beyond doing any favors for Ashley. She was just enjoying being back in the game. She didn't know what she was going to do with what she found out. Probably nothing. Yet the game was afoot and Annette felt that old familiar thrill. With Bill outside fueling the generator, Annette called up another environmental group's web page. She copied the source code and pasted it into a text editor for manipulation. This was going to be very interesting.

69

To say that the morning had been a whirlwind thus far would have been a gross understatement. Throughout the limo ride from the hotel, Zach, Julie, and Martha had each taken turns coaching Ashley, reminding her of things that she should and shouldn't do.

"No matter what they say or how they say it, be respectful," Zach said.

"Yes, be respectful but don't let them push you around, either. Dobbs particularly will try to bully you. Don't let her," Martha interjected.

"Don't be afraid to use a little charm and give a smile to the freshman senator. Our sources tell us that he likes the ladies. I know it probably rubs you the wrong way to do it, but any ally we can get will be a big help," Julie added.

And on and on it had gone. The ride to the Dirksen office building had seemed like it was over in only a couple of minutes. Now, in what seemed like no time at all, Ashley was passing through security and walking rapidly down the marbled hall trying desperately to keep up with Martha. Martha was all business today. Ashley could tell she was in a zone. This was what she did and she was very good at it.

Ashley hid her disappointment. When she'd been told that she would testify before Congress, she'd assumed that even though Senator Dobbs' office was in the Russell building, she would walk the historic halls of the Capitol and give her testimony there. She was slightly embarrassed when Zach condescendingly told her that committee hearings did not take place in the Capitol, but rather at Dirksen, which was a relatively clinical looking, rectangular building, indistinguishable from dozens of other government buildings they'd driven past. Still, Ashley's heart was racing.

When she walked into the committee hearing room, the first thing she did was look for Hunt. He'd said he'd be there in the gallery, though he wasn't sure when. They'd seen the Smithsonian Friday, done brunch and the Zoo on Saturday, and attended a church service together yesterday. Ashley had foolishly scheduled her departing flight for the evening after she was scheduled to testify. When she'd made up her travel schedule, she hadn't envisioned meeting Hunt and had assumed that she would want to get back home as soon as possible.

Even if she had scheduled another day, Hunt was going to have to travel today as well. He'd told Ashley that he had interviews scheduled with some senators and he would have to work around their calendar. Tomorrow he was to be in Canada for some interviews there. If the two didn't see one another within the next few hours, she wasn't sure when they would have another opportunity. She realized Hunt hadn't arrived in the hearing room yet.

The next thing that struck her was how empty the room was. There was a balcony for the press and their TV cameras, but on this morning, no one was manning a camera and only one or two reporters sat in the balcony seats. Someone was already testifying and Ashley was on schedule to be the second witness of the morning. Despite the ongoing testimony however, most of the senators' seats were empty as well, including Chairperson Keitha Dobbs' seat.

Julie led the way down a row of wooden chairs like those in an old movie theater and the others followed in single file. Once they were seated, Ashley wasted no time in whispering to Julie, "Where the heck is everybody? I thought this hearing was a big deal."

"It is a big deal." Julie leaned close to Ashley's ear. "Something's not right. This is only about the size of the crowd you'd expect in a routine committee hearing."

"You've got to be kidding me," Ashley's whisper was getting a little more intense now. "There can't be more than twenty people in here. Do you mean to tell me that is all that normally show up at these things? "

"That's the way it normally..." Julie stopped mid-sentence and looked up as if she'd just seen a rampaging grizzly bear. Ashley turned to see what Julie was looking at. Her eyes landed full in the wilting gaze of Martha Claiborne who was sending a clear mental message for them "be quiet!"

They sat there silently while they listened to the man currently testifying on behalf of a large corporate manufacturer of windmills. He was being very respectfully received. The senators seemed to like his assurances that it would be possible to power much of the country with wind power if he could just be provided enough research funding. Ashley had read quite a bit about wind power even before coming to D.C. She wondered when the man was going to tell the committee that in order to replace one power plant like SPG alone, you would need windmills covering half of South Dakota, and a constant wind.

Ashley took a deep breath and for the first time really took in the room. As they'd walked down the hall earlier, Julie had told her that this building had first been occupied in 1958. It had been needed at the time in order to accommodate the ever-growing responsibilities of Congress and the burgeoning federal government. As Ashley looked around at the darkly paneled walls, she was surprised at how small the room was. The few senate hearings she'd caught on C-Span seemed like they were in huge auditoriums. Except for the balcony, this one looked not much bigger than the county court back home.

Though the hearing room was small, it was only one of dozens in this seven-story building. Julie had shared that the Dirksen building was one of three senate office buildings, including the more famous Richard B. Russell building where Dobbs' office had been. Ashley couldn't help but think about Independence Hall in Philadelphia, which she'd toured as a little girl, and how great men had accomplished great things in that small space. Then she thought about how the senate conducted all its business for generations in just the Capitol building itself. She wondered if the founding fathers would be happy with the sprawling complex now required to conduct the so-called business of the federal government.

Finally, the man currently being questioned finished his testimony. Ashley's heart rate began to rise once again. She would be next. Suddenly one of the doors behind the senators opened and Keitha Dobbs entered the room. She made quite an entrance considering it was already the middle of the hearing and she was late. She passed by one senator after another placing a hand on a shoulder here, or whispering some inside joke in an ear there, until she came to her seat. She pulled out the large leather chair reserved for the chairperson and, once seated, rolled it up to the microphone.

"Will the vice chair yield the gavel?"

"The vice chair yields, Madam Chairperson."

"First of all, let me thank our witness for his time," Dobbs smiled broadly at the windmill guy. "I regret that I missed what I'm sure was a fascinating testimony. I was tied up in another committee this morning. I'll get the transcripts from my staff and do a thorough review, Mr. Smith."

Ashley's attention was momentarily drawn to Zach who

rolled his eyes as if to say, "Oh yeah, right. I'm sure she will read every word this guy had to say just as soon as hell freezes over."

Dobbs continued, "As there are several other important committee meetings going on today and as several members of this committee have been asked to meet with the President this morning, I am going to declare a recess of these proceedings until after lunch today. At 1 p.m., we will hear from the witness from the Greenpeace organization. As for the two of you that were scheduled to testify this morning," Dobbs looked up briefly and gave a halfhearted smile, "the committee would like to thank you for your time and for your willingness to participate in this very important part of the workings of your federal government."

Without looking up again, Dobbs stacked some papers in front of her and carried them beneath one arm as she glad-handed her way out the door through which she'd entered moments before.

Ashley looked around. Zach let his head drop and stared into his lap, dejected. Martha was silently grinding her teeth and looking intently at the empty chair Keitha Dobbs had just vacated. Julie was looking sympathetically at Ashley.

"What the heck just happened?" Ashley asked.

"You just got trashed, that's what just happened," Zach said.

"Zach, that's enough," Martha snapped. She turned to Ashley. "Ashley, I'm really sorry. You've given this your all and worked really hard. I'll try to get your testimony rescheduled but that probably won't happen. I hope you'll look back on this as a great learning experience."

"Do you mean to tell me that this is it? Are they just going to cancel on me like this?"

"I'm afraid so," Martha answered. Julie placed a hand on Ashley's arm as if to comfort her.

She pulled her arm away. "No, I don't want to calm down! They can't do this."

"Actually, they can." Zach said. "This is a senate hearing, not a court. She's the chairperson. She can do virtually anything she wants as it relates to this hearing."

"Do you mean that I sat in that room and read and studied and prepared and now she's just going to tell me 'Thanks, but no thanks. Hit the bricks'?"

"It stinks, Ashley. It really stinks," Martha said. "I'll grant you that. This usually doesn't happen to our clients. In fact it's only happened a couple of times before."

Ashley stood up. "So are we done here? Now that I've wasted two weeks of my life, can I go home now? I do have a job of my own to do, you know."

She wanted to storm out of the chamber and slam the door but that was difficult to do with full effect since she'd have to climb over Zach and Martha to get to the aisle. Then when she got to the door, she found it was dampened by hydraulic door hinges, so she couldn't even have the satisfaction of slamming it. As she exited, she looked into the gallery one last time. No Hunt. She didn't see him step in through an upstairs door just as she exited the room. He would sit there for a few critical moments before he realized that the room was emptying out and the committee was adjourned.

"She's pretty ticked," Zach said.

"I don't blame her," Julie said.

Martha had too much to do to dwell for long on what had just happened. She'd already moved into damage control mode. "Julie, go after her. See if you can talk her into delaying her flight until tomorrow. Take her on a tour of the Capitol. Give her the gold-plated version. Take her out to lunch. You can use one of the firm's private rooms at The Pine. We might need her again somewhere down the road. After lunch, get her back to her hotel. Zach, we're on Capitol Hill and we're going to make the most of it. Come with me, we've got people to see."

70

Ashley walked quickly down the hallway. "So much for my being brought here for God's purpose," Ashley said, under her breath. "Guess your instincts weren't so good on that one, Hunt." Almost as soon as the words left her mouth, she felt bad for having said them.

She had no idea where she was going. She only knew that she wanted to chew nails and right now, right or wrong, her ire was directed toward Martha and the others. At that moment, she felt that they'd participated in making a fool of her. She just wanted to get away from everyone for a few minutes. She turned left down a hallway where people were standing around talking in groups of two and three. She recognized a couple of the faces as those of reporters she'd seen on TV. They were apparently interviewing senators or staff members. She took another left down a different hallway. She was beginning to realize she was walking in a circle around the perimeter of the hearing room she'd just left, when she froze in her tracks.

Charles Fagan! He was standing with his arm affectionately around the waist of the Chairwoman of the Senate Committee on Climate Change, Senator Keitha Dobbs.

70

71

Julie walked out the door of the hearing room and couldn't see Ashley in either direction. They'd been placed under strict orders to have their cell phones off prior to entering the hearing and after trying Ashley's cell, Julie realized that she'd not yet turned hers back on. She had a chance at heading in the direction that Ashley had gone. She chose the wrong way.

72

Ashley was paralyzed. What was the guy who kept a combat knife under his car seat doing talking to a U.S. Senator? And why did the senator look so happy to see him? One thing was certain; this was not the place to try to make sense of it all. So far, he hadn't seen her. He was too busy slathering on the charm for Dobbs. Ashley took a step backwards and was about to turn and walk away when a voice called to her.

"Young lady, did you have something you wanted to say to me?" The voice belonged to Dobbs and it was clear she was issuing a challenge. She stiffened with fear. She didn't want to turn around. Then she thought to herself, "I don't owe this woman anything. Who does she think she is? Why should I endanger myself just because she summons me in the hall?"

"Ms. Miller, is it? Was there something you needed?"

This lady is going to tell that creep who I am right here, she thought, terrified.

"Ian Flannery," Dobbs said. "Meet Ms. Miller. Ms. Miller thinks you're very stupid for believing that we must do something about global warming."

Before Ashley could respond, she saw the smile fade from the face of the man she had previously known only as Charles Fagan. They locked eyes only briefly and Ashley saw the same deadly look that she'd seen that night in his car. Without hesitating further, she turned her back on the pair, accelerated her pace, and headed back for the main hallway.

73

Flannery could barely contain himself. As Dobbs had spoken, he'd turned to see the woman whom he felt had betrayed him two weeks earlier at the service station. His fists clenched and unclenched as he imagined them closing around the woman's throat. Then, just as quickly as his temper had flared, he forced himself to regain control. He swallowed hard in order to force his voice to sound even and calm.

"What did you say the lovely young woman's name was?" he asked, attempting an air of detached interest.

"Something Miller. I can't remember her first name. Something southern sounding. Made me think of Gone with the Wind. Oh, that's it! Ashley. Ashley Miller. She came by my office. Some utility Neanderthal who wants to keep burning coal until we destroy the planet. She was supposed to testify this morning but I decided that she probably didn't have anything to say that the committee needed to hear."

74

Ashley was gripped with fear. She tried to calm herself. *What has the guy really done to you other than give you a dirty look?* But calm would not come. Every fiber of her being screamed that she was in danger. She had to get out of this building and out of this city.

She searched frantically for her cell phone as she walked. She pushed open the door to the hearing room only to find it empty. Her fingers fumbled as she tried to turn her cell phone on even though she'd done it a thousand times before. She messed up twice while trying to speed dial Julie's number. Finally, the screen on her phone said, "calling Julie." "Come on, come on," Ashley said as she continued to walk toward Security.

"Hi, this is Julie' I'm not able to come to the phone right now…"

At that very moment, Julie was wandering aimlessly through the halls trying to call her. Next Ashley tried Hunt. She could see the security checkpoint at the entrance to the building just ahead. Hunt's phone also rolled straight to voice mail. He was in the middle of an interview just a few doors down, but Ashley couldn't know that either.

"Hunt, it's Ashley. I need to talk to you as soon as possible. Please call me." She closed her phone and walked up to the first security guard she saw. Before she could speak, she felt someone grasp her forearm. The guards face lit up.

"Why, Mr. Flannery, he said. Didn't see you come in this morning. How are you, sir?"

"I am quite well. And how is that son of yours?"

Ashley turned and stared full into the face of the man whom she was certain wanted to kill her. He obviously knew these guards, too. She had to get out of here and away.

"He's enjoying college. Thank you for asking. And thanks once again for helping him with that scholarship, Mr. Flannery."

Ashley yanked her arm away and said, "Excuse me," as she pushed past the guard.

"Well, she was kind of rude wasn't she, Mr. Flannery? She seemed angry with you."

"I stood her up on a date the other night, Paul, I'm sure you remember those days well. I'd say you had your share of women." He forced a broad smile and elbowed the middle-aged guard.

"Oh now, Mr. Flannery, that might be true, but some of these folks know my wife. Don't go getting me in trouble."

The guard slapped Flannery on the back as they both stood and watched Ashley exit the building. The guard did not notice the bitterness present in his companion's eyes, just as he didn't know that he had inadvertently given her a two-minute head start.

75

Walter Davidson had his cab parked and idling along the curb at the corner of A Street and Third. He was just around the corner from the Dirksen building, so when Ashley frantically dialed his cell as she walked outside, he was able to swing around onto Constitution Avenue and meet her within a minute.

"I jes had a feelin' you was gone need ol' Walter before this day was over, Miss Lady," Walter said as she climbed into the cab's front seat.

Flannery exited the building calmly but as soon as he was out of sight he began to run. He couldn't be sure but he thought he'd just seen a redhead in a cab pulling away. He gritted his teeth and slammed a fist into the palm of his other hand. He snatched his cell out of his pocket and used the walkie-talkie feature. This was getting out of hand. It was time to involve others in his team in capturing the liar, Ashley Miller.

76

"Oh thank you, Walter. Thank the good Lord you were close by." Ashley was as out of breath as if she had run a marathon.

"He prolly had somethin' to do with it. You look like you seen a ghost! What's wrong?"

She told Walter everything that had happened, being careful not to leave out how hard Flannery had grabbed her arm and the deadly look in his eyes.

"I kept telling myself I was being paranoid before, Walter, but I was right in the first place. This guy wants to kill me."

"I'm takin' you straight to the police station."

"So we can tell them what, Walter? He hasn't done anything illegal."

"I seen a man runnin' up the sidewalk as we drove off. Looked Arabic. I think that was your guy. If he's chasin' you, we need to get the law involved."

"Well, he's not going to catch me now. This man schmoozes with senators and is on a first name basis with Capitol police. What chance do I have in this town if it is my word against his? No, I just want to go to the hotel, get my stuff and try to get an earlier flight out of here. I often see the sheriff when I go to the gym back home. He's kind of a friend. I can trust him and he knows he can believe me."

"Naw, naw, that ain't a good idea now, Ashley. You don't know what or who you dealin' with. You don't know how dangerous this man is."

"I know, I know." She was near tears now. "I can't believe all this is happening. I need to think. Just please get me to my hotel and let me get my stuff and check out. The senator gave him my name. He may be able to find my hotel that way. In the meantime, I'm going to start calling the airlines. My flight was this evening. I'm going to try to get it moved so I can fly out as soon as possible.

Walter stepped harder on the accelerator. "If you think he might find your hotel then let's get you out of there now."

Ashley took a moment to sigh deeply. "Walter, are you an angel?" she asked, sounding rather pitiful.

Walter laughed. "Man I can't wait to tell my wife and kids that one. No. No, ma'am. I ain't no angel, but I am one of God's people. And God's at work all around all of us all the time. And He uses His people in that work. Yeah, I'd say He's the one what told me to wait on that corner for you. I done told you before—you a treasure, Ashley. God lookin' out fo you."

God is at work all around you. Those same words from Hunt echoed in her head. It was the second time she'd heard them in a day. So why did God seem so far away just now?

77

Adeem, the one man who wanted to kill Flannery, aka Muhammad, more than any other, had been dispatched to the airport to wait for the American redhead. Nadeem and Abraz had already located her hotel and were on their way to her room. A hotel worker from their mosque was scheduled to meet them there and let them in Ashley's room. It had been over an hour since she'd last been seen by Muhammad speeding away in a cab. He'd been so intent on making sure it was Ashley that he'd failed to get the license plate number.

Now Adeem waited reluctantly in the passenger drop-off area. The chances of him even seeing this woman with the throngs of people streaming into the terminal were slim to none. More than that, he had no stomach for kidnapping a woman only to cover up for Muhammad's lustful weaknesses. But he did see her. There, pulling up now in a dark green, Crown Victoria. Adeem had to admit that Muhammad had good taste.

78

"While you been talkin' to airline folks, I been listening in on the weather channel on the radio. Miss Lady, y'all got a awful bad storm comin' your way down there where you from. It might be good you getting' out of here now. They startin' to talk about cancelin' flights."

"Oh great," Ashley said. "That's just what I need. Just please, Lord, get me out of this town. I love you to death, Walter, but other than coming to visit you, I don't think I ever want to come back to Washington, D.C. again."

"The time you done had, I can't blame you. It's a pretty good place most times, though. You come back up sometime and me and the wife will show you a good time. And this ain't goodbye. I got your cell number. We'll stay in touch. How 'bout that?"

"That would be great, Walter. If you don't call me, I'll call you."

"You got a deal. Now here we are. This terminal a busy place. Don't go steppin' out in traffic. These folks'll run you over soon as look at ya."

Ashley got out and turned to take her larger rolling case from Walter. Back at her hotel, the two of them had wildly thrown everything into her luggage and, though they didn't know it, got out just ahead of Muhammad's men. Now as Walter pulled the trunk lid closed he looked up to see a tall, svelte Arabic man walking rapidly toward Ashley. Ashley hadn't yet seen him and Walter didn't take the time to warn her. Instead, he stepped between Adeem and Ashley, blocking his path.

Adeem, having already alerted Muhammad, held a syringe in his hand. When the drug in that syringe was administered, it would render Ashley unconscious. Adeem stopped when he was just inches away from Walter. The two men were nose to nose. Adeem knew that he needed to do this quietly and not draw attention. He didn't need to create a scene. He hadn't expected this from the cab driver.

"Listen, old man," he began with a mild accent. "Right now you and I don't have a problem. You might want to..."

He never finished the sentence. Without saying a word and while remaining completely calm, Walter hit him with a quick, devastating elbow to the jaw. Adeem, caught completely by surprise, buckled at the knees and his eyes rolled back in his head.

"What's this?" Walter asked Adeem. "You wanna take a nap in da back of this ol' man's cab. I don't mind that a bit. Lemme get your fare money out for ya."

With Ashley's rear door still open, Walter eased Adeem into the back seat, fished two twenty's out of his pocket, put one twenty back, and then slammed the door. He looked around. No one seemed to have even noticed.

Ashley stood there staring, her mouth agape.

"What you lookin at?" Walter said. "You think they give them Silver Stars to jes anybody? Miss Lady, you gotta forget this plane ride. You got to get to the first policeman you see. Somethin' goin' on here," Walter hadn't noticed that Adeem had dropped the syringe between the curb and the rear tire of the cab. "This man was comin' for you and I'd say he knows that Flannery guy. I don't know what all we into here."

"I'm scared. Other than you, I don't know who we can trust in this town. I don't know how deep this guy's influence goes," Ashley said.

"Den you go and get on this plane and get to that sheriff friend of yours. I ain't sure who to trust round here right now either."

"What are you going to do?"

"Oh, him? Don't you worry 'bout him. Me and him 'bout to take a little ride. When he wakes up, he gonna be finishin' his nap all warm and cozy in a pretty little dumpster I know of not far from here. Or maybe in jail. I got to think. I ain't sure what I'm gonna do with him."

79

Muhammad was speeding in the Jaguar to the airport where he was to meet Adeem in the parking deck and take the unconscious woman. She would wake up just long enough to receive her punishment, then he would kill her and turn her body to ash.

80

Ashley took a deep breath as the plane angled up from the runway. She'd begged, cajoled, and pleaded, and finally gotten a seat on another airline to Nashville. She'd have a connection in Memphis and, with the drive, wouldn't get home until 10 p.m., but at least she'd be home. She was supposed to be at work tomorrow but instead she'd drive directly to the sheriff's office and tell them everything. They may not have jurisdiction but they would know whom to call.

She thought once again about Flannery and the fact that he'd been in a small town near a nuclear plant. Her instincts screamed at her that he had some ill intentions. Then again, he did have some connection with Keitha Dobbs. Maybe he'd gone to Vidalia for some type of environmental protest or meeting.

Maybe he's just a militant environmentalist that has a creepy attitude toward women, she thought.

She pulled out her cell and tried to check with some people at the plant. She'd received voice mails about Shelton's plan to bring a national news crew to the plant. Now she wanted to see what had happened with the news crews and

Shelton's charges. Unfortunately, the flight crew was already instructing the passengers to put their phones away. She'd try again when they touched down in Memphis.

82

Walter sat staring at the still woozy Adeem. They weren't at a dumpster. Instead, they were in a garage only two blocks from the run-down, inner city apartment where Muhammad had planned to assault and murder Ashley only two weeks prior. Walter had grown up in this community when it was not nearly so run-down, though it had still been a tough place to grow up. Through hard work, he'd earned the ability to leave this neighborhood long ago. Still, he'd returned here to establish his taxi service after retiring from the Army. He had a couple of employees and he felt bringing business to the area was the best way for him to give back.

Now he sat inside the dingy garage on a stool before a spotless workbench. Walter couldn't afford to put much money into the outside of the garage, but he took great pride in the inside of the building. He did all of his own maintenance on his cab and the two others he owned that his two employees operated.

Adeem tried to clear his head as he sat on the concrete floor of the garage, his back resting against the front wheel of Walter's cab. He first looked at Walter with confusion, and then shaking his head rapidly, he looked again. Now he set his jaw and fire began to return to his eyes. He started to feel for his shoulder holster and then realized that his hands were bound tightly behind his back.

"Zip ties," Walter said, pulling a large black plastic tie from a workbench cubby and holding it up. "Every garage gotta have a pack a these."

"You caught me off guard earlier. You got in a lucky shot. I am telling you, old man, you have no idea what you're into," Adeem said angrily.

"Oh, I got an idea what I'm into and it's all bad. And I don't know so much about lucky. I got in a good shot, but I ain't ready to jes call it luck." As Walter spoke, he stood, walked over to a forty-year-old yellow refrigerator and took out a cold can of Coke. He popped the top, stuck in a straw from a nearby drawer and, dragging an old wooden crate over to Adeem, sat the Coke on it. "You can lean over and drink outta this. The sugar will hep clear da cobwebs."

Who was this guy? Why would he give a Coke to someone that just tried to kidnap one of his passengers? Despite his confusion over the matter, Adeem leaned over and took a long drink from the straw.

"You are probably a nice old man," Adeem said. "Why don't you take me down the road and dump me. I'll take care of myself after that. I won't track you down."

"You know," Walter said, "a whole lotta men would laugh in yo face when you say that. But I ain't gonna do that. I ain't gonna let you go neither, but I kinda believe you. See, Adeem, they's good in you."

Adeem looked startled.

"Oh, I went through yo wallet a bit. I found yo fake ID and yo real ID. A man can't be too careful who he hangin' out wid."

"You don't know anything about me."

"Oh, *now* I do," Walter said, "Yeah, I do know some

things. I know I wasn't lucky back there. I won two boxing championships fo da entire seventh army back a long time ago and I know you hesitated. And when you did, I taken my shot. So da question we got to deal wid is this; why did *you*, prolly a trained fighter, hesitate when you was standin' in front of a seventy year-old man?"

"I didn't hesitate! I was naïve, that's all. I underestimated you."

"Naw, naw...this sound good. This is what you can tell yo buddies wherever y'all hang out. But you sho 'nuff hesitated." Walter leaned in close. "You hesitated 'cause you got some good. You got good in you, son. It may not get out much but you got good in you. Somewhere, sometime, you was loved. You was taught what was right."

Adeem looked even more confused. In that instant he had a flashback of himself sitting in his home with his mother and father. He was helping them peel fruit that the family was going to enjoy for dessert. His sister and brother were there. Everyone was laughing at the antics of his little brother. There in the garage, Adeem's eyes began to well up with tears.

"Yep...yep..." Walter laughed. "You sho did tell me, yes, you did."

Adeem gritted his teeth now. "What are you talking about you crazy old...you think you can figure anything out about me just because I might have hesitated a little?"

"Oh naw, not jes 'cause you hesitated, I been praying 'bout you since I put you in da cab back at the airport. I noticed you hesitated. *He* tol me da rest," Walter said holding his index finger toward the ceiling. "Now come on, I can't dump you on da side a da road. Me and you got ta take a little ride. I know some cops. They'll know what to do." Walter was heading to roll up the door of the garage. He stooped down to open it.

Adeem marveled, wondering why he suddenly recalled that scene from happier days when Walter said there was good in him. He'd never had that memory before. He rarely had any memories of his family. His own bitterness had clouded them. Now he wanted to see that mental picture again. He looked up at Walter. For a moment, he started to warn Walter about the transmitter inside his watch. But what good would that do now? Adeem knew what had to be done to Walter.

The door came up abruptly with a good shove. Then Walter turned his back to the darkness outside and placed a hand on the left rear fender of his cab. "Now," he said, "you gonna get in this cab da easy way or we gone do this da hard way? 'Cause it don't make me no difference. I...."

Walter fell forward with a thud. As he lay there, a trickle of blood began to wind slowly around the back of his ear and down his neck.

83

Ashley landed in Nashville to find out that she'd missed a call from Annette. Annette rarely called her, so she knew she'd probably found something significant. She called back and listened as Annette told her all that she had found.

"That group you asked me to look into from your buddy's business card, Crystal Moon?"

"Yes," Ashley said.

"I was already aware of them by the time I got the message you sent through Connie. They've been sending money for a couple of years to your ex. This is all getting way too scary."

Ashley gasped. This bordered on overload. She couldn't take it in. "Annette, do you think Shelton sent this guy after me?"

"No, I don't think it's anything like that. In fact, I doubt they even know each other. From what I've been able to tell, Crystal Moon is a multi-million dollar outfit. Shelton's small potatoes. He's just one of many small fish this organization is feeding—no pun intended."

"I've got to sit down," Ashley said as she plopped down in a seat at the nearest gate. "This is blowing my mind. I'm going to the cops as soon as I get back there."

"Well, you'd better hurry. The counties north of us are already being hit hard with ice. They're starting to close some roads coming in this direction. By the way, if you're going to the cops, you can't mention me or anything I've told you. The stuff I did for you is highly illegal."

"I think I have enough to tell them now without involving you, so don't worry. All of this sounds too crazy and I'm not at all sure any of it adds up to a crime. The authorities may think *I* am crazy. Listen, I'll talk to you sometime tomorrow."

"Hey, one other thing," Annette broke in. "Things might be looking kind of bad for your guy, Shelton."

"He definitely isn't my guy, but how do you mean?"

"There's a rumor all over the plant that Mike and Leroy spent some time pouring over video from the security cameras. Apparently, our cameras have some super zoom capability and they were able to get a shot of Shelton on the day they were sampling. Seems they have a pretty good close-up video of Shelton taking something out of his pocket and putting it into the sample basket. We're hearing that they've actually sent the tape to the FBI for enhancement. They think Shelton planted that endangered fish."

A moment later Ashley hung up the phone, her head spinning.

84

Muhammad was waiting impatiently for his flight to depart. He'd stood at the bank of computer terminals and watched as one by one the status of flights leaving Washington to anywhere in the Midwest changed from "departing" to "cancelled." He'd been assured that nothing was flying in our out of those areas for at least the next twenty-four hours. The television in one of the airport kiosks was declaring it the winter storm of the century for the Midwest. Now he waited for the one flight he'd been able to find. To St. Louis! He'd have to rent a car and drive from there.

He'd used his connections to find Ashley's home address. Just as he'd suspected after George's call, she was affiliated with the plant that was being shut down. He'd worry about how to avoid paying out the million-dollar reward for getting coal-fired units shut down later. He'd always expected to get out of paying the money on some technicality.

He thought briefly about George. He actually liked the young go-getter. He'd feel a little bad when he had to kill him in a few short weeks. First, he'd take care of this woman and then go underground until it was time for the strike.

He'd neutralize this problem and then join them. When they emerged, it would be the perfect time to bring The Great Satan to its knees.

85

Ashley tossed the keys to her pick-up truck on the kitchen table and watched them slide off the far end. "Great," she said. "just great." As she'd driven carefully along the slick road to her driveway she'd been heartbroken to see a "For Sale" sign in Ray's front yard, the house dark and abandoned. She was worn out from the stress of the day but she knew she was also too wired to fall asleep. She couldn't turn her mind off, couldn't stop trying to think her way through all that was happening around her.

She'd planned to see the sheriff as soon as she got home. Now she felt less scared since she was back in familiar territory. More importantly than that, it was very late and she was exhausted. She'd see the sheriff tomorrow in hopes that he could make some sense of all this.

As if the flight delays and looking at every man that she encountered in the airports with suspicion wasn't tiring enough, the drive from Nashville had been treacherous. Even that far south, sleet and freezing rain were already making the roads slick. As she traveled west and north, things had only gotten worse. Since she'd already had five missed calls from her mom, she decided she'd better call her and let her know that she'd finally made it home from the airport.

38

86

Now it was Walter who felt woozy. He opened his eyes to see that it was no longer only he and Adeem in the garage. There were two other men standing nearby. Adeem was rubbing his wrists, which had been freed from the zip tie. He took a gun with an extended barrel that was handed to him by the third man. It was equipped with a silencer. Walter began to pray for his family. He wasn't ready to leave them but he wasn't afraid to die. He was prepared. Before he finished his prayer, his vision went black.

87

Muhammad was beginning to think that Allah was against him. Sheets of ice were covering the roads and the interstate had been closed to all but emergency vehicles. His rental Mustang had nearly slipped off the road multiple times. Now he was stuck in a fleabag motel, waiting. He had no control over the situation, and that realization was almost more than he could bear. He would wait here until daylight. By then, hopefully the roads would be cleared. There had to be a way for him to get to Ashley. He didn't know how much she knew, but he knew that he was running out of time. Ashley Miller had to die. And it had to be soon.

88

Ashley walked into her bathroom, opened her medicine cabinet and swallowed two over-the-counter sleep aids. She thought about fixing something to eat or a mug of tea but she was too tired to make the effort. She would never know that Shelton Leonard had spent two nights in her home. He would never confess to it and he'd done a thorough job of restoring everything in her house to normal. Ashley kicked off her shoes and fell into bed, clicking on the small TV on her dresser as she did so.

The TV was tuned to a news network and she stared at the screen completely disinterested, the volume muted. She watched the images on the screen, waiting for sleep to overtake her. A half-hour passed and finally her eyelids became so heavy that she could barely keep them open. She felt herself drifting off into blissful sleep when suddenly the picture on the screen jarred her awake. There on the television stood Keitha Dobbs with a man that the caption identified as Aaron Hatcher, the former senator that Hunt had told her about.

Ashley tried to shake the cobwebs from her brain and reached for the remote. By the time she'd turned the volume up, the narrator was talking about a controversial move the two were undertaking with the help of the White House and the EPA. Ashley didn't get it all, but it was something about forcing a temporary shutdown of some of the least efficient coal-fired units in the country, which, in the assessment of the host, was nothing more than some sort of PR maneuver. The pair intended to prove to the country that existing hydro, wind, and solar power could make up the lost generation. They were calling the effort Smartpower USA.

She couldn't listen to the rest. She could barely keep her eyes open and her brain felt as if it were in a fog. She snapped off the TV and immediately fell into a fitful sleep.

89

She woke with a start to the sound of a gun going off. At first, she doubted what she'd heard, but then she heard it again. This time it sounded like a larger gun, maybe a shotgun. She turned and saw that her alarm clock was flashing 1:30. The power had gone off an hour and a half ago for some period of time but was now back on. The noises were coming more frequently now. Just when she was beginning to think about Ian Flannery, and becoming really scared, she heard a loud crash outside.

She reached around for a flashlight but she was already starting to realize that the sounds she was hearing were not gunshots. She made her way to her bathroom window. It was covered in a heavy frost. She raised it so that she could get a clear look outside. The property around her house had been transformed. Every surface was covered in a thick layer of ice. Only a foot or so from the window, a large maple tree that had been standing near the corner of her house had fallen. She was able to reach out and grab a nearby limb. It was frigid to the touch and the twigs on the branch shattered like glass. The entire limb was encased in at least a half-inch of ice.

The popping and cracking that she'd thought were gunshots were actually limbs breaking off trees all around the area. She closed the window and turned off the flashlight as she observed her yard in the darkness. Every two or three seconds another limb would fall or an entire tree could be heard falling with a thud in the woods behind her house. She began to realize that there was a great risk of a tree falling on her house, yet she felt that she was much safer indoors than she would have been if she had stepped outside.

Suddenly, she began to hear the cracking and groaning of what was apparently a very large tree beginning to fall. Instantly the sky lit up in a blue glow. Ashley was nearly blinded as the transformer on the power pole at the end of her driveway exploded. A huge oak was toppling down onto the power lines almost as if it were in slow motion. As she watched, powerless to do anything about it, the tree took out her power lines, snapped two power poles, and crashed down on top of her pick-up truck, crushing it. The sound was deafening as the transformer blew, the tree fell, and the ice coating all the limbs exploded into a shower of crystalline slivers once the tree hit the ground.

"Oh no! I loved that old truck." Then she realized that the house had gone dark again. It was time to find the camping gear.

About two hours later, going on very little sleep, Ashley was barricaded in her small den. The kerosene heater was driving the chill away, at least in that room. She had a kettle for tea going atop the heater and she was trying to read by the light of her dad's old Coleman lantern.

90

Muhammad shivered with cold. He was regretting his decision to leave the motel and press on towards his victim. His rental car had slid off the road and into a ditch that ran along the side of the interstate. For hours, he'd alternately run the engine for warmth and then shut it off to conserve fuel. Gas stations everywhere were closing because there was no power to run the electric pumps. He'd been unable to refuel prior to the wreck. Now his gas gauge was so low that he'd decided to try and tough out the cold a little longer.

He'd watched the rearview mirror for approaching cars most of the night. None came. The interstate was officially closed and besides, no one was getting out on a night like this. There was no snow; there were only sheets of this wretched ice. It was nearly impossible to maintain traction.

Finally, with the first light of morning just beginning to break over the horizon, Muhammad saw headlights approaching. He already had a plan. As the vehicle drew closer, he could see that it was a four-wheel drive pick-up. The driver eased slowly to a stop and a tall man emerged, clad in heavy boots, a fur lined cap, and camouflage coveralls. He shone a bright flashlight toward Muhammad's car.

"You all right in there? Are you hurt?"

Muhammad waved and gave a thumbs-up signal. He turned on the key and rolled down the window.

"I'm not hurt, but this door is stuck against the embankment. I can't get out. I was hoping you could pull me out," he called. The door was barely stuck and he could easily have opened it. He wanted the man to pull him toward the pavement so that he could drive away before the man saw his face.

"Well...it's slick up here, too," the man said. "I could probably back up to that little slope where the ice hasn't settled as bad. Maybe I can get enough traction there to pull you out with my winch. You look cold. You're turning blue. Let me see if I can get that door open and you can warm up in my truck until I can get your car hooked up and all."

"No, that's not necessary."

"No, hang on there, I don't mind. Just hope I don't bust my rear-end sliding down this hill here," the man said as he stepped gingerly toward the stuck car.

A moment later, the well-meaning man was standing at the car door.

"You shove with your shoulder and I'll give it a yank. It don't look that bad from out here."

"I don't want to damage the door," Muhammad said testily.

"I don't think we'll....one...two...hey, there she goes. There, you can get out now."

"Thanks," Muhammad mumbled.

"Boy, you sure ain't dressed for traveling in this weather. Is that all you got is that little light jacket?"

"I didn't see the weather report. I didn't know it would be this cold." Muhammad said over his shoulder as he practically skated up the bank and along the shoulder of the road. He was getting very annoyed with this hick.

He got into the idling truck and watched the man pull the winch hook out and toward his rental car. Then he warmed his hands by the heater vent as he watched him lay on his back on the wet icy ground as he tried to find a place to connect it to the car. Muhammad was more perturbed than ever now. After all the women he'd used in his life, he couldn't believe this one causing him so much trouble.

And now he was going to have to go to the trouble of killing this redneck. That, and the ensuing work he'd have to do to make it look like a car accident, would set him back at least another two hours. And as near as he could estimate, in this weather it would take him a minimum of four more hours to find and kill the woman.

91

"I was going to do him for you but I figured you'd want the reward from Allah for yourself," Nadeem said in Arabic. "After all, you're the one that was sucker punched."

Adeem looked at his comrade. He couldn't hesitate this time, even though he was reluctant to pull the trigger.

"I was very close to freeing my hands anyway," Adeem replied. "The result would have been the same for the cab driver."

"Grab that tarp over there," he said. "I don't want to have to do a big clean up afterwards."

Walter woke again as his body was jostled roughly. He fought to stay conscious. He wanted to at least put up a fight. He didn't want to go out just laying there motionless. Oddly, at that moment, Walter found himself wondering if *he* would be considered a martyr. Was his dying to help Ashley a form of dying for his faith? He flailed weakly at the two men as he tried to push their hands away. He wished he could clear his head. He wished he could make his limbs do what he wanted. He didn't want to die this way.

He didn't know where he was. He knew this city as well as anyone, but he didn't recognize the vacant lot where he now lay. Only at that moment did he feel the shards and gravel cutting into the side of his face. He hoped that someone would find his body. His family would need to be able to bury him if they were to have closure.

He decided to do the only thing he could do in that moment. He decided to follow the example of his Lord and Savior Jesus Christ. As Jesus was on the cross, He had prayed for those who were crucifying him. Walter forced his eyes open wider. He wanted to make eye contact with Adeem as he prayed for him. As the men fumbled with his limp body, he could only catch glimpses of him as he held the pistol extended at his side. Each time he got the chance, Walter looked into Adeem's eyes and fought to remain conscious and focused in his prayer. It was as he was praying for forgiveness for Adeem and praying that he would find peace, that he thought he saw tears welling up in the man's eyes. Then his prayer stopped and he watched helplessly while Adeem extended the pistol in front of him and aimed carefully.

Dear Jesus, please receive my spirit, Walter thought. He watched the gun buck in Adeem's hand silently...once.... twice....then he felt the two men who had been pushing him onto the tarp fall on top of him.

92

When Ashley awoke, it was already eight o' clock in the morning. It seemed much earlier. She'd fallen asleep on her couch under several quilts. She'd barricaded herself, the kerosene heater, and the camping gear in her den and sealed off the rest of the house. That kept this room a bearable sixty-one degrees according to the thermostat on her wall. She sat up, still a little foggy from a night of frequently interrupted sleep and the after-effects of her mild sedative.

She decided to call her parents and see how they'd made it through the night. Her landline was dead along with the electricity. She reached for her cell phone and was about to dial when she noticed that there was no signal. That was unusual because she normally had four bars in her house. She wouldn't be able to contact them. The house was quieter than Ashley could ever remember it being. The television and internet were, of course, out of the question because of the power. After a few minutes of sitting in silence, Ashley felt very alone. She began to rummage around in some drawers using the dim light from outside. The weather was still grey and overcast, although the freezing rain had stopped.

She found a spare flashlight and was pleasantly surprised to find that the batteries were still good. It took considerably more effort to locate an old transistor radio she'd been given for her tenth birthday and a 9-volt battery to go in it. She got the radio on just in time to hear the DJ promise some news and weather updates after the next song. Before the song ended however, the radio station seemed to go off the air. No other stations would come in. Ashley assumed they were losing power as well.

"Oh, well," she said as she stepped back into her den and closed the door. "My little corner of the world." She looked around for something to do. She walked to her bookshelves and pulled down a novel that she'd read a couple of years before. Then she decided she wasn't in the mood for that so she tossed the book onto the coffee table. She looked around the bookshelves again when a family heirloom caught her eye—the Bible her grandmother had left to her.

She entertained herself for a few moments by going through the pages and pulling out an old photo or two or a yellowed newspaper clipping her grandmother had placed there as far back as 1963. She found a small red flower that was pressed flat at the beginning of the book of Romans, the same book that Hunt had quoted when they were together at the coffee shop. She thought about Hunt and the things he'd said about her having a purpose and the verse he'd shared from Romans. She thought about the flower and how she'd been the one to pick it for her grandmother on a walk home from church one Sunday. She couldn't have been more than seven or eight years old at the time.

She recalled times when she sat on her grandmother's lap, rocking in an old oak rocker, as her grandma read to her from this same Bible. She stared down at the pages and wondered when it had happened. When had she begun to take this book, those walks to church and the worship there, and her relationship with Jesus for granted? She couldn't remember. She only knew that she had.

As high school activities began to take more and more of her time, then college life had proven so busy, it had become easier to skip church a Sunday or two. Soon she was going weeks at a time without attending. She had begun to neglect praying as her grandmother had taught her. She couldn't remember the last time she'd really sat and read the Bible. She began to read now. She read from the same book that Hunt had quoted.

She began reading in the first verse of the first chapter. She stopped and stared out the window after she read,

"For I am not ashamed of the gospel for it is the power of God for salvation to everyone who believes...the just shall live by faith."

For the first time in years, she remembered when she'd invited Jesus into her heart as a twelve year-old girl, kneeling in front of her grandmother's rocker. She remembered her grandmother's passion for God's message of hope in Jesus and how she had "told folks about Jesus" every chance she got. Then she remembered going under the cold clear water of a creek only fifty miles from where she now sat. The pastor had baptized her that day as the congregation of her little country church sang, "What a Friend We Have in Jesus," their voices blending beautifully there on the creek bank under the maples and oaks. She couldn't help but feel a little ashamed that she'd never really nurtured the relationship with Him that began on that day.

She read on, *For since the creation of the world His invisible attributes, His eternal power and divine nature, have been clearly seen, being understood through what has been made...*

Her eyes began to tear up as she read in the margin, alongside this verse, what her grandmother, with her beautiful handwriting, had written:

"God's natural revelation—God reveals Himself to us through nature. We can know that He is real and all-powerful when we see His glory manifested in His creation."

She began to cry softly. It was not just at the sight of something her grandmother had written and that she'd never seen before, but at the symmetry of it all. Hunt had quoted to her from this very section, only a few lines further down in this same chapter. Now with the pressed flower and the note in the margin, it was almost as if God was speaking to her. It was as if He was simultaneously sending her a message from her past and her present. But what was the message?

A little further down she read what could happen in the heart of men when they turn their backs on God and even deny God's existence: *They became futile in their speculations...*

She thought about Keitha Dobbs and her adamant insistence that global warming would surely be our doom. She looked out the window and the ice-encrusted world. She shook her head in disbelief as she read some more: *Their foolish heart was darkened...*

She looked next door at the now empty and cold house that Ray and his family had vacated. She thought about Emma and hoped she was safe and warm somewhere. She wondered if Keitha Dobbs and Aaron Hatcher ever thought about people like Ray when they were driving energy costs skyward for the sake of some supposed yet poorly indicated threat.

She read further still, reading about all the immoral and vile behaviors that ultimately result when men deny God and look only within themselves for what is right and moral: *God gave them over...to impurity...for they exchanged the truth of God for a lie...and worshipped the created rather than the Creator.*

She set the Bible down on her coffee table. Within the span of just three weeks, she'd experienced betrayal at the hands of her ex-fiancée, met another man that she knew she may very well be falling in love with, foolishly gotten into a car with a stranger who now seemed to want her dead and who also was a part of an organization that was sending Shelton money, nearly testified before Congress, and been chased down a dark alley fearing for her life. Now she was stranded in a record-setting ice storm. If God was trying to tell her something, He certainly was going about it in dramatic fashion.

Just a couple of days ago she'd been standing in the middle of the Washington Mall being convinced by Hunt that she would do some great thing for God. Instead, when her moment had come, she hadn't even gotten to testify. Now she was sitting here, wrapped up in quilts, wearing old sweats, and thinking that God was talking to her.

Walter must have been right. You are a real treasure. She laughed at the thought.

93

Ashley looked at the flickering light of the kerosene heater and decided she'd better check the fuel level. It was nearly empty and she dreaded going through the refueling process because that meant she'd have to put on her coat and head to the garage. She decided to eat some breakfast first.

She turned the heater on low to save fuel, and then removed the teakettle full of water she'd placed there the night before to heat and took it to the kitchen.

She made herself a cup of instant coffee and sipped it as she looked out her kitchen window at the netherworld of ice-covered limbs. She cringed at the sight of her pick-up, crushed by the large hardwood whose trunk had landed right in the center of the cab the night before. She knew it would take days, maybe even weeks, to clean her yard and she wondered what the rest of the community looked like. She thought about trying to get the Mustang out and make it to the plant. Then she realized that would be impossible for one person to do, so she walked back to the relative warmth of the den. She sat down with her coffee and curled into a ball on one end of the sofa. Once again, she stared outside.

It was deadly quiet in the room and Ashley wished the radio station would come back on the air. She wished she could talk to Hunt, or better yet, she wished that he were here with her. Thinking of Hunt once again brought her back to their conversations and to what she'd had just read in her grandmother's Bible.

"I don't think someone who nearly got themselves killed by stepping out with a total stranger is quite ready to do anything for God," she said aloud. The sound of her own voice in the deadly quiet room nearly startled her.

"But you didn't get killed, I sent Walter."

Ashley looked around the room. She was certain there'd been no audible voice but the thought had come into her head as clearly as if someone had spoken. Suddenly her mind was beginning to race. In her mind's eye, she went back to that night. Walter had pulled up to the alley at the perfect time. He'd told her that he normally would've been home by then.

"I ain't no angel," Walter had said. "But I *am* one of God's people. God is at work all around us and He uses people in that work."

Again, she thought back to the gas station that night when she'd been so terrified as she waited in Ian's Jaguar. She'd needed an opening, some way to get away from that car without Ian seeing her. She could see him now. She could see the irritated look on his face as he waited for that elderly lady at the cash register. She hadn't thought of it before, but she remembered taking one last look at the door to the store as she headed around the corner to the alley. The elderly lady had been coming out. Something about the lady stood out but Ashley had forgotten what it was.

It was her necklace. Hanging around the neck of that woman was a large golden crucifix. And the woman had been dressed in white. She was a nun! Had God sent her too? Had he sent two of His people to save her? Perhaps God *did* want her in Washington for some purpose.

"How many people do you suppose were in Washington that night that would have known anything about a nuclear plant in Vidalia, Georgia?"

It was that voice in her head again. Or maybe it was a voice in her heart. No, no it was all wrong. God wouldn't have been involved in something that required her to run off with a stranger.

Suddenly she remembered the card. Flannery had dropped a business card in the restaurant that first night. She grabbed the flashlight and headed for her room. She frantically searched her purse and luggage. Finally, she found what she was looking for—the card that had fallen from Ian Flannery's pocket that night at the restaurant. The card looked expensive with raised, gilded type. On the back was written "Holiday Inn, Vidalia Georgia." For the first time it hit her—everything that she needed to know about this man was on this card. It might be that she never needed to get into that car in order to learn what she needed to learn. From the card, she could have made the connection to Crystal Moon and to the nuclear plant.

She grabbed a legal pad and began rapidly jotting down the thoughts that were now spilling from her mind:

- Ian Flannery may have visited a nuclear plant.
- He had a combat knife in his car.
- His eyes say that he has a violent streak.
- He was helping to fund Shelton.
- Shelton tried to fraudulently shut down units at SPG.
- Flannery is somehow affiliated with Senator Keitha Dobbs
- Dobbs proposes shutting down several coal-fired plants for a week in February.
- Crystal Moon uses a crescent moon symbol.

I don't know where I'm going with this but maybe there is something I'm supposed to figure out, she thought. Maybe Flannery really was a terrorist. Maybe he was going to try to spread radiation by blowing up that plant. "If that's the case, then where does his relationship with Dobbs come in?" she asked aloud.

She jumped as someone loudly banged on her front door. Her heart began to race. She walked slowly towards the kitchen window. From there she could see someone standing outside the door. She grabbed a large kitchen knife. Then the front door flew open, banging against the doorstop. Just as she had that night in the alley, she could feel her pulse in her throat. She clutched the knife tightly.

94

"You must really be hungry," a voice called out. "You're already standin' there with your silverware in your hand."

"Dad!" Ashley exclaimed. "You nearly gave me a heart attack. How on earth did you get here?"

"My old '56 Ford," he said. He was clutching a paper bag of groceries tightly to his chest. "Your mom said you might need some more food. You didn't convince her on the phone that you'd be fine."

"You mean to tell me you rode twenty miles in that old truck of yours with no heat? Why didn't you bring the car?"

"'Cause the truck had gas in it and I wanted to leave what gas was in the car for your mom. Plus, I didn't know how the roads were gonna be. If something was going to go in the ditch, I wanted it to be my truck, not your mom's new car."

"You look like you're about to freeze," Ashley said and wrapped her dad in a big hug. His face was cold against her cheek and he held the groceries out to the side to keep her from crushing them.

"It did get a might nippy," he said. "A fella just has to sort of hunker down into his coat."

He kissed his daughter on the cheek and set the groceries down. "By the way, I don't know if even the two of us could ever fix that truck of yours. I am afraid it's a goner."

Ashley smiled, "Yeah, I think the old boy could be considered totaled."

"Sweetheart," her dad went on. "I'm glad you're home but I almost wish you were back in Washington till this mess passes. I'm tellin' you, I've never seen anything close to this. The whole state has been hit hard. I saw power lines down from here to home. They're sayin' that power may be out two weeks or more. The stores are runnin' out of food and there's no power to drive the gas pumps so you can't even get gas for your car. I found one place that was still sellin' kerosene, so I got us both five gallons. I was afraid somebody was gonna knock me in the head for it before I could get it here. It's crazy, I'm tellin ya."

"Wow, I can't believe that. It's like we're suddenly thrown back into the 1800s," Ashley said. "Daddy, take your coat and gloves off and sit with me. I'll fix you some coffee. I've got some things I need to tell you."

"I'll sit a while but I can't stay long. I don't want to leave your mom by herself tonight and I need time to stop up the road on the way back. I saw a brand new Mustang off the road a mile or two from here. Nobody was around, but I want to see if the owner needs help when I go back by."

The two sat side by side on the sofa, holding mugs of coffee, a quilt across their legs. Ashley told her dad everything. She told him about meeting Hunt, Walter, and even the way she'd met Ian Flannery. She told him about her disappointment at not getting to testify and that she'd seen Flannery talking to a U.S. senator in the Capitol.

"Well, you've got the right idea now," her dad said. "As soon as they get your cell phone working, you need to get in touch with the law. Sounds like they'll have a whole lot of things to look into. I sure hope I get a chance to meet this

Walter fella. Sounds like a wonderful man."

"He is wonderful," Ashley replied. She got the list from the coffee table and went over it systematically with her Dad.

"What are you thinking?" he asked. "You think this Flannery is some sort of terrorist? You think he's going to try and blow up that nuclear plant or something?"

"I don't know. It seems far-fetched, I know. Even if he could get through all that security, the reactor would be so shielded it would be almost impossible to scatter radiation with any kind of explosion."

"Well, there is that, I suppose," her Dad said. "But I was thinking more along the lines of what would a terrorist be doing at the Capitol building talking to a senator?"

"I know. This is why I was so hesitant to go to the authorities in Washington. Nothing makes any sense."

Just as the two were contemplating this, the radio crackled to life.

"This is J. J. Johnson with KBQI in Woodland, Kentucky. Ladies and gentlemen, we are sorry for the delay in getting back on the air. Very quickly, here is the situation. Power is off to thirty-seven counties in this area. We're broadcasting to you now using our emergency generator. We do have systems in place to be able to broadcast in these situations but the sad truth is we've so rarely used the generator that it's not proving to be as reliable as we'd like. We hope to stay on the air for about thirty minutes now to get you some news and updates. We'll be announcing places where you can go for a hot meal and shelter and then we'll have to go back off the air for some additional generator maintenance. Folks, this is an unprecedented storm and we're just going to have to work together to get through it."

"Wow, the TV and radio stations are even having troubles," her dad said. "You just don't even think about that. No TV, radio, phones, no power for the gas pumps."

Ashley held up her hand as the DJ went on. "Hang on a minute, Dad. He's coming back on."

"Ladies and gentlemen, this is one of the first things we need to address. There have already been some altercations at grocery stores and gas stations. Police just had to break up a small riot at the Food Mart. Officials are asking us to remind you to please remain calm. Food supplies are running out but they're going to try and truck some in here as soon as possible. Likewise, the National Guard is coming in to help with fuel supplies. Please remain calm."

"Twenty-four hours into this and folks are already losing what little mind they've got," her dad said. "Can you imagine what it's gonna be like in ten days?"

Ashley looked out the window at the now dead power lines entangled on her demolished truck. All the jumbled thoughts, all the seemingly disjointed bullet points on her legal pad, suddenly began to snap together like the final pieces of a jigsaw puzzle.

95

"It's the grid. He's after the grid," Ashley said as she stared out the window."

"What are you talking about?"

"The grid! The electrical grid. Don't you see, he doesn't need to get through the security at the nuke plant? He isn't trying to blow up the reactor or spread radiation. He just has to take out the transmission lines which might be as much as a mile outside the protected area of the plant."

"I'm not sure I'm following you."

She was no longer talking to her dad but to herself. "Shelton doesn't necessarily have to be in on it. I would guess he's not in on it. He's just a willing dupe. He thinks he's saving some fish and collecting an award or something. He doesn't see past that. He doesn't see how he's being used."

She was pacing now and tapping the index finger of her right hand against her lips. She was still connecting dots but the connections were coming faster.

"That would also explain why he was with Keitha Dobbs."

"Who?" her dad asked, a little irritated at being left out of what was clearly an exciting revelation to his daughter.

"She was just on television last night before the power

went down, talking about Smartpower. He and Hatcher have convinced her to force units off-line. At the same time, Shelton was trying to force two of *our* big units off-line. If he waited for a cold day, when demand was high and then took out the transmission from the nuke plant, the whole grid might go down like dominos."

Her dad clutched both her forearms. "Slow down a minute, you're getting all worked up. Now what are you talking about? You're not making any sense here."

"Okay, it's like this. Just say it's a normal day, no ice storm like now. You and Mom are at home and you use a certain amount of electricity. You have lights on, the TV, maybe the stove. You have no idea where the electricity is coming from. It might be from my plant here close by, but it could also be from a plant three states away from here. All of the power lines all over the country are connected. The electricity may flow from just about any plant.

"But then, say that the plant that was supplying your power goes down. Instantly your supplier of electricity changes. You start getting power from some other source. It's all handled by the suppliers and much of it is automatic. Let's say your power was coming from a plant to the north. When that plant goes down and the switch is made, your power has to come from, say, the east. Now there is more power coming through the eastbound lines and a small amount of heat builds up in them.

"If it's just one power plant that's affected, there's no problem. All the extra power can flow from that other direction. But say a second plant goes down from the west. Now three times as much power is flowing from the east and the lines get hotter. A few years ago, something like this happened in the Northeast and one section of the grid after another began to fail. As more and more sections failed, more strain was put on the remaining sections and they failed. It became a vicious cycle. Soon almost the entire east coast was in the dark. That problem was fixed in a few hours. What this guy has in mind could keep the grid down for weeks. You think people are getting panicky now after one day. Think of what it would be like over a period of weeks."

Her dad picked up the thought. "No cell phones, no communication, gas would run out pretty quick because of the electric pumps. Heck, there wouldn't be any refineries working, there would be a run on food..."

"This guy has got Keitha Dobbs and Aaron Hatcher doing a political dog and pony. With this Smartpower stuff, they think that they're going to take a few token units off just for show. At the same time, Flannery has encouraged Shelton's group and who knows how many others to get a few other units off here and there. That puts strain on the grid.

"If a really cold day comes along and millions are running their heat full bore then that adds more strain. In conjunction with that, if Flannery takes down the transmission lines at such a large nuclear plant and instantly pulls that load off the grid at just the right moment of peak demand, the grid will fail. The entire nation could be facing what we're facing now because of the ice storm. Even government and military communications would be affected. It could easily create mass chaos and panic."

"I hate to say it, Ashley, but this all sounds a little crazy to me. I mean it's just too far-fetched. You can't..."

Ashley pushed her dad's feet off the coffee table. "Put your boots and stuff back on Daddy, I need you to fire up the truck."

"I just started getting warm. I was going to have another cup of coffee."

"You can have another cup when we get into town. Now help me get some of those limbs dragged out of the way. I've got to get the Mustang out." Ashley said.

"Get to town?" her dad said incredulously. "The Mustang? You're going to take the Mustang out in *this* weather."

"Well, I sure as heck am not going to ride in that slow truck and that's the only other vehicle we've got. I'll have to risk it. I'm going to have a talk with the sheriff."

96

Nearly an hour later, Ashley was sweating under her winter coat as she hooked the heavy towing chain around the main trunk of the tree that had fallen on her truck. She and her father had been hacking and dragging limbs at an intense clip since they stepped outside. Now her dad pushed the gas pedal on the truck and eased the tree off to one side of the driveway. He shut off the engine and hopped to the ground.

"That ought to about do it. Why don't you go in and fire up the Mustang? Get the engine warm. I'll pick up some of this little stuff and toss it on the pile back by the woods."

Her dad began to pick up some leftover smaller limbs and stack them in the crook of his arm. Ashley stepped into the garage through the smaller side door and pulled off her gloves. She didn't plan to open the large garage door, which would let in a cold blast of wind, until she was ready to leave. It was the first time she'd seen the Mustang since she'd returned from Washington. She patted the hood as if greeting a reliable old steed. She knew that her dad had probably come by and run the Mustang's engine while she was gone. Still, in this cold, she decided to spray a shot of starter fluid into the carburetor to help the engine come to life.

Once that was done, she eased the hood closed, and slipped behind the wheel. She pulled out the manual choke, knowing just the right amount it would need for a cold start, and feathered the accelerator pedal. "Come on, baby," she said. "Show off in front of Dad and fire up on the first try." She turned the key.

THUNK!

The noise outside the driver's window startled Ashley. She turned toward it to see her father, his palms on the car's roof, sliding down the side of the car, smearing the glass in his own blood.

97

Earlier that day, Muhammad Raschi had parked his car along the side of the road. When Ashley's Dad had stopped momentarily on his way to deliver groceries to his daughter, Raschi had been hiding in the nearby woods. As the truck took off, Raschi returned to the rental car. He then drove a little further down the road, got out again, and did the necessary reconnaissance of the area around Ashley's house, deciding how he would kill her.

He was in position in the woods behind her house, the silencer secured on his 9mm Glock, within ten seconds after Ashley had stepped into the garage. Muhammad had not seen her and he assumed she was still in the house. The presence of her dad in the yard had only provided a momentary obstacle. He'd walked right toward the spot where Muhammad was hiding with an armload of limbs.

Muhammad had unceremoniously shot David Miller in the vicinity of his heart, the silencer effectively doing its job. Miller's knees had buckled and he had collapsed to the ground in a heap. Muhammad then jogged rapidly to Ashley's rear deck where he'd expertly picked the lock on the back door. He was now standing in Ashley's kitchen.

His heart was racing. He was so looking forward to taking this woman back to the woods. He would make her suffer before she died for her insolence and for all the trouble she'd caused him. He'd wanted to control and kill this woman from the moment he saw her. He was still angry with himself for nearly compromising an operation that he'd planned for years because of his insatiable lust. He couldn't afford to think about that now, however. Now he was the consummate professional, a highly trained killer. He took a deep breath and focused his powers of concentration. That is, until he heard someone outside trying to start a car.

98

Ashley choked back a scream as she got out to help her dad into the passenger seat. She ripped the scarf from around her neck and tried to fashion a crude pressure bandage. She hoped he could stay conscious long enough to apply pressure to his own wound as she drove him to a hospital.

Adrenaline surged through her body as she miraculously maintained calm and carried out what she knew had to be done. Within seconds of seeing her dad, she'd realized he had a gunshot wound, that Flannery was somewhere nearby, and that she'd be next if she didn't get them both out of there.

"Come on, baby. Come on!" she urged as she turned the key. The starter jumped to life but the engine didn't start. "Can't flood it, come on, Ashley, you've done this a thousand times," she said. It was as she was about to try a second time that she realized her dad was trying to say something.

She leaned her ear close to his lips, "Too much choke, run the choke in a quarter..."

"Dad," Ashley said, amazed that even at a time like this her dad insisted on giving her driving tips, "I've got this. I don't have too much choke." She hit the starter again and the engine roared to life. She gunned the accelerator way more than she normally would have in these temperatures. For the first time since she'd rebuilt the car, what was best for the Mustang was not foremost on her mind.

Absent-mindedly, she hit the opener on the garage door. Nothing happened since there was no electricity. At that moment, she saw a shadow appear at the bottom of the garage door. Without hesitating, she shoved the gearshift into first and raced the engine.

99

Muhammad ran towards the garage door. When it flew, half of the door hit him like a giant sledgehammer, sending his body skittering across the ice-encrusted ground and slamming his shoulder into the side of the house. He felt pain shoot through his shoulder and down his arm. He was too stunned from the blow to get up and reach for the pistol that now lay ten feet to his right.

Ashley saw his body go flying along with the thin aluminum of the garage door. She nearly panicked as the Mustang's tires began to spin at the end of her driveway. Within seconds however, the tires gained enough traction to shoot her out onto the pavement. The roads had been treated with a melting solution and with the temperature now approaching 32 degrees, the road in front of her house was mostly clear. She'd reached the end of her road and was making the ninety-degree turn toward the highway when she checked her rearview mirror again.

Flannery was running awkwardly up the road in the opposite direction. There was a 2009 Mustang parked there. He held a pistol loosely in one hand and Ashley knew he'd be coming for her.

"Hang on, Dad. You keep fighting. I'm going to have you to a hospital before you know it," she said. Then she thought, *That's got to be a rental. It doesn't look like a GT but it may have an eight cylinder.* She was in full race mode now. She fully realized that this race wasn't for a trophy—this was a race to save her and her dad's lives.

She turned onto the highway in a cloud of tire smoke as she brought the Mustang's rear-end around in a controlled slide. She would have a mile and a half of straightaway before the first set of curves. *His car will have better handling than this one but I can out-drive him,* she thought. *But it's the straightaway where he might catch up.*

She looked over at her dad and her eyes filled with tears. Blood had soaked through the scarf and his complexion was growing increasingly pale and waxy. "Dad!" she shouted. "Dad, can you hear me? You hang on. We've made the highway. We can be there in twenty minutes."

She gritted her teeth and tried to press the accelerator through the floor. She glanced at the gauge needles. She was driving over one hundred and ten miles per hour. If she hit ice at this speed, they both might die. She also knew that if she slowed down their death would be certain.

As she approached the first set of curves, she checked her mirror again. He was there and he was closing fast. "He's closing on me," she said to her dad, hoping he could still hear her. "Now we'll find out what this guy can do."

She slammed the gearshift into third and jerked out the clutch. She'd never been through these curves this fast. As she exited the last turn, she accelerated back up through the gears, the pedal to the floor. She had another straightaway coming up, only this one was only about three-quarters of a mile. She didn't see Flannery's car until she was nearly to the next set of turns. She'd increased the distance between them significantly. It was at that moment, she realized Flannery didn't have the skill to catch her.

The mirror on the passenger side door of her Mustang exploded. “Oh no,” she exclaimed. “He doesn’t have to get close enough to run me off the road. He only has to get close enough to shoot me or my gas tank.” She was still talking to her dad but he’d now slumped over and was nearly falling down into the floorboard. She knew she couldn’t take the chance of pulling over for help and she couldn’t bet both their lives that Flannery would continue to miss once they reached the next straightaway. She had to stop him somehow.

She forced herself to concentrate, forced herself to think about every inch of the route she’d driven in this car hundreds of times before. Suddenly, she knew what she would do. Just ahead, there would be a bridge over Panther Creek. The bridge was about one hundred yards long and was notorious for icing over every winter.

She entered another series of curves that took her out of Flannery’s line of sight and allowed her to gain some space between them. As she exited the last curve, tires squealing, she could see black ice shimmering on the surface of the bridge. Panther Creek was swollen out of its banks and was interspersed with patches of ice as well.

She gripped the wheel even more firmly, aimed her car at the centerline of the bridge, and held her breath. She roared across the bridge, being careful not to change either direction or speed even slightly.

The Mustang fishtailed but didn’t strike the guardrails. She felt the tires grip once again as she reached the road on the far end of the bridge. Just past the bridge was another sharp curve. She pumped her brake pedal hard, bringing the nose of her car almost to the pavement. She slid into the curve, coming to a near stop halfway through. Instead of stopping, she flung the Mustang to the shoulder and simultaneously stomped the accelerator and cut the steering wheel hard to the left, slinging the back end of the car around in a cloud of tire smoke and sending her dad against the passenger door.

"I'm so sorry, Dad, but I don't know what else to do," she cried.

Now, facing the way she'd come, Ashley stopped and waited.

"I have to time it right. I can't come at him too soon or too late," she coached herself.

Within a couple of seconds, she thought she heard Flannery's car. She stomped the accelerator and popped the clutch, heading right at Flannery down the middle of the road.

Flannery looked up, startled to see Ashley's white Mustang barreling toward him on the far end of the narrow bridge. She was driving down the center of the road in a suicidal game of chicken. He didn't know how to react.

"Come on, hit that brake pedal, you..." Ashley let her voice trail off as she gripped the steering wheel with all her might. Flannery's Mustang entered the bridge on one end as her car entered on the other. She gritted her teeth in anticipation of the impact.

Suddenly, Flannery's car went into a spin. He'd flinched and turned the wheel or hit the brakes or perhaps both. The car careened wildly into one guardrail, seemingly gaining speed in an ice-induced spin. When the right front fender struck the opposite side of the bridge, Ashley got more than she'd hoped for. Flannery's car went airborne over the guardrail as her Mustang raced beneath it, untouched, to the other side of the bridge.

100

Muhammad Raschi regained consciousness with his car upside-down and under water. He began to breathe rapidly and felt a sharp pain in his ribs from the effort. He fumbled with the seatbelt latch, finally freeing himself. He reached for the power window button but nothing happened. He grabbed wildly at the door latch as water covered his nose then eyes.

He had little strength, and the door seemed to be wedged closed. He kicked at it with all his might as he struggled to turn himself upright while breathing through his mouth. He panicked. Gulping in a large swallow of the ice-cold creek water, he began to cough violently. The seatbelt was undone but something was still holding him in place. It was then that Muhammad realized that his legs were pinned beneath the steering wheel and that he would die here, hanging upside down.

He didn't think of his plan to destroy the U.S. electrical grid, a plan that would now be discovered and stopped. He didn't think of Allah or his promised virgins. Instead, as his lungs filled with water, he thought he saw the face of Adeem's baby sister—the three year-old girl whom he'd ordered murdered in the desert long ago while he forced her brother to watch. She was staring at him with pity from inside a brilliant white light.

101

Ashley stepped out into the cold fresh air and breathed deeply. Though the roads had thawed, the ornamental trees that surrounded the hospital were still bent nearly to the ground by their own covering of ice. She walked deliberately toward one of them and grasped the end of a twig. She let the ice melt and water run between her fingers until she could feel the tender bud beneath. In that moment, she felt a kinship with the bud. They had both been freed from something that had enveloped them.

Her father was going to make it. He'd received four units of blood during surgery but the doctors felt all indications were positive and they were expecting a full recovery. She continued to walk, knowing that the deputy sheriff assigned to her would be her shadow for the foreseeable future. The authorities had agreed to take a break from the questioning. The interviews being conducted in a counseling room of the hospital were not over. They were only getting started.

She didn't know where she was going or why she was walking, she just wanted to be outside. She wanted to be away from everyone, even if only for a few minutes. Finally, she found herself standing alongside the Mustang. It didn't look too bad considering all it had been through. She knew she needed rejoin her mother in the post-op waiting room. She wanted to be there as soon as they would let them see her dad. But she didn't want her mom to be nearby the first time she talked to the FBI and CIA agents who were now on their way to the hospital.

The stress of all she'd been through finally hit her. Her knees began to shake violently and she had to hold onto the fender of the Mustang to remain upright. It was as she stood there, leaning heavily on the hood of her car, that she felt someone come alongside her and place one arm tightly around her shoulders and the other on her arm, holding her firmly.

She turned to look into the gently smiling face of Hunt Finley.

"What? How on earth did you get way down here in this weather? You're supposed to be in Canada or somewhere."

"Alaska actually. But I heard there was a great story here about a beautiful damsel in distress, so I came running," Hunt answered.

"How did you..."

"Hey, I'm a reporter. I have instincts. Plus, I got a call from Walter and he filled me in on as much as he knew, which was that some guys were following you and trying to kill you. You know, just your standard stuff."

Ashley smiled. "So did he tell you to rush down here and save me?"

"He probably would have, if I'd given him time. But before he had a chance, I told him I needed to hang up on him so that I could start working on a flight. He just said 'Good boy,' But before he hung up, he told me something even scarier. He told me that he was in the hospital too, recovering from a pretty serious concussion."

Ashley gasped and covered her mouth with one hand. Hunt told her about how Walter had been found by his wife, barely conscious back in his garage. There was no sign of Adeem or anyone else. There was no trace of any blood other than Walter's anywhere. Walter had told everything to the police but it seemed that, with no evidence other than the knot on his head, they didn't believe him.

"The police think he'd a bad enough head trauma that he'd hallucinated the whole thing. I'm sure you'll be getting questions from these guys," Hunt tilted his head towards the deputy, "about Walter as well. The good news is Walter is going to be fine. His biggest concern was you."

Ashley let herself fall against Hunt's chest. She felt awful about her dad and about Walter. Hunt pulled his coat around her and wrapped her in an embrace that rapidly began to drive away the chill from both her body and spirit.

They stayed like that for a time before Ashley spoke up again. "Did you fly all the way down here from Alaska?"

"Can't be any more than a few thousand miles. I knew all those frequent flyer miles would come in handy some day."

The two began to talk and before she knew it, the words were tumbling out of Ashley's mouth—about what she'd seen, what she'd suspected, and the palpable fear that had gripped her during her ordeal. She'd been afraid she'd die but she'd been driven forward by the love of her father and a burning desire to stop Flannery's plan. It was a drive and a motivation that she never knew she was capable of.

"It's the first time in my life that I felt like I had a small sample of what it must feel like for soldiers who fight for their country. I didn't think about it consciously, but I knew I was fighting for something larger than myself. I knew I had to make it."

"There's no difference in the bravery you showed and what patriots before you have shown."

"I'm still shaking. I don't feel very brave."

"Some great man once said that courage is not the absence of fear. It is taking the needed action in the face of fear, or something like that," Hunt said.

"The TV was on in the waiting room," Ashley replied. "The story is already starting to get out that a powerful lobbyist was tragically killed in a car accident. What if I come out looking like the villain in all this? Hunt, what if I end up in jail?"

Ashley looked up into Hunt's eyes. He placed his hands on both sides of her face. The familiar warmth against her cheeks made her reminisce about their first kiss, only now Hunt kissed her forehead and then kissed her lightly on first her top lip, then the bottom.

"Don't even think like that," he said. "I used my press credentials and got one of the deputies to talk to me. He wouldn't come right out and say it, but they have a pretty good idea who the real villain is. I think somebody in the CIA is already beginning to connect some dots. There'll be no charges against you, I'm pretty sure."

"I hope you're right."

"Hold my hands," Hunt said.

Ashley took both Hunt's hands, a look of curiosity in her eyes until Hunt began to pray aloud for her. She'd never had anyone other than her grandmother pray for her. As he said *Amen*, Ashley repeated it. They opened their eyes to see the sheriff's car approaching on the distant highway. His blue lights were flashing with no sirens. There was a black Chevy Suburban following closely behind.

"That'll be them," Hunt said.

Ashley sighed deeply. "I'm tired, Hunt. I don't want to do this."

"I don't blame you. You can do it, though. You're going to be fine. And I'll be here waiting for you when they're done talking to you. I'll be right here for as long as you need me."

Ashley smiled up at him, kissed him, and then led him toward the deputy.

"I guess I'm ready," she said to the officer.

The deputy led her back into the hospital where they were using a counselor's office as an interview room. She would be in there for over two hours.

Hunt stood outside and watched the Suburban pull up. He watched the very serious looking agents walk inside. He was scared for Ashley. The truth was, he was scared to death for her. He wasn't worried about criminal charges. It was just that Ashley couldn't possibly realize the hornet's nest she would soon be in the midst of. She couldn't know the depth of misguided passion that some felt on the topic of global warming. He had only recently begun to realize the magnitude of money that was at stake. Many powerful people all over the world must surely have a stake in keeping the public in a near state of panic over global warming.

He was already getting calls to the effect that Keitha Dobbs and others were planning on doing everything they could to present the now-deceased Muhammad Raschi to the public as Ian Flannery, dedicated environmentalist. They were going to try to make him into a martyr for the green movement. Right now, Hunt's biggest fear was that they would try to destroy Ashley if she said anything different.

As a reporter, he knew that Ashley was in very treacherous waters. But he also knew that she had the truth on her side. She'd done the right thing. She'd been very brave. She had stopped a terrorist-induced catastrophe. No matter how the media tried to spin things, those facts couldn't be denied. He wished he could be in the room holding her hand. Since he couldn't, he did the next best thing—he bowed his head and said another prayer for her. When he finished, he looked up at the sky and saw the sun's rays breaking through the clouds for the first time that day. The ice would start to melt soon. Hunt smiled, knowing without a doubt that Ashley was not alone in that room.

EPILOGUE

Spring was in the air and a bright yellow butterfly sunned its wings on a smooth rock in the middle of Panther Creek. Unbeknownst to it, the female madtom catfish was feeding along the bottom only three feet beneath the surface. She'd enjoyed much better success this year and was now followed by a small school of her hatchlings. Her mate waited patiently at the mouth of their new home, his head swollen to approximately the same size as the tunnel opening that served as a front door. In the event of danger, he would swim backwards, sealing the opening with his own head and protecting his mate and offspring inside.

His mate had once lived in the river. Instinctively, on the day she'd watched her lone surviving offspring disappear into a yawning steel tunnel, she'd swam to escape. She'd not been concerned about escaping the tunnel; it was no threat to a healthy fish. She'd swum to escape the bass that had inflicted the mortal wound on her offspring.

During her escape, she'd found the mouth of this creek where it dumped into the massive river. She swam upstream and inadvertently found a habitat in which she could thrive. She would remain there the rest of her life. For now, as she fed she kept one eye on her school of hatchlings and the other on alert for predators.

At that instant, she saw the shadow that was a near daily threat to her and the others. This time it was not a bass but a much larger mud cat. The mud cat was a distant cousin but was a grave threat nonetheless. She whisked her tail sharply, abruptly. In a millisecond, her offspring instinctively followed. They swam with all their strength toward the silvery fortress that had become their home.

Due to the quick reaction of the female, they made it to the door with relative ease. True to his instincts, the male reacted just as quickly and filled the door with his head, sealing them in. The underside of the algae-covered dome vibrated at the impact from the mud cat. Some of the algae broke loose and rained down like snow on the occupants. After a couple of futile attempts to overturn the silver dome, the mud cat swam away in his lumbering fashion. He would head back down the creek in search of other, easier prey. Their fortress had saved the madtom family once again.

The female remained in place for a time, using her fins to hold her gently in place in a kind of suspended animation. She had no concept that the source of her home was man. She was merely an opportunist and made use of this readymade habitat accordingly. Had she had the mental capacity however, she could have observed the dome from the water above it. There she would have seen, at the dome's center, an embossed horse, rearing its forelegs majestically. She might have deduced that her home was actually the wheel cover from a 2009 Mustang. It had been left behind by the salvage operation to recover the rental car company's property. The female madtom and her young were the inadvertent beneficiaries of Muhammad Raschi's one and only real contribution to the environment.

AFTERWORD

"WELL, LET'S SEE, you have depicted a tie between those who are most concerned about climate change, with a plot that is part Communist and part Islamic extremist in nature, and thrown in a dose of paganism. Good story, but if this ever gets published, people are going to think you're a conspiracy nut!"

That was the basic reaction of a few friends and loved ones when I showed them a rough outline of the plot for this book. As I worked on the manuscript, I sometimes questioned myself. I thought perhaps that this is going a bit far.

The genesis of the plot, however, came about from watching press coverage of the international negotiations on the Kyoto protocol. Kyoto, like the more recent Copenhagen proposal, suggests that we must severely curb CO_2 emissions, particularly within the United States. Conversely, we will drive the capital costs of energy much higher. "Energy costs will necessarily skyrocket," President Obama said when referring to implementation of these treaties and their corresponding policies.

Many economists have shown a strong link between affordable, reliable energy and economic health and growth. Economic development in turn is infinitely more effective than charitable giving in helping the world's poor. Therefore, as I followed Kyoto I asked myself the following: *What would motivate individuals from so many diverse cultures and countries to do something that was completely contrary to their best interests, achieved no benefit for them or others, and would cost their nations billions if not trillions of dollars?*

During this same period, I was struck by another disturbing trend in our culture. While visiting the offices of the EPA for a meeting, I observed a large display of pictures decorating the lobby, drawn and colored by elementary class children from various schools. In a minimum of 80 percent of the pictures, the theme was the same—two or three stick figure children attempting to play outside. However, in the background a rectangular industrial plant with large stacks belched out gigantic plumes of black smoke. The stick figure children coughed, wheezed, and cried.

As adults we've read one novel after another, seen one movie after another, where industry and those who work in it are depicted as careless dolts who would poison a baby seal if it meant making a single additional dollar. In these inaccurate depictions, some environmental do-gooder usually arrives on the scene to save us all from the pirates and cutthroats of industry. They always seem to utter the same phrases: "follow the money trail," or "always ask yourself, who benefits, who profits?" I will delve more into those questions in a moment.

What have we taught our children? What have we been taught by our entertainment culture and in our own public school experiences? Is industrial development always bad? In a world approaching seven billion people, is there nothing positive to be said about the health and economic benefits of an industrial base? We celebrate this base when we reflect on how our productivity rescued the world from the tyranny of the Nazis—how hypocritical we are now.

As I completed my manuscript and scheduled my vacation so that I could call on publishers, I continued to be concerned as to whether my plot tying the Green Movement to Communism and radical Islam had indeed gone too far.

However, in January 2010, long after my manuscript was shipped off to potential publishers, Osama Bin Laden made the following public statement:

"Discussing climate change is not an intellectual luxury, but a reality. All of the industrialised countries, especially the big ones, bear responsibility for the global warming crisis."

Does anyone reading this assume that Bin Laden is terribly concerned with the presumed fate of the polar bear? Or is it much more likely that, like the villains in this story, he is rubbing his hands together merrily over the willingness of some to shoot themselves in the economic foot in a futile attempt to curb a mythical man-made influence on climate change?

Then a few months later, I saw a *60 Minutes* documentary on the vulnerability of the U.S. electrical grid and the interest that some militant Islamic groups have shown in that vulnerability. I began to feel less like an alarmist.

I read the following quote in the *Washington Times* (January 17, 2011) from top NASA scientist, James Hansen. After comparing the U.S. to "barbarians," he said, *"I have the impression that Chinese leadership takes a long view, perhaps because of the long history of the culture, in contrast to the West with its short election cycles. At the same time, China has the capacity to implement policy decisions rapidly. The leaders seem to seek the best technical information and do not brand as a hoax that which is inconvenient."*

It sounds as though Hansen finds the model of Communist tyranny preferable to our federalist republic—the same system that affords him a living. I wonder if the millions of mass-murder victims of the Mao regime would agree. Setting that aside, it also appears that Hansen is unaware that recently, the Chinese exploding economic machine was bringing a brand-new coal-fueled power plant on line every single month. None of these new plants has a fraction of the pollution controls of our U.S. plants. All the while, Hansen and others propose that we shut down our own aging (but reliable, safe, and comparatively much more environmentally friendly) coal plants and allow U.S. citizens to suffer the stiff economic price of doing so.

As of this writing, I don't feel much like a conspiracy theorist anymore. The alarming truth is that the goals of climate change alarmists dovetail quite nicely with those of Communists and radical Islamists, namely, the diminishing of the United States as a world power. Unfortunately, that is not all.

In this story, Shelton stops after finding a madtom catfish that he thinks he can use as propaganda and drops to his knees and thanks Gaia. Gaia was an ancient Greek goddess; from her we derive our concept of "Mother Nature." In that culture as well as later pagan cultures, she was said to have given physical birth to the sea, air, and land. Imagery featuring Gaia was prominent in some of the displays at the Copenhagen conference on climate change, which was attended by world leaders including the president of the United States. Learned men have come up with the *Gaia hypothesis,* wherein the earth is seen as a large living organism.

Dr. James Lovelock is one scientist who believes the results of global warming will be catastrophic. He is credited with being the originator of Gaia Theory. In an op-ed that ran in *The Independent* on January 16, 2006, he wrote, "*Perhaps the saddest thing is that Gaia will lose as much or more than we do. Not only will wild life and whole ecosystems go extinct, but in human civilisation the planet has a precious resource. We are not merely a disease; we are, through our intelligence and communication, the nervous system of the planet. Through us, Gaia has seen herself from space, and begins to know her place in the universe.*"

Dr. Lovelock's mention of humans not being a disease must surely be a reference to the accusations of others who have fully embraced his theories and gone so far as to conclude that humans are something akin to parasites on the organism that is Gaia.

Let's agree to begin an experiment tomorrow and keep it going for five business days. Tomorrow, as you begin your day, make some mental notes. As you open your bath products, as you open the packaging on your breakfast foods, as you put on your clothes and shoes, as you listen to your car radio, pass billboards, look around the office, thumb through a magazine at lunch, or watch some evening television—count how many times a day you are given the message to "go green." I can tell you that a Google of the term "using the new green technology" instantly brings up three hundred and seventeen million hits. Our culture is currently obsessed with it. At the same time, reasonable and highly competent scientists have raised serious and valid questions about climate models and the data that is fed into them. So how can we explain this phenomenon?

As a Christian, I am particularly struck by the discounting of any role for the God of the Bible. Allowing for the fact that many in the global warming movement do not believe in God, are we to presume that He is currently sitting up in heaven wringing his mighty hands and saying, "Oh my, now they have built factories and are emitting CO_2. What a surprise! Whatever shall I do?" Is there no allowance among global warming researchers for God's sovereignty over the earth and humans that He created? No, of course there isn't.

In the final analysis, this book is a work of fiction. It was originally written to explore some "what if" scenarios. Although initially I was a bit concerned that perhaps the story would be seen as having gone too far, now, with the passage of time, with Climategate, books on Gaia, and repeated quotes from global warming alarmists (I have only included a fraction of them here), my fear is that the story does not go far enough.

I return the reader to the question raised above by so many anti-industry movies and novels:

If we insist on continuing to enact the law of diminishing returns upon our culture with one draconian environmental regulation after another, if we bow to third world political pressures to take extreme legislative actions to curb fossil fuels while powerful nations that may wish us harm do nothing, if we diminish human beings in a futile attempt to save a mythical Gaia, then who benefits, who profits? Perhaps we should follow the money trail.